# Circle of Three

# Circle of Three

Rohit Gore

GRAPEVINE INDIA

Grapevine India Publishers Pvt. Ltd.
Plot no.4, First Floor
Pandav Nagar,
Opposite Shadipur Metro Station,
Patel Nagar,
New Delhi - 110008
India
grapevineindiapublishers@gmail.com
contact@grapevineindia.in

First published by Grapevine India Publishers in 2012



Typeset and layout design: A & D. Co.



Printed and bounded in New Delhi

# *Acknowledgements*

*Most importantly, to the person I am forever indebted to – my wife Pranita. Thank you for standing beside me throughout. Her sacrifices and never wavering support is what makes me write.*

*Heartfelt thanks to Grapevine India's Sachin Garg and Durjoy Datta for deeply believing in this novel and for their critical inputs to make it better.*

*A special gratitude is due for Devaki Khanna for her inspired and painstaking editing.*

*Big thank you to friends Deepa Aithal, Shruthi Krishnamurthy, Vikram Jain and Vinay Nayak for beta reading this novel and giving very honest feedback. Their encouragement and enthusiasm is a constant.*

*Special thanks to my agent Kanishka Gupta of Writer's Side Literary Agency for always championing my books.*

*To my wife Pranita*

# Part 1

## Chapter 1

## Three Birthdays

Ria was certain that two events would take place. The coffee she had put on the gas flame would boil over, and she would kill herself.

There wasn't much she could do about either. Several incidents had occurred to make these two future events possibilities beyond question. Perhaps she was exaggerating when she put together *several events* and the coffee boiling over. All she had done was to pour the milk from the container, switch on the burner to medium flame, add two teaspoons of sugar, sprinkle one spoonful of Nescafe (the coffee had to make a perfect mound on the spoon) in exactly fifteen seconds on the surface of the milk, and stir her favourite concoction for twenty seconds. She planned to keep it on the flame for two minutes, exactly. Any more or less, and the coffee tasted burned or underdone. There were, in all, six actions.

The suicide—and she was shocked to think of the word—had become a certainty because of the other several minus six incidents or actions. All that had happened in the last few years had made it a certainty, but it was set in motion exactly thirty-three years ago when she was born, on 13 October.

The milky coffee spilled over the sides of the vessel, making a loud sighing noise, and extinguished the flame. The brown liquid charred on the burner within moments. Ria wondered if her death would be as quick and violent. She promised herself it wouldn't be as messy.

She didn't want her suicide to be a spontaneous act, although it was very tempting to get it over with. She could feel herself dying every day, with every moment. But she had come to hate spontaneity. It had to be planned.

She couldn't move for a long time from the reclining chair in which she sat. She could smell the leaked gas from the burner, which spread in the kitchen, filled it up, escaped it and corrupted the air in the living room of her three-bedroom flat. Outside, the light had faded. All she had to do was to press any of the switches. She looked at the row of buttons—fan, tube light, exhaust fan, refrigerator. Which one would kill her?

*No, it had to be planned.* She vowed not to fall into temptation.

Ria got up from the chair, opened the windows and turned off the burner.

It had to be two months after this date—sixty-one days.

She wondered how many people had decided on their birthdays the date and time of their own demise. It was creepy and she had never liked anything creepy. She thought that people who watched horror movies, like *The Saw,* were complete nitwits.

All she now had to do was to make a list of things to do before she ended her own life. She smiled at that thought, pulled out the chair from under her desk and sat down. She had never written a To-Do list and ironically, this would be the last thing she would write. Ria had always believed that writing was for her scripts and plays, not for something mundane, which the mind was too lazy to remember. She had written a script for a film or a television show almost two years ago. There was no paucity of scriptwriters in Mumbai; she knew that those who not so long ago used to line up outside her house had found better writers. She switched on the table lamp with shaking hands, fearing the house would explode, leaving the list unwritten.

It didn't.

Aryan stood at the door of his flat for a long time. He could hear people laughing and crying and dancing. Some were even vomiting. The nauseating smell of alcohol and all kinds of smoke was wafting out of the open door.

A man stepped out of the neighbouring flat down the aisle and motioned to him.

"I am going to call the police again if you don't make your moronic parents stop that ruckus," the man said.

Aryan shivered a little as he recalled what had happened the last time his parents were hauled up by the police. Funnily, the cops were more drunk and stoned than the people in the house. They had slapped around a few of his parents' guests. One of them had actually gulped a few large swigs from a bottle of vodka, calling it *angrezi daru*. It had been a long night.

"Can you give me fifteen minutes before you call the police?" Aryan asked.

The man sighed as though doing him a great favour.

There was no choice. He had to step into the house and either stop the stupidity or spend another night sitting on the wooden bench outside the police station.

*No thirteen-year-old kid should have these kinds of choices, especially on his birthday.* He was, perhaps, the only child in the world who would want his own birthday party to end, or better still never have a birthday party. He wanted everyone to forget that 13 October was the day he was born. His birth had been a mistake anyway; his parents had said so. They hadn't said it to him directly, but they had yelled it often as they fought in their bedroom, believing that he couldn't hear them.

He looked at his watch and cursed himself for wasting precious minutes. The man, wearing pyjamas with a design of sunflowers on them, was looking at him with his arms folded and eyebrows raised. Aryan thought of telling him he looked silly in those clothes, but thought better of it. He gave the man what he thought was his most reassuring nod and stepped into hell.

His parents' guests were in various stages of drunkenness and undress. A few were kissing and feeling each other up. It took a minute or so before his eyes adjusted to the darkness and then they stung because of the smoke. He had taken a deep breath before coming in, but he knew he wouldn't be able to hold on too long. Ms Mathur, his class teacher, had said more people died because of second-hand smoke than the actual smokers. He desperately looked around for his parents. Theirs was a three-bedroom flat—his parents' room, his own room and a guest room, although they seldom had anyone staying over. However, the room did have its uses—either his mother or his father stormed off after a fight to sleep there.

After looking everywhere in the flat, he found his parents in *his* room. His mother was sitting on his bed with a cigarette in one hand and a glass in the other, pulling off the usual miracle of not spilling the wine even though the glass was tilted at an impossible angle. She had said it was her definition of 'holding a drink'. She was completely drunk. His father was sprawled on the floor in what looked like his own vomit. He rarely needed fancy glasses.

"Gagan was feeling a little drunk," his mother said. Her voice was so slurred that had Aryan not heard her talk like that a million times before, he wouldn't have understood a word or the nasty sarcasm in it.

"Happy birthday, Aryan. Did you have your piece of cake?" she asked with a sudden smile. Aryan had never liked her smile when drunk. It was as if she actually wanted to cry. He could see the fine lines and wrinkles when she scrunched up her face like that.

He nodded and said, "Mr Malhotra says he is going to call the police."

"Ask him to go screw himself!" she slurred.

Aryan could never learn not to flinch when she swore, particularly when she was drunk. Somehow, she always managed to utter the swear word perfectly.

"He had his mobile phone in his hand," he said, "and was about to dial."

That made her pause. He was sure the memory of the recent scuffle with the policemen was fresh in her mind.

She looked at her glass for a few moments, then looked at his father's loudly snoring form and repeated, this time without the slur, "Ask him to go screw himself."

He stepped out to the living room and found his way to the

audio system that was blaring some weird music. He switched it off.

It took the people some time before they realized the music was gone. Aryan knew he had barely a few minutes before Mr Malhotra would call the police.

"Who shut the music?" Someone shouted.

"What's this kid doing here?" Another demanded to know.

Aryan screamed, "My father wants you all to leave!"

"What? The party has just started!"

"You are all freeloading morons. His words, not mine," he said, "So take as many bottles as you want and leave! His words, again. And the police are on their way. Just like last time!"

The party wound down with loud groans and horrible curses, but everyone had heard the last part. They all grabbed a bottle or two and filed out of the house, grumbling. A couple even called his father vile names (*something*-sucker). He didn't mind.

After the last man had stepped out of the house, Aryan peeked out and looked at Mr Malhotra. The man in silly pyjamas nodded at him. He nodded back, grateful for his patience.

Aryan knew none of his parents' friends would remember this incident. He wouldn't meet many of them a second time. They were all wannabes. He didn't know what the word 'wannabe' exactly meant, but it was used in a very derogatory sense by his father. The house was still reverberating with the fading music and it would take days for the nasty smells to seep out of the walls.

He knew it would be of no use to talk to his parents in their current state but a great worry was making his stomach churn. It wouldn't be the first time his father would sleep in his own vomit. However, Aryan had learnt recently that choking on vomit can kill a man, especially a very drunk man. He tiptoed back to his room and peeked inside. His mother had dozed off on his bed. Her glass was empty and lying on the floor. She had burrowed her face in his pillow. His father was still on the floor, but he could hear his loud snores now that the house was steeped in silence.

Aryan went to the guest room, which wasn't too messed up. It had a few empty bottles flung on the floor and it didn't smell too bad. He curled up under the bed sheet and lay awake for a long time, battling with a thought. Finally he decided to act on the thought and walked back to his room. His parents hadn't changed their positions. He quietly opened the cupboard and pulled out two blankets. One was his favourite when he was seven. It had a Mickey Mouse and Donald Duck print. He hadn't used it since what felt like a thousand years.

He covered his father with the other blanket and walked up to his mother to cover her with M&D (Mickey and Donald). He paused when he saw that his pillow was drenched in her tears. She was crying without making a sound.

He covered her with the blanket.

"Aryan," she said in a whisper, "you hate me, don't you?"

He tucked her in, kissed her wet cheek and said, "Goodnight, Mom."

"Did I wish you *happy birthday*?"

"Yes, you did."

"Did your father?"

"Yes, he did too," he lied.

"Liar," she said and smiled, "Mommy is going to make a lovely cake for you tomorrow."

He nodded and kissed her again. Within moments he watched her drift into sleep, though she continued to weep.

All Rana Rathod had hoped for on his sixty-third birthday was to have one more fan, one more human being 'liking' his Facebook page. He accessed the page after the crappy internet connection had ditched him for almost three hours. He cursed when he saw that the number of people liking his author page, the one he had spent countless hours creating, was still seven. It had been seven three hours ago; hell, it had been seven for the last year. Every fan was older than fifty. One of them, a man who displayed his yellowed teeth in his photograph, had posted on the wall, "Many happy returns of the day, sir! 13 October, wow! You certainly don't look sixty-three. You look fifty-five!" There was a stupid smiley at the end of the comment. Rana wanted to punch the man on his face and wipe that yellow grin off it. He didn't look fifty-five. Perhaps forty-two—forty-five if he'd had a bit much to drink the previous night, but certainly not fifty-five.

What the hell was wrong with the world? He'd hired the best photographer to take his pictures (the arty-looking goateed guy had told Rana he looked quite a lot like Amitabh Bachchan), created a natty website with heavy animation and extracts from his bestselling novels, and opened accounts on Twitter and Facebook where he posted his status every half an hour. All the comments on his Twitter and Facebook page were his own, except for the grinning man with the deformed teeth telling him he looked fifty-five.

Didn't everyone say the internet was the best way to market yourself? Lying bastards.

Maybe what were lacking were photographs of the jackets of his novels. Re-energized by that thought, he rushed to his bookshelf and pulled out all his creations. These included *The Traders of Death, The Last Dead Body, A Loaded Revolver* and many more. He had loved the cover pages –violent but seductive, depicting men with sinister faces and women with suggestive expressions interspersed with guns and blood. He laid them on the floor, like a collage, and got his camera. It was a Nikon DSLR, on which he had spent a fortune. He clicked a number of pictures, transferred them onto his PC and then uploaded them onto his Facebook, Twitter and MySpace pages, his website and every other web presence he had painstakingly created.

Rana waited, but nothing changed for the next six hours. Finally, he stopped refreshing the page.

Didn't people remember his great novels? His publisher had abruptly stopped reprinting them fourteen years ago, but his fans were still alive, weren't they?

Rana poured himself a Glenmorangie on ice. This was a drink his private detective in the books, Dev Chakravarthy, was known to enjoy. He stood near the window as the sun set and wondered bleakly about the various options for celebrating his birthday. The local disco club was out of the question, after he had been kicked out the last time. It hadn't been his fault. The woman, who had complained about him to the bouncer, had already downed the several drinks he bought her. Rana had quickly gotten bored with her, particularly because of her relentless complaints about her husband and her gaudy, runny makeup that made her look like a mime artiste. He had tried to move away from her, politely at first and forcefully when she tried to grab him. That hadn't gone too well with the parasitical cow. The bouncer, never too keen to question the story she told of being molested by Rana, had lifted him as though he were an old rug and flung him outside the club.

Drinking alone in the neighbourhood bar was tempting, but he had done it too many times of late and it made getting up at five in the morning for his daily five-kilometre run too difficult. He had checked all his online female friends (he thought they were females) and sent them chats obliquely asking if they wanted to meet him in person for the first time, considering it was his birthday. Nobody had responded. He had concluded that they were all either busy or out. Why else wouldn't one want to talk to a great author?

After a long time, he decided it wasn't such a bad idea to visit the disco. The bouncers changed very often, and even if the same giant was around, he had seemed too brain dead to recall anything. Rana opened his wardrobe and sifted through the neatly pressed and arranged clothes. He chose a shiny black shirt. It contrasted nicely with his well-trimmed salt and pepper beard. He sprayed the scent on himself several times. The musky odour enveloped him in its familiar pungency. There would be women in the disco and he was sure the perfume would knock them off their feet, if they were still standing after looking at his handsome rugged face.

Rana stepped out of his flat on the second floor, took the stairs, stepped into the noisy, clammy night of Mumbai and hailed a taxi. The rickety cab stank of stale sweat and unprocessed tobacco.

When he told the driver where he wanted to go, the man gave him a surprised look.

"Is there a problem?" Rana asked.

"No problem, sir," the driver said and started driving. Rana leaned back on the seat. Wading through the Mumbai traffic in the night was the worst thing one could do on one's birthday. The bloody bikers were scurrying around the road, which was blocked by cars that were as numerous as cockroaches on a kitchen floor. Everyone honked in this country, even when they were at the red signal. Rana hated the noise and wished he had taken his own car—a ten-year-old Maruti Esteem sedan, which made oddly complaining sounds, as though always reluctant to go where he wanted it to. He wished he could somehow be able to drink a lot and drive safely.

After a few minutes of twitchy silence the driver said, "Are you going there to get your grandson or granddaughter back, sir?"

Rana looked at the man staring at him in the rear-view mirror. His conjoined eyebrows, like a long fat earthworm, were stretched in a quizzical arch.

"No," Rana said.

"Then?"

"Why don't you just drive and keep your mouth shut?"

"Sorry, sir," the man said and didn't ask him any more questions.

There was a long queue of people wanting to get inside the disco. Everyone, particularly the girls, looked at him first with curiosity, then with suspicion and finally with giggling ridicule. Rana thought they were like the mannequins—porcelain white and dressed as though they couldn't afford clothes. He had known such girls once, a little too intimately. A few girls whispered in each others' ears and laughed. He wondered if they knew him, knew his books. Or perhaps they had just visited his Facebook page. He smiled, silently congratulating himself that the collage trick had worked.

When he reached the end of the queue, the same giant who had thrown him out of the disco just a week ago was blocking the entrance.

"I am not going to ask you for ID, old man," the man said in a retarded drawl.

"Good," Rana said and started walking towards the door.

The ogre, who resembled Shrek in those Disney movies, put a palm as big as a full chicken on his chest and said, "Where do you think you are going?"

The man wasn't all that brain-dead after all.

"Get out of here, before I twist your neck," he said, somehow making his drawl sound menacing.

"You can't do that. I have a right," Rana said, hating his slightly quavering voice.

"No, you don't," the man said and pointed at a billboard that said 'Right of admission reserved', "I reserve your fucking right. Now get out of my sight and stop holding up the line."

The giant gave him a tiny push that was enough to make Rana almost sprawl on the ground. Everyone in the queue behind him laughed, including the porcelain girls. Rana put his hands in his pockets, turned back and walked away with as much dignity as he could muster, which was very little. The sound of laughter grew.

As he was climbing the stairs to his flat, he was stopped by Vinny.

"Yo, Rana. Why are you walking like an old man?"

"They kicked me out of the disco."

"Again?" she said with a fake surprise.

"Yeah," he said, suddenly feeling very tired.

He had never asked Vinny what her actual age was. His guess was between twelve and sixteen, although there were times when she looked and acted a lot younger or far older.

"Those phony bastards," she said, "Anyway, happy birthday, young man."

"Thanks," he said, "Didn't think you would remember. And stop calling me young man."

"Well, I am not your family to forget. You haven't messed up with me like you have done with them. So, no harm in remembering it, old man," she said.

Rana smiled.

"Sorry. Raw nerve?" she asked.

"Maybe," he allowed.

She looked at her watch and said, "Well, I got to go now.

Have a stupid exam tomorrow. I hate this education system. It is making me a human."

Then she was gone.

Rana thought a little about what she had said last. When he couldn't make any sense of it, he assigned it to many such things he had heard from her. He climbed the remaining steps and got into his flat. It smelled of strong coffee, as it always did. All the lights in the flat were on—he could never enter it in the dark. The doctor had said his eyesight was not as good as it used to be. Damned doctors. After checking the status of his chat (no one had responded) he got out of his clothes. The shirt reeked of the taxi, as if his musky perfume was a thin veil easily torn by the unwashed sweat in the cab. He thought it was good he didn't get inside the disc. The smell would've surely forced some girl to gag in disgust. He laughed at that thought. It reverberated in the empty house, as if several unseen beings had laughed with him.

Chapter 2

# Three Hearts Filled with Darkness

After sitting at the study table for two hours, all Ria had was a list with three small tasks on it.

1) Clean the flat thoroughly. There are some beautiful memories in this house. I can't leave it just like that.

2) Create a charity from all the money in the bank.

3) Return the library books.

She read the list again. Maybe the first one wasn't such a small thing after all. Buying the flat had been the fulfilment of a dream just five years ago. It deserved to be in nice shape after she was gone. And what was she going to do about the one room in the house she had locked up forever? She shivered a little. That room would have to be cleaned too, even though there was no chance of a speck of dust entering it.

Even the second task was not small in nature. The money wasn't insignificant—was it twenty or forty lakhs? She decided to get all the due diligence done before she created the charity. Perhaps the third task—returning the library books—was minor. The library wouldn't mind losing a few books to a suicidal woman's negligence. But why should they lose their property?

The doorbell rang. She hadn't opened the door for many people in the last few weeks and definitely not for anyone in the last two days. She waited, hoping the visitor would just go away. The milkman, the newspaper boy, the grocer, all the usual people had deserted her a long time ago. The person at the door was persistent. After five rings she got up, walked up to the door and opened it without looking through the peephole, on the verge of shooing away whoever it was. She knew it was a mistake the moment she saw who stood at the door.

"I need to talk to you," the woman said.

She had always dehumanized her by calling her 'the woman'. It was as if she was some inanimate being that had acquired life just for the sole purpose of destroying hers.

"If you want to hit me just do it. But for God's sake, please talk to me once," the woman said a little too loudly. Ria saw a kind of madness in the woman's eyes, as though she had thought the worst would happen and was terrified about it. For a moment, Ria thought she was looking in the mirror. Perhaps she, too, had the same look on her face.

"So talk," Ria said, disbelieving the viciousness in her own voice.

"Can I come in?" the woman said.

"No you can't!"

"Please, it would be terrible doing this here."

"You deserve it," Ria said.

She had imagined saying such things to the woman for a long time, all the time thinking she would feel better after saying them. All she felt was a sickening hollowness in the pit of her stomach. It was as if she was talking from a script which had seemed very good when she had written it, but played out badly when enacted.

The woman looked around the aisle that led to Ria's flat. Nobody was there, but Ria knew the people inside their homes could hear everything.

"Okay. I know you are right, and I deserve every horror that I am going through," the woman blubbered, "I wanted to say that I am sorry. I am so sorry. I can't even describe how sorry I am. It's been just. . ."

The woman couldn't complete her sentence, because Ria had slapped her. Her face had the stunned hurt look that an animal has that doesn't know why it was hit. It was the repetitive apology from the woman that got to Ria. She was as shocked as the woman, this being the first time she had ever hit anyone.

"Get out of here," Ria said in a whisper, the hollowness in her stomach threatening to consume her entirely, "Get out before I really kill you."

The woman suppressed a sob and said, "Ria, he loved you more than he loved me. He always did."

For some reason, Ria found it hilarious and she started laughing. The woman took a step back, as though expecting Ria to lash out again.

Through fits of laughter she said, "You have the gall to walk in here, stand at my door and tell me that my dead husband loved me more than he did you?"

It was as if her married life had been some damned race and she had just about edged out the second best runner. In any other situation, if someone had said it to her, she would've really found it worth using in one of her scripts.

"I am sorry," the woman said, "I just don't know..."

Ria slammed the door on her face.

She sat down on the floor. The woman's shuffling was still audible through the closed door. Ria closed her eyes, vowing not to cry. After a few long moments, during which she felt the woman's presence outside the door, she heard her footsteps walking away.

"Why did you do this to me, Raj?" she whispered in the silent house. The only man, Raj, her husband, her soul mate, who could answer that question, was long gone. She couldn't move from the floor for a long time. The bitterness she tasted in her mouth was revolting. She knew what hatred tasted like. She hated that woman; hated every single moment the woman had stolen her husband from her; hated her own naiveté that made her aware of Raj's betrayal only after his death.

She had wanted to scream at Raj, wanted to ask him what made him desert her. And what made him forget about their Varun? Their only son, who thought his father was his hero.

*Varun . . . Mom is sorry . . . so sorry.* Focus on the list. That's all that mattered now.

She must've said that to herself a hundred times before she thought she had regained the strength she needed to stand up.

When she got up, she decided to find out everything she

could about the charity to which she should donate her money. Or maybe setting up a trust was a better idea?

Aryan knew something had happened to his father, something very bad.

He used to come home very late at night. After he got home, he would sit on the couch with a glass full of his favourite scotch and call everyone a *chutiya.* His boss, the CEO, was the biggest *chutiya* of all. The only thing the boss had done was to be the slave of the Board of Directors and get all the promotions (his father's words). His co-workers were big *chutiya*s too. They were a bunch of bloodsucking leeches and did nothing else but suck up to the CEO. The donkeys working under him were worthless *chutiya*s and were responsible for his bad performance. The politicians were a bunch of *chutiya*s who were ruining the country. The actors and actresses were *chutiya* buffoons who were merrily making money at the expense of all the other *chutiya*s of the country. The doctors, the bureaucrats, the television anchors, the shopkeepers, the neighbours and even the people on the road, every single one of them was a *chutiya.*

Aryan had rarely heard his father call anyone a non-*chutiya.* He hadn't known the meaning of the word until three years ago when Sanjay, his bench-mate in school, had told him what it meant. Aryan had thought it was a terrible word, but had found it very funny. The next time his father had gone about calling the world full of the c-word, he hadn't been able to stop laughing. Aryan had imagined the world full of beings that looked figuratively like the meaning of the word.

Nowadays, his father came home at night and said nothing. He just drank a lot and sat on the couch, staring vacantly at the muted television. Aryan heard the word 'recession' a lot and how it was making everyone's job insecure. It seemed his father was suffering because of the recession. The word recession didn't sound all that sinister to him. It was unlike menacing words like genocide or Armageddon or annihilation.

He had never heard that word before it became the most talked about. It was suddenly everywhere. The newspapers were full of it; the television channels couldn't stop talking about it; and even Ms Mathur said she was worried about it. The only other boy he could ask about it in school was Sanjay and he had told him his father, a businessman who owned hardware shops, was the most stressed out man because of it.

His mother's job, though, was a different story altogether. It seemed the only industry unaffected by the recession was the restaurant industry. She worked in Mumbai's most famous five-star hotel restaurant and had recently become the head chef there. She was also the star of a cookery-based show on television. Everyone said she looked marvellous on the small screen, as though she was born to do it. There were times when he didn't see her for days. She never returned before midnight and worked even longer on Sundays when he had no school. The only way he was sure of not being an orphan was listening to the late evening ranting of his father. With that too ceasing, the silence in the flat was absolute.

Sometimes, Aryan wondered if his father even remembered him. And now, this recession had made sure that there was no real hope. Every day, he looked at his father and felt a gut-wrenching worry. Gagan Khosla had once been a fit and boisterous man, who could run several kilometres without breaking a sweat. Now, he looked like a deflated balloon, with a rapidly developing pot belly and unshaved beard that made him look a little crazy, like the bums on the sidewalk.

Aryan missed Sakhu-mai. Sakhu-mai was their maid, who had raised Aryan in the perennial absence of his parents. When he was five or six years old, he had even started addressing Sakhu-mai as Dadi-ma, grandmother. One day, his mother told him not to do that. Sakhu-mai should be called Sakhu-mai, is what she had said. Aryan had asked Sakhu-mai if it was okay not to call her Dadi-ma. She had smiled and said he should always call her Sakhu-mai, because that's what she was. He had always wondered why she had tears in her eyes when she was smiling.

For the last couple of years, Sakhu-mai looked as if she was starving. She was always tired and had breathed as though she was drowning. Aryan had asked her repeatedly what was wrong with her, but she had stubbornly refused to tell him. Almost six months ago, she had said something to his mother, which had shocked her. After that, Sakhu-mai had hugged Aryan tightly, kissed him on his cheek, walked out of the door and never returned to their house. Aryan had demanded to know from his mother what she had said the next day. Finally relenting, his mother had told him that Sakhu-mai had cancer and she couldn't work anymore for them. Aryan had cried all night. His mother had said he shouldn't worry because she would find another full-time maid very soon. He had thought of telling her that that wasn't the reason he had cried, but didn't.

Aryan hadn't told either of his parents that he regularly visited Sakhu-mai every two days. She lived in a shanty-like house on the outskirts of a nearby slum. Her niece, who was crippled and walked with crutches, took care of her. Sakhu-mai never had children of her own. Aryan's mother, apparently, had created some kind of fixed deposit for Sakhu-mai. She received some money every month from it and it was supposed to be enough to take care of Sakhu-mai and her niece. Looking at the bad condition in the shanty, Aryan didn't think the money was enough.

Sakhu-mai didn't recognize him anymore. She wasn't even conscious when Aryan visited her. He and Sakhu-mai's niece sat silently next to her heaving, aching body. Aryan held the hand of the woman who had fed him for years, hoping she would get some comfort. He didn't think it helped her.

His mother hadn't found another maid.

Something even worse had happened on the day after his birthday. It seemed his father had been told he had just three months to either get the figures (his father was always under pressure because of the figures) or quit the company. His mother had said that Papa's company was using a polite way to fire him. Aryan had overheard his parents talk about it that night. It must've been the first time they had talked to each other in a long time. His mother had listened to his father silently, which was unusual for her. All he heard her say at the end of his father's monologue was, "I can feed all of you, literally and figuratively." It was his father's turn to stay silent after that.

Aryan hated the recession. It was making life too complicated for him. He already had too many things to deal with—Samar Singh Sangwan being not the least of his problems.

He was walking to school, staring at the pavement and thinking about the recession, when he was intercepted by Samar and the Rebels. That was the name of Samar's gang. Aryan though it was cheesy and unimaginative, but never said so to anyone. The Rebels were a bunch of thirteen-year-old kids with permanent scowls on their faces and tattoos made from fountain pen ink on their thin biceps and bony chests. But they were a nasty bunch of boys. He had seen them do terrible things to other kids like him. He had managed to stay out of their way for a long time, but somehow Samar had spotted him a few months ago despite his best attempts to make himself invisible. Since then, their interactions had been an unending torture.

"Oye, Ponchu," Samar said to him. The leader of the Rebels had never called Aryan by his name.

Aryan cursed under his breath for walking with his head down. He could've seen the Rebels from a distance and could've found a different route. Now, there was a serious possibility of getting a bruise or two. The recession was going to get his father fired and him beaten.

"Have you done what I told you to?" Samar said with his face inches away from Aryan's, giving Aryan a stomach-flipping view of his yellow teeth and purple gums.

"No," Aryan said, hoping his voice didn't sound too shaky. He was afraid of the Rebels. Everyone was. But unlike everyone else, Aryan had never spoken to Samar in a scared voice. He knew the day that happened, the fragile agreement between them, in which Aryan did most of Samar's homework as protection against a beating from the Rebels, would be broken. He would still have to do the idiot's homework, but he would also get beaten up.

"Then we have a problem, don't we, Ponchu?" Samar said in an affected voice.

Aryan wanted to laugh. Samar had seen too many Hollywood movies of late, and had started talking like Don Vito Corleone from *The Godfather*. He even suspected that the sudden fluffing of Samar's cheeks was his attempt to look like Marlon Brando by stuffing them with chewing gum.

"Didn't I tell you, that a day will come when I'll call upon you to do a service for me?"

Aryan wanted to tell him that he had been asking him to do his assignments for a very long time now. But there were times he couldn't do them. And besides, it was a really bad recital of a great line from *The Godfather*.

"I am sorry Samar," he said, "My parents had a party yesterday and I couldn't find time to do it."

Samar leaned forward with gritted teeth and said, "This is your final warning. You do it again and I will reshape your face in a way your parents won't be able to recognize it." His breath smelled of endlessly masticated chewing gums.

The other boys scowled at him and when they couldn't distort their faces any further, they all walked away.

Aryan stood there for a few moments to gather his breath and to wonder if he should include Samar as a character in the story he had been writing for months now. He hadn't told anyone about the story. It wasn't a story anymore. It had crossed thirty thousand words. So, it had officially become a novella. He liked the word novella. There was something cute about it.

He decided to think about it while he did Samar's assignment that night. He also decided that he had to do something to help his parents with the recession. The first thing was to stop using the spare car with the driver to go to school. He would end up saving a lot of petrol. Besides, the driver, Jeevan, was more interested in chewing tobacco and dozing off.

Rana thought enough was enough and decided to confront the bloody publisher in his office. The man had refused to answer any of his emails or phone calls for several months.

Unprofessional, discourteous bastards. It was time for their greatest author to teach them a lesson. He barged into the new, lavishly decorated office of Croons and Jain Publishers. They had very recently published a series of children's books that had become a rage not only in India, but all over the world. Those books were being hailed as the first truly international crossover of Indian talent. The author of the books was a seventeen-year-old boy who had become a millionaire. Rana thought the books were crap and was sure they weren't written by that snotty kid who was now being considered the greatest author of India. Phony morons.

"I need to meet Raman," he said to the receptionist who gave him a blank stare.

"Raman Jain," he repeated.

She nodded her head and asked him to sit down.

He bristled and fidgeted for hours.

"Is he in the office?" he asked the receptionist every fifteen minutes.

"Yes. Please remain seated," she said every time without looking at him.

He wondered if she was a robot programmed to say the same thing. All she had done to everyone who had come to the offices was asking them to sit down. This was the problem in this damned country. Nobody gave a skinny rat's ass for someone else's time.

Raman Jain's father had signed him up as an author when he was a young twenty-eight-year-old writer and the elder Jain was a middle-aged failed publisher. The elder Jain had told him once that it was the proceeds from the sale of Rana's books that made him dream about becoming the biggest publisher in India. Fifteen years ago, the elder Jain had formed a joint venture with the world's biggest publishing company, The Croons International, and since then everything had changed. Sometimes, Rana wondered if he even got a new brain in his son's head as a part of the joint venture agreement.

After almost three hours, he saw the short and rotund Raman Jain, so unlike his father, walk out.

"Raman! Raman!" Rana got up and called after him.

Raman turned around and Rana thought he saw the man grimace with disgust when he saw him. For a moment, Rana wondered if Raman wanted to make a run for it. What must've stopped him was Rana's supreme fitness. Rana could outrun people half his age.

"We need to talk. I have been waiting for hours and your receptionist won't even tell you about it. How are you, son?"

"Fine," Raman allowed, making a big show of looking at his watch.

"I thought we should discuss the reprints of the novels," Rana said.

Raman put his egg-shaped head down for a few moments and then nodded, as though he had made a decision.

"Look Ranasahab, you were a very good friend of my father's. But my father is dead and he has been dead for fourteen years. You are a hopeless writer. You always were and I could never understand why my father indulged you. So I don't want to reprint those crap novels you have written. Ever," he said, uttering each word very slowly, as though he were talking to a mentally disabled person.

Rana couldn't say a word.

"Please don't disturb me again. I believe I have tried to tell this to you in a nice way for several years, but you just don't understand. I don't want to see your face again. Ever," he said, turned around and was gone.

There was absolute silence in the lobby. Even the robotic receptionist had her mouth agape. Everyone looked at him with pity, making his humiliation complete. Rana couldn't remember the last time he felt so disgraced.

"I was his father's first author, you know," Rana said to no one in particular, surprised that he could even speak.

When he didn't get a response, he walked out. The shame of being insulted by an abomination of a man like Raman Jain was unbearable. The elder Jain, who had suddenly died fourteen years ago, had always treated him as family. After his death, Raman Jain had promptly removed Rana from his author list, cancelled the contract and stopped the reprints of his novels. Rana had always feared that it would happen, but was still stunned at the speed with which Raman had severed a relationship that had lasted decades. Raman had told him that his books weren't selling much in the market; that people were moving on from him; that nobody wanted to read detective fiction anymore in India, at least not a Detective Dev Chakravarthy novel who, Raman said, was so totally out of tune with the modern world. But he had never said Rana was a hopeless writer until now.

It was time to vent out the anger Rana felt at the world.

When he reached the bowling alley, the bunch of boys he usually played with was already there.

"Hey, Rana," called out one of the boys who had spiked hair like needles protruding from his scalp.

Rana raised his hand to him.

The other kids quickly surrounded him. They were all between nineteen and twenty-one.

"What happened? You look majorly pissed off."

"I wish I could just kill my publisher," Rana said.

"Man, don't tell us. We feel the same about many people in our lives, especially our parents and professors and politicians."

They all laughed and high-fived.

"Let's start a game," Rana said, feeling a little better.

Rana thought he played a great game. He beat all the kids but one. He was second by just a couple of points.

"Rana, man, you are just so cool. We wish our fathers were as cool. And they aren't half your age."

The kids laughed. He had met them a few years ago in a disco when they had sniggered at him, calling him *tharki buddha*–horny old man. He had challenged them, and won by downing seventeen shots, four more than the next best and then walking in a straight line when none of them could. Since then, they had revered him.

Rana said his goodbyes and walked out of the bowling alley.

You are a hopeless writer! You are a hopeless writer! You are a hopeless writer!

He couldn't get that voice out of his head. It had also acquired the whiny nasal tone of Raman Jain and it was getting more and more shrill. There was no way that could be true, was there? By the time he had reached home, he had made up his mind to start writing again.

He announced that on his Facebook, MySpace and Twitter pages and also made a grand entry of it on his website. Of course, as always, nobody responded. He opened a new MS Word file on the computer and named it 'new novel'. And then he sat on his chair without writing a word for the next five hours.

Chapter 3

# Three Tragedies

Ria stepped out of the house feeling like an alien in a world she had once taken for granted. She had drawn all the curtains inside the house and had lost track of time because the light in the flat did not seem to change. The bright sunlight hurt her eyes, giving her a shock. She was certain everyone would stare at her when she walked down the stairs of her housing society.

People did pass her by, but nobody gave her a second glance. Some people, such as Mr Wadhwa on the second floor, the bald, pipe-smoking old man with a naughty smile who had always ogled her, and Geeta Johari on the first floor, the young woman with a beautiful body and a pockmarked face who had always glared at her, now pointedly avoided looking her way.

It is a curious situation to live through a tragedy, she thought. At first, everyone wants to comfort you with a visit and a few words of wisdom on how to cope with grief, but eventually, they all go away. It is almost as though they want to take a good hard look at you, because you're going through hell, so that they can then feel better about their own lives. Once that is done, they don't want to acknowledge the tragedy, lest it came too close to their lives. Some avoid it because they had made promises in the heat of the moment—she recalled Mrs Sharma's offer to cook for her every day—and later, in a much calmer state, they realize they've made a stupid mistake.

She decided to take the local train. It would be nice to save every paisa she had. Now that she had decided to donate all her money, she didn't think it belonged to her anymore. Just six months ago, it wouldn't have occurred to her that she could take a train to go anywhere in Mumbai. The local trains were a medium of transport she had left far behind, not because she was a snob, but because other mediums had opened up—like the childhood friends she had unconsciously let go because she had moved on, made new friends and got used to them. She had gotten used to driving everywhere and the trains had ceased to exist. In a way, she realized, these two months would force her to get in touch with the kind of person she had been once, which would then help her die easily.

She shivered a little at that thought.

When she reached the station, she thought she could breathe a lot better. There were no familiar faces in the sea of people. She was just one more statistic here. There were so many people with so many tragedies. Her grief was insignificant, mundane compared to it all. Or maybe she was experiencing the numbing of her senses, which was a result of travelling in the local trains of Mumbai. It felt as though she were no longer a person but a part of the machinery of the train network.

She closed her eyes as the train moved along to an ancient rhythm. Her senses were slowly getting used to the smells, the conversations and the sensation of being surrounded by the people around her.

When she opened her eyes, she looked across at the boy who was staring at her. He was wearing a school uniform and it felt as though his entire body was twisted savagely amidst the crowd of people in the train compartment. But it seemed he was oblivious to it. She wondered if she knew him.

The train slowly ploughed into the station. In a violent and sudden heave, the mass of people in the compartment lunged at the exit. Ria couldn't take her eyes off the boy. Already perilously entwined in the crowd, he was thrown out of the exit, as though he was something regurgitated by a giant beast. The boy fell on the ground and before anyone could realize this, his fellow passengers had stomped on him on their way out.

"No!" Ria screamed.

Somehow, their fellow passengers responded to her primal cry and at least stopped stepping on the boy. She waded through the crush of sweaty, harried commuters and reached him. He was bleeding profusely from a wound on his chin. His white school shirt actually bore the prints of people's shoes. Suddenly, everyone around them was awakened into a collective concern. A few people helped Ria get the boy back on his feet. She hauled him out of the onrush of bodies that was trying to get into the train.

Blood was gushing from his wound.

"Are you all right?" she asked.

The boy gazed at her sheepishly.

"Your wound looks nasty," she said touching his chin. The area around the gash was fast turning black. The boy flinched at her touch.

"Let's get you bandaged," she said, "are you hurt anywhere else?"

"No," the boy said.

She was a little surprised when she heard him speak. His voice was that of an adult.

She waited for him as the nurse bandaged his face in a medical clinic near the train station.

"What's your name?" she asked when they stepped out of the clinic.

"Aryan," he said in a tiny, embarrassed voice.

"Why are you travelling alone on a school day?"

"I was going to school," he said, avoiding her eyes.

She knew he was lying. In all probability, he was skipping school.

"Let's get you to your school, shall we?" she said.

The boy abruptly stopped in his tracks and demanded, "You think I am lying, don't you?"

"Of course you are," she said turning on him.

"I don't want to go to school in our car because I want to save money," he said.

"What?"

"The recession is here, you know," he said.

She stared at him, wondering if he was trying to be clever.

There was a frightening sincerity in his eyes. Frightening because she thought he truly believed in what he had said and was prepared to do anything to ward off the recession.

The absurdity of the situation somehow made her smile. She was shocked when she realized it.

"You think I am joking?" the boy asked, shaking his head as if she were a five-year-old girl, "You have no idea."

She couldn't control it any longer and laughed. It made her feel wonderfully light-headed and wrenchingly guilty.

The boy looked at her as though she had gone crazy.

"So where do you want to go? School or home?" she asked after controlling her laughter.

He pulled the straps of his bag onto his shoulders, his bloodied chin jutting out defiantly.

"I am not a baby," he said, "I can decide on my own."

"You sure can. I think someone who can fight the recession by taking the trains is very wise indeed," she said and laughed again. The light-headedness returned; the guilt didn't.

He fidgeted around a little and then looked at her. It was as if the boy recognized a certain desperation in her laughter and smiled back. And after a few moments, he joined in her laughter.

"So there," she said as they stopped the taxi in front of the school, "Promise me to take the school bus in the evening now that you have made me travel by taxi, something I didn't want to do today."

"Why didn't you want to take the taxi?" he asked.

She wondered if he would understand. Perhaps not; her reasons for saving money were not as simple as his.

"Because I am saving money, but not because of the recession," she said. The kid smiled with lovable embarrassment. He had hardly said anything through their ride from the clinic to the school.

"For what, then?"

"Because . . . I just felt like doing so," she said.

The boy nodded, as though he understood her, and stepped out of the taxi .He looked at her through the window of the taxi, without bending. He was a short child.

"Go on, then," she said pointing at the school.

"All the best," he said.

"What?"

"All the best," he said and walked away from her.

She leaned back on the seat as the taxi turned back to take her to the lawyers' office and wondered what the boy had meant when he said that. Why would he say 'all the best' to her? What was his name? Aryan, right. She thought it was a sweet name.

It was that day of the year when Rana had to do the most humiliating thing in his life. This was the day when he had to go to the offices of his family's lawyers to give an account of his activities during the past year. The leech-like lawyers reviewed every penny he had spent in the year, as though it was their money he was splurging. It was his family's money and he wasn't splurging any of it.

He was sitting in front of the most annoying lawyer in the offices of Lakhani and Shah.

"Hmm," the fat bastard Lakhani said and leaned back on his chair, as though he were about to pass judgment on Rana's fate and would enjoy doing so. Rana hated the damned lawyers. All of them need to be stood in a row and shot one at a time.

"So Ranasahab, how is your writing going on?" the corpulent son of a bitch said.

"Fine," Rana had decided to answer everything in monosyllables. The last time their argument had escalated into such a violent quarrel that he had lunged across the mahogany table to hit the moron. Lakhani had screamed like a little girl, calling his brothers in arms. The black-coated clowns had restrained Rana, after which he had stormed out of the office.

The family wanted him to apologize. He had refused. His trust allowance was cut by twenty percent the next day.

The lawyer smiled, as though he understood the course of action Rana had decided to adopt. Lakhani's little Hitler moustache was quite strange. It had hair pointing straight ahead rather than downwards, like a black toothbrush. The man sweated as though sitting on the cushioned chair in the air-conditioned office built on the vast sums of money taken from his family was hard work. He spoke in wheezy sighs, which added to the anger Rana felt towards the lawyers.

"Apparently, your expenses are on the rise, Ranasahab."

The tone in which he said *sahab* was such as though he actually wanted to say freeloader. Rana felt like punching him on his double chin.

"So?"

"So, nothing. It's just an observation. You are very close, though. Very, very close. I would suggest not increasing your expenses any further."

When Rana said nothing, the stinking heap of lard chuckled and said, "Do you still frequent those expensive discos and bars? Alcoholism is a problem, you know. A disease."

Rana took a deep breath and said, "Done?"

"Yes," the lawyer got back to his paperwork as though Rana had merely been an irritating distraction.

Rana got up and got out of Lakhani's cabin.

He was wondering how to deal with his writer's block when he saw her. She walked into the lobby, as though she was in some kind of a trance. Her eyes had the kind of haunted look he had seen in someone else's eyes forty years ago. It was as if he was looking at the doppelganger of someone who had been the only true love of his life.

She spoke to the receptionist as Rana looked on. The receptionist told her to go in his direction. He thought he couldn't move. He watched as she walked towards him, her eyes not even registering his presence. She walked past him, opened the door of Lakhani's cabin, and disappeared inside. He thought he was going to faint and clung to a table nearby to stop himself from collapsing.

It can't be.

Aryan wondered what had possessed him to say something like that. All the best? It had seemed to be the right thing to say at that moment. This habit of his—of blurting out the first thing that came to mind—had caused much annoyance and awkwardness in the past. He recalled the time when the history teacher had asked the class to name the greatest moment in India's history and he had said "cheap mobile phones", when the right answer was "Independence". The frustrating thing was, he knew the right answer. But the "cheap mobile phones" response felt most appropriate at that time and he had ended up blurting it out. The history teacher hadn't liked it one bit.

When Aryan reached home in the evening, his father was sitting in front of the muted television, watching a cricket match with glazed eyes. Mom called it his 'hate-this-life' mood. He had a glass in his hand and a cigarette was stuck to his lower lip. Aryan thought the cigarette had extinguished midway and his father hadn't even realized it, as in many times in the past. The ashtray on the table was overflowing with cigarette butts.

"Hello, Papa," he said, bracing himself for the questions about the wound.

"Hey champ," his father said without taking his eyes off the television. "Your mother will be a bit late today. Some bigshot's reception," he said with a snort.

His father had a sarcastic smile on his face. Aryan thought of telling him that Mom was telling the truth, that she was responsible for cooking for the reception of Norway's visiting Prime Minister, but thought better of it. He walked into his room, grateful that he didn't have to answer any questions. His father had never asked him any questions of late, certainly not any in the last one year. Aryan didn't like the word *champ.* Aryan Gagan Khosla wasn't a champ in anything.

The wound had swelled up under the bandage and was truly hurting now, although, he had kind of liked to have it. Everyone in the class had looked at him when he had walked in, including the girls. His bench mate Sanjay had stared at him in awe. When Sanjay had harassed him for the details, all he had said was he had got into a scuffle. It made him sound mysterious and mean. Technically, he had been right. Sanjay had looked at him with narrowed eyes and had called him a lying pansy. Aryan had stuck to his story.

*All the best?*

He was sure she had thought of him as a nutcase. And what was her name? He had forgotten to ask her name! Of the hundreds of people on the station platform, she had helped him get back on his feet and he hadn't had the basic manners to ask her name and thank her properly. He wondered if he would ever meet her again. Didn't she say she lived very near to his school? Or had he heard it wrong, considering how entranced he had been with her?

When the pain woke him up in the night, he thought of getting a glass of water. He saw light in the living room and decided to have a peek. His mother was sitting on the lounge chair, staring vacantly at the ceiling.

"Come out, I know you are there," she said.

He stepped into the living room.

When she saw the bandage on his face, she rushed to him and held his face in her hands.

"What happened? Did anyone hurt you?" she demanded.

"No, I fell," he said.

"Fell? Why do you lie to me, Aryan? Remember the bond?" Her voice was louder, almost intimidating.

Of course, he did remember the bond. He wanted to tell her that she had forgotten it. It was a promise they had made to tell each other everything when he was seven years old. He had always honoured the promise till a few months ago, when he started visiting Sakhu-mai. She had never done so. But it was she who always reminded him of it.

"I do," he said.

"Why didn't you call me at work?"

He hadn't called her because there was no way he would've reached her in the kitchen. Once, many months ago, he had accompanied her to the hotel's restaurant. The massive din and the sheer frenzy in the kitchen had been scary. The chefs weren't allowed to carry their mobiles there (his mother's own diktat). And even if they were allowed to, he was sure they wouldn't be able to hear the ringtones with so much noise in there. Sometimes he wondered what would happen if he was dying and everyone was trying to reach his mother. She would be cooking a salmon dish while he was taking his last breath.

"I am sorry," he said.

"Is it hurting?" she said.

He shook his head to say no. It was hurting badly.

"Did your father see you?" she said.

He wished the interrogation would end and she would head off to bed. It had been a stupid mistake to walk into the living room. Her brow was deeply furrowed and she was actually speaking through clenched teeth. All these were very bad signs. It would mean a massive showdown between his parents and he would be the reason for it, something he had managed not to be for a long time.

"Invoke the bond," he said.

It meant she had to do what he wanted, no questions asked. That had been the rule, and she had used it almost every time. It would be perhaps his first in the last year.

She twisted her lips. Perhaps she knew what he wanted very well.

"Don't ask Papa about it, please," he said.

She kneeled down in front of him and touched her forehead to his (she was an extremely tall woman, everyone in her family had been—tall and beautiful).

"Sometimes I wonder if we deserve you. If *I* deserve you," she said.

He said nothing.

## Chapter 4

# A Prayer for the Three

When Ria stepped out of the law offices of Lakhani and Shah, she looked at the old, distinguished looking man, who was staring at her as though he had seen a ghost. Eighteen months ago, she had been in the stare-worthy category. Those eighteen months had aged her in decades.

She thought it wasn't as bad as she had feared it would be. A boy and an old man had stared at her throughout the day. It meant she was holding on. At least, it wasn't obvious that she was a walking suicide. She would need every ounce of that strength for the next sixty days. Although melodrama had been an integral part of her scripts, she didn't want any of it in the last days of her life.

"Excuse me," the old man said, as she had expected he would. She was forever labelled a buddha-magnet by all her friends. For some unknown reason, she had always managed to attract the attention of older men.

She paused and looked at the man.

"Are you, by any chance, related to Nina Kumar?" he said.

She thought there was a childlike hope in his eyes, as if he desperately wanted her to be related to Nina Kumar. She knew she would've loved to be, only if to continue seeing the twinkle in his eyes.

"Sorry," she said and smiled, "Never heard that name."

His smile faded and was replaced by a look of sad disbelief.

"Who is she?" she couldn't help asking, but wondered why she did so.

"She was . . . well, never mind," he said in a pained voice.

Ria knew the man wanted to tell her more. And he would've if she had asked him to go on. But she didn't. No melodrama at the end. She started walking ahead.

"It's a miracle," she heard the man say. "I can't believe you could look like that."

She turned back, feeling slightly irritated, believing the man was trying to hit on her. A familiar wave of dislike rose up her spine, the kind she had when men resorted to desperate measures, like telling her that she looked exactly like their grandmothers. She was about to say something nasty to the old man, when, perhaps sensing her intention, he raised his hand in a gesture of surrender and pulled out his wallet. He fished out what was an old photograph and gave it to her.

It was a picture of a much younger version of the man. The same aquiline nose and sad but striking eyes. Although he hadn't changed much, apart from the salt and pepper beard, and a few lines on his large forehead.

But she couldn't speak when she saw the woman with him in the photograph and she understood the emotions on the man's face. It was a miracle, as the woman smiling in the photograph looked exactly like her.

Ria looked at it for a long time, trying to find a feature that would make the woman in the picture distinct from her. When she couldn't find any, she looked up at the man who had a distant, faraway look in his eyes. She mutely returned the photograph to him, turned around and started walking away.

Rana felt a physical pain in his heart as she walked away. It had to be some cruel joke. Why else would he come across a woman who looked, talked and even walked like Nina? She even had the same heartbreaking dimples when she smiled. He closed his eyes and took a deep breath, believing he was having a hallucination. When he was going to open his eyes, she would be gone, if she even existed in the first place. She still hadn't found a taxi when he opened his eyes.

For one frightening moment he had thought of running after her, calling her Nina and holding her hand. To touch her, just to ascertain if his body, too, thought she was Nina. But that scary moment had passed, and thankfully she had found a taxi.

He watched as she opened the door of the cab, got in, spoke to the driver and determinedly looked ahead, as though she had decided to get away from him. He had surely frightened her. It would've scared the hell out of him had someone done that to him. Maybe it was better this way. She was going away, never to be seen again. Perhaps he would remember this incident as a strange anomaly, something he wouldn't believe happened after a few days.

But he had seen her dimples. He had seen her eyes. And they were Nina's.

He would never forget her. Now, two people would haunt him forever who looked exactly the same—the first, his dead love; the other, a complete stranger.

In the calm of the night, he sat in front of his computer staring at the blank document for hours. The ability to put words together had deserted him. The little voice in his head that could tell stories was mute. His body shook every few minutes; a state he was in for weeks after Nina's death. That was when he thought there was nothing left in his life worth living for. A whole life without her had seemed so very incomprehensible.

He had come out of it. Sometimes he had wondered if he had come out of it too soon. He had just snapped out of it, and had never paused to think what Nina's death did to him. At least, not in the way she deserved. He had told her she was the one, hadn't he? Although she had called it cheesy, laughed and told him that if she died the next day, he would fall for the first beautiful woman on the street. He had been very offended then, but he had done what she had expected him to do–fallen for the first beautiful woman he saw on the street—not literally, but in spirit—with disastrous results.

Hours later, he could neither stop shivering, nor could he write a word.

In the early hours of the morning, as the rising sun lit up the eastern sky, he knew what he had to do.

"I have taken a day off today," Aryan's mother said as she handed him a cup of chocolate milk in the kitchen, "and I want you to take a day off too!"

Aryan thought she looked as if she hadn't slept the whole night. He hated the stupid wound for that. She had no make-up on her face and she wore a very loose orange dress. These were all very bad signs. It meant only one thing.

"We are going to Jaya's today!"

Aryan wanted to smile but the wound and the prospect of another visit to Jaya's meant he couldn't. Jaya *mata,* the woman who called herself the mother of the entire world, was his mother's spiritual guru.

"Look a bit more enthusiastic, young man," his mother said with her arms folded.

"I am very enthusiastic," he said. He would gladly have another face-off with Samar and his Rebels rather than go to Jaya's.

"That's not possible," she said with a sarcastic smile, "because your face doesn't say so."

"I might've a surprise test today in the school," he tried.

"I will talk to your teacher, don't worry," she said.

The last time she had talked to his teacher was three years ago.

"The wound is hurting a little," he tried again.

"That's why we are going to the doctor's first and then to Jaya's, though I think she can cure everything. What do you think?"

"Okay," he said.

She shook her head in exasperation and said, "Aryan, all I am asking you to do is come with me to my guru's place. And you are making such a big fuss about it."

"Sorry, Mom," he said, "I will come."

When they reached Jaya's, there was already a big crowd—perhaps two hundred people—in the hall of her *Dhyan and Prarthana Sthan,* her Hall of Meditation and Prayer.

They had gone to the hospital to get a dressing for his wound from a doctor who was his mother's patron at the restaurant. Incredibly, the wound was hurting even more after that. Aryan had thought the doctor was more interested in showing off his knowledge of cooking than in treating his wound. He hadn't liked the way the doctor touched his mother's hand or shoulder every now and then. Men generally did that to her, especially at those big parties his parents took him to.

"Oh ho! Look who is here today after a very long time! The little prince and the queen," Jaya said.

She was a big corpulent woman who was famous for two things—kissing the people who visited the centre anywhere on the face (she had proclaimed her lips were the fastest route to Nirvana) and being extremely cheerful. And for some unknown reason, she always called him 'prince'.

"*Pranaam,* Jaya*ji,*" he said with folded hands and touched her feet. She grabbed him with surprising force and planted a wet kiss on his cheek. He desperately tried to not rub it.

"Jaya, Mata," his mother said as she, too, folded her hands and touched Jaya's feet. Aryan thought Jaya always liked it when someone called her Mata.

"We are in trouble, Mata," his mother said with tears in her eyes.

"Sheila, there are no troubles in the world. They are only there in your mind," Jaya said leaning back on a big, drum-shaped pillow. She was sitting on the softest of the mattresses on the floor. Aryan thought she looked like a big fat whale sunbathing on the beach. *You should respect your elders,* he said to himself in order to stop bursting out into laughter, or more damningly, stop himself from actually saying it in front of so many of her maniacal followers.

"I and my son are drifting apart. We don't talk to each other the way we used to. I no longer know what he thinks. He closets himself in his room. God knows what he does in there."

Aryan was dumbfounded. He had no idea his mother would embarrass him like that in front of so many people. He looked at the followers who were supposed to be deep in prayer, but were eagerly listening to the conversation between Jaya and his mother. Many of them had knowing smiles on their faces. Aryan just wanted to disappear into thin air. He wanted to at least tell them it wasn't exactly what they were thinking.

"He is embarking on his own spiritual journey, Sheila. I see a deep awakening of an ancient soul in this boy," she said.

"Oh, Mata! Does that mean I can no longer talk to my boy?"

"You can. And you will. Just give him some time. Let him be," she said, "the Almighty is watching both of you. Now come, pray with us."

"Come, Aryan," his mother pointed him towards a few empty places and they sat on the cold marble floor. He had always wondered, *if Mata can sit on such a cosy cushion, why should her followers sit on the floor?*

The next person who spoke to Jaya was a cancer patient, who started crying when Jaya said her name loudly. Jaya kissed her on the lips and hugged her fiercely. Aryan thought his mother had taken a lot of Mata's time by telling her about her inane problem when there were people with such tragedies in life. He wondered, for possibly a hundredth time, if he should tell Jaya about Sakhu-mai. He had a feeling Jaya wouldn't be able to help her. What she needed was good medical care, which cost a lot of money. Creating money out of thin air wasn't one of Jaya's many documented miracles.

"What happened to you? Why are you making that face?" his mother whispered.

"Can we go now?" he said.

"No, we need to pray and find the emotional connection. Didn't you just hear what Mata said?"

"Can't we pray at home?"

"Can't we do this? Can't we do that? I am so tired of your attitude, Aryan. All it takes is closing your eyes and finding peace within. Is that so difficult for you to do?" she hissed.

"No," he said.

"Well, do it then!" she said, closed her eyes tightly and began humming the prayer Jaya had authored for all her devotees. The prayer portrayed Jaya as the reincarnation of Goddess Durga and how one's problems disappeared when they prayed to her. Aryan had tried to learn the prayer, but had never managed to.

Every time he closed his eyes he thought people were snickering at him. Ancient soul? What did that mean?

"I worry about my sister a lot, Mata," a woman said to Jaya.

Jaya got into a long monologue about worry and how pointless it was and its evils. It didn't seem to have satisfied the woman. Finally, Jaya asked her to bring her sister to the Sthan, which the woman said was not possible because her sister wasn't a follower. She added that she feared for her sister's mental condition as she had suffered a terrible tragedy eighteen months ago. Aryan had seen Jaya regularly bless the photographs of people her followers brought with them. The woman took out a picture and handed it to Jaya, who raised it high in the air.

"Everyone," she said, "please pray for our sister here. She is suffering right now."

Aryan was stunned when he looked at the picture. It was that of the woman who had helped him at the railway station.

## Chapter 5

# Three Coincidences

When Ria reached home, she felt as though she had run all the way back. Her legs gave way the moment she opened the door of the flat and she collapsed on the sofa like a deflated doll. She couldn't understand why she had acted the way she did. There was no real reason to get involved with the boy and with the old man. The lawyers had agreed to create a charity using the money she had saved. The buggers hadn't even paused and asked her why she wanted to do it. She had to take care of two more things in the list, and then she would be ready for her final goodbye. Had she set too long a deadline? The lawyers had said they would get everything sorted out in a couple of weeks. She was sure the house wouldn't take more than three weeks to clean, even if she wanted to dust and scrub every single nook and cranny. The library would be open at nine in the morning the next day to accept their books. So, could she make the deadline more reasonable? Say, one month? The word deadline couldn't be more apt. She smiled at that thought. So many smiles in such a short span were bizarre.

As if on cue, to balance it, she got a call from her sister. She had switched on the mobile phone after a long time, hoping the lawyers would call her and tell her it was all done.

"Hello," she said.

"Why are you doing this to me? You have cut everyone off. Are you discarding me, too, now?" She heard her sister's voice, which was like her own. Everyone had told the two sisters that they sounded exactly the same. But that's where the similarities ended. Anju was a total fantasist, and as their parents had said, a little empty-headed.

When Ria did not reply, she heard Anju say, "You and I are the only family left now, aren't we?"

It would've sounded terribly nasty had someone else said it. But such subtleties escaped Anju.

"Uh-huh," Ria said, biting back some angry words. What she said had no effect on Anju.

"We prayed for you today," Anju said, as though she had pulled off a grand coup.

"Oh," Ria said.

"All two hundred of us. Mata prayed for you, especially. She called you a sister! Would you believe that? She has rarely done that to anyone. She kissed your photograph, too!"

"That's nice," Ria said grimacing.

"Why that tone, Chimni?" Anju said, using Ria's childhood nickname. It meant a sparrow in Marathi. Her father used to say Ria looked as cute as a sparrow. She had never understood that because she had never thought she was cute and neither did she think she resembled the little bird. The name had stuck for a while in her childhood. She had fought a long and hard battle to get rid of it. The only living person who dared call her that was her big sister, and Anju never quite understood her younger sister's dislike for such a "pretty nickname".

Ria wondered if she was being needlessly rude to Anju. Her sister hadn't changed for thirty-six years and she wasn't going to change ever. Anju was doing right by the only person in the world she could call family. They were inseparable when they were children, with Anju taking her role of elder sister a little too seriously. Nobody had dared to hassle Ria in the school because Anju was the biggest bully. There were times when she had beaten up boys older than her because they had the audacity to trouble her Chimni. Although Anju was responsible for Ria learning many things she shouldn't have so early in her life, she truly loved Ria. Anju was always on the verge of becoming unbearable; but Ria knew Anju would kill and die for her.

"Tai, thank you for asking Mata to pray for me," she said, calling her elder sister.

"You are welcome! You will see how the power of two hundred people praying for your well-being works for you now. You are going to have a very good time very soon," Anju said.

"Great," Ria said mustering as much fake enthusiasm as possible. She was sure Anju wouldn't know the difference. Ria felt a sudden pang of sadness imagining how her Tai would react after her death. Anju would weep and wail; she would truly be the only one left of the family after Ria was gone.

"I love you, Tai," Ria said.

"Me too," Anju said, "Anyway, how do you know Sheila Khosla's son? Are you writing a cookery-based show script?"

"Who?" Ria asked.

"The celebrity chef, Sheila Khosla," she said.

"I don't know her."

"Her son knows you. He was most curious to know what happened to you and was asking me many questions. Even asked me where you lived. Cute kid, a little sad-looking, though. When I asked him how he knew you, he buttoned up. Interesting. Had a big bandage on his chin," Anju said.

Ria closed her eyes and wondered what was going on. How could this kid (what was his name...Aryan, right?) meet her and her sister within twenty-four hours?

*All the best.*

"I helped him when he fell out of the local train yesterday, Tai. I didn't know who he was. Did you give him my address?" Ria said.

"Uh-huh. That's not what he seems to have told his mother about the injury. He is just a kid! It's not as if he is going to stalk you or something if I gave him your address. And what were you doing at a train station?" Anju asked. She had an unhealthy and intrusive interest in the little details of people's lives. Many years ago, she had eagerly handed over Ria's mobile number to a young actor who had harassed Ria for many days. So much so, that Ria had to threaten him with police intervention if he didn't stop stalking her. Incredibly, the young actor had graduated from television shows and was the current Bollywood heartthrob. Ria had screamed at Anju for sharing her mobile number. Her sister had never stopped pointing out that the actor was immensely popular and so cute.

"Oh, Anju . . . I need to go. I will talk to you later," Ria said.

"Hey! Wait, when are you coming to my place. . .?"

Ria didn't allow her to complete what she was saying and disconnected the phone. She switched it off, lest Anju call her back.

This was unbelievable. She was actually worrying about the kid lying to his mother. What prompted the son of a big-shot celebrity chef, who was the current television darling, to start worrying about recession? And why was she getting worked up about it all? Kids fall all the time and get injured. She felt like crying at that thought. Perhaps there was a little bit of her sister in her too—that callousness.

The woman she saw in the photograph the old man carried with him was dead. She had seen it in the man's eyes. The woman had died very soon after the photograph was taken. Ria hugged herself tightly. She felt irrationally jealous of the woman. There was a man who carried her photograph in his wallet and her image in his heart for decades after she was gone. She had a feeling that the old man wasn't the only one haunted by the woman's death. There were several people who still remembered her. In a way, she was still alive. There was no one who would remember her like that. Anju would, but she was a survivor, what with her impressive record of countless flings and two divorces. So she would move on. Who else? The producers who had ceased calling her the moment she told them she wouldn't be able to write any new scripts? No. The television and film actors who had become household names thanks to her dialogues, and who had started thanking a different scriptwriter in their interviews? No. She had never hogged the cameras and so was sure the general public didn't even know who she was. There are not too many scriptwriters as famous as Salim-Javed in the last fifty years.

To cut a long story short, she wouldn't haunt anyone's memories like the woman in the photograph did. The one man she had thought would've never forgotten her was dead. He had had an easy way out, that cheating bastard.

Maybe it was better this way. When you are gone, there ought to be no trace of you. Why should anyone suffer because you decided it was time to let go?

Rana fidgeted as he waited in front of his least favourite place in the city: the offices of Lakhani and Shah, Attorneys. It would've been unthinkable a day ago that he would return to this lair of fools twice in two days. But there was no other way to find the woman he had met here. He hadn't slept the whole night wondering how he could get her contact details without these wolves becoming suspicious of him. After all, he was an old man asking about a young beautiful woman. His kind of an old man. He already felt like a creep, trying to surreptitiously find out about her. What if these guys don't tell him anything about her, but let her know that a man was asking around? Lakhani would surely add his own vile adjectives to it. Would it be a slimy old man or a dirty old man or a womanizing horny old man? She would surely get her guard up. She might even tell the lawyers that she had already been harassed by him. The fat bastard Lakhani would have a Cheshire cat grin on his face and wouldn't wait for a moment before he called up the bloody family and let them know details of his latest escapade with heaps of garnishing, and give them something new and nasty to say about him. He shook his head. There was no point in imagining the what ifs? Either he tried to find out about her or sat in front of the damned computer to lose his sanity.

He touched the wallet in his pocket, which had Nina's picture in it. It felt reassuring, as though he had asked Nina about it and she had said it was the right thing to do. Nobody else mattered, anyway.

The only person whom Rana didn't loathe was Lakhani's secretary. She was in love with him. She had been in love with him for the last twenty years. Twenty years ago, she had told him his books had been her constant companions. That was a time when the Detective Dev Chakravarthy novels were a rage. The elder Jain's plan to reduce the price of the books below fifty rupees had worked wonders and the books flew off the shelves in the bookstores. The women had loved those novels. And he had loved the women.

Madhu, Lakhani's secretary, no longer the curvaceous woman she had once been, stepped out at one every afternoon for her lunch. A hundred metres from the office, there was a little Udupi restaurant where she religiously gulped sambar-rice. He hoped she would follow her routine that day too. If Lakhani's secretary refused to tell him, he had no other way to find out. No plan B, as the detective in his novels, Detective Dev Chakravarthy, usually said to his side-kick, Inspector Lamba.

She did step out at exactly one and headed towards the Udupi restaurant.

"Hello, beautiful," he said as she was about to gulp her first morsel.

She looked up from behind the mound of gooey rice on the spoon.

"What are you doing here?" she asked, angrily.

He thought she sounded more annoyed than surprised to see him. She *did* love him still, didn't she?

"I just thought I would sit with you and have some lunch," he said, smiling as sweetly as possible. This was something Dev Chakravarthy did frequently with women.

"I don't have time for this," she said, frowning and twisting her lips.

"Oh come on, there is an empty chair in front of you and as far as I can see, nobody is sitting in it," he said, continuing to smile.

"You have some gall to talk like that to me," she said, "Get the hell out of here now before I scream and call the people around to get you beaten up."

He knew she loved him. All this was a façade to tease him, make him grovel a little.

"Darling..." he couldn't complete his sentence, as she got up, muttering an expletive under her breath, picked up her purse and started walking out of the restaurant.

"Hey, Madhu, wait," he said and ran after her.

"Stop following me, you selfish son of a bitch! I almost lost my job because of you five years ago," she said.

Was it five years ago? It seemed a lot less than that when he had convinced her to get an inside view into what his family said to Lakhani about him. She had told him and he had, of course, used it. It struck him suddenly that he had never bothered to talk to her properly after that, barely acknowledging her whenever he walked into the lawyers' office.

"It helped me a lot, Madhu," he said. She had told him his brother was planning to claim the house in which Rana stayed. Rana had quickly put a legal trap in place, which made it impossible for his greedy brother to stake a claim.

"And then you act as if you don't even know me! I risked everything for you," she said, as she turned around and walked away.

Five years ago, she had been forty, recently widowed and vulnerable. Now she was just bitter. He almost wanted to tell her that she, too, had used him then. Why else would she come to his flat every night? She needed to vent her grief and he was available. Why did she think there should have been some kind of denouement for their relationship? What did she expect? Flowers every week?

"I am sorry," he said catching up with her, "I didn't think it had been that long."

"I don't want to talk to you," she said.

"All I want is one small thing," he said.

She shook her head, her lips drawn in a tight line, a drop of sweat nestled on the tip of her nose.

They were very close to the lawyers' offices. It was now or never.

"I am dying, Madhu," he said

That stopped her. She looked at him out of breath.

"What?" her voice was slightly wheezy.

"I am dying. And there is nothing I can do about that," he said.

She looked at him with narrowed eyes and said, "Liar."

"There was a woman who came in to meet Lakhani

yesterday. I just need her contact details," he said, "She could actually save me."

"This is nonsense. You think I am a fool?"

"No. But it's the truth, Madhu," he said quietly, "And I am desperate."

She looked at the office, looked back at him and said, "You promise never to trouble me again?"

"I promise," he said, meaning it.

"I will call you and give the details to you," she said and walked away.

He knew she would and she did.

After school got over, Aryan stepped out on the road, and instead of getting in the car to go home, he started walking on the footpath. He knew Jeevan, the driver, would wait for a while for him and would simply turn back. It wasn't the first time he had avoided going home right after school. In the last three months, he had visited Sakhu-mai so many times, but Jeevan hadn't bothered to report this to his parents. It was an unspoken pact between them—Jeevan got to laze around and use the car, and Aryan didn't have to tell him what he did.

He hoped he would be able to find Ms Ria's house. He had run after the crazy-looking lady who was Ms Ria's sister at the Sthan yesterday. She had looked at him with deep suspicion when he told her that he knew her sister, but didn't know her name. The lady had asked him so many questions in such a short time that he had felt as if he was in a viva voce. His mother hadn't stepped out of the Sthan immediately, perhaps a little stunned by the abrupt manner in which he had run after Ms Anju. He had known she wouldn't do that in front of so many people chanting Mata's name. It had given him enough time to ask the woman for Ms Ria's address. His mother had admonished him and apologized to the woman. The woman had recognized his mother and sought her autograph. Aryan knew his mother always loved giving away autographs and that had helped reduce her anger at him.

Ms Ria's sister couldn't have been more different. She looked a little like a witch, with her grey, cat-like eyes and sallow cheeks. She made him think of a naughty witch who was always up to some mischief. When he had asked his mother why Ms Anju's cheeks were so sallow, she had said perhaps she smoked a lot. Then, she had said, that was beside the point. His mother wanted to know what he was thinking when he had bolted out of the Sthan hall, running after the wild-haired woman.

Now that Aryan thought about it, he knew it must've looked a little weird. It would have done nothing to help his already growing reputation of being a little nutcase. Not a harmful weirdo, like they showed in the movies–all chained up in a mental hospital or carrying a chainsaw—but the kind of weirdo you can laugh at.

His mother had refused to talk to him for the rest of the journey home, which was fine with him, considering how angry she had been. He had wanted to tell her she had embarrassed him far more. She had opened the door of the house and walked into her bedroom. Fifteen minutes later, she had stepped out, all decked up. She had told him she was heading for work, as he had managed to ruin any peace she was going to find that day. He had shrugged.

He was wondering what he would say to Ms Ria when he met her, when he felt a tap on his shoulder.

"Always lost in thought," Samar said to him.

Now this was embarrassing. Even his bench-mate Sanjay would have had the wits not to repeat the same mistake twice, when he was under constant threat from the Rebels. He wondered when he would break the habit of wandering around, his mind lost in thought. Maybe he should have used the car after all.

"Where is my assignment?" Samar demanded, uttering each word as if he was chewing them.

"Sorry Samar. Couldn't do it today either," Aryan said pathetically, bracing himself for a blow.

Samar raised his hand. Aryan flinched. When the blow didn't land, the boys started laughing at him.

"Tomorrow the assignment is due, Ponchu. I want to see it in my hands before the prayer starts. It's an option you can't refuse," Samar said.

Aryan was almost tempted to tell him that the *Godfather* dialogue didn't fit, but said nothing.

When the boys left him, he resumed his walk. He had to make a choice between doing Samar's assignment and finding Ms Ria's house. Doing Samar's homework meant freedom from the idiot for at least a week. What was he going to do after he found Ms Ria's house? Perhaps he would ring the bell, tell her he forgot to say thank you the other day. And then what? Perhaps he would say he meant absolutely nothing when he had wished her "all the best".

He decided to find her house.

Her sister had told him she lived in a flat in the Chiraag Building Society. It wasn't too difficult to find. It was a collection of buildings that were as grey as the sky above. He walked inside the gate of the building society where a security guard was yawning. The guard abruptly stopped his grotesque display of the innards of his mouth and looked at him with narrowed eyes. Aryan walked inside the building with his head down. He had learnt that sometimes the head-down-lost-in-thought walk had its advantages. The guard didn't stop him.

He walked to the basement of the building. There were a few steps that led to a rather grimy looking lift.

A man with a salt-and-pepper beard was waiting for the lift. Aryan stood next to him, still in his lost-in-thoughts pose.

The lift arrived. The man opened the double door and got into the tiny box. Aryan hesitated for a moment, wondering if he should get in with the old man or not. What if the man was a resident of the building and asked him who he was?

The man was looking at him with a small frown on his face. He had a very sophisticated look. Aryan thought he would be either the principal of an engineering college or a scientist.

The man nodded for him to step in. Aryan did.

"Which floor?" the man asked, after the lift had started its ascent.

"Umm...six," he said.

The man pressed a button with the number six on it with a slightly surprised expression. He didn't press any other button. Aryan knew he was in trouble. If the man lived on the sixth floor, he would surely be wondering who this boy in a school uniform was. Aryan frantically thought of an excuse but none came to mind. Should he tell the man that he actually wanted to go to the seventh floor? That would make him sound like a suspicious character. When he couldn't think of any excuses, he decided to face whatever came his way. The man now stared ahead, as if Aryan had never been there. The lift moved at an agonizing crawl, increasing the anxiety Aryan felt in his stomach.

When the lift stopped, Aryan stepped out quickly, hoping the man would press the button for another floor. But the man followed him out.

Ms Ria's sister had told him that Ms Ria lived in flat 6B. He stole a glance at the man, wondering if he would walk towards any other door.

Frighteningly, the man followed him and now, they both stood in front of 6B.

The frown had disappeared from the man's face. Aryan thought the man was just as unsure as he was. He had deep lines on his forehead as he stared at Aryan. If ever there was an opportunity to walk away, this was it. Aryan couldn't decide what to do. Like a fool, he stood in front of the door. And the man stood beside him.

The clock ticked along in Aryan's head, something he was used to imagining when attending mind-numbing classes in school. They must've stood there for at least a minute. After which, the man gave a tiny shrug and pressed the door bell.

Nobody opened the door.

The man pressed the bell again. Aryan heard the bell ring inside the house.

When the door was flung open, Ms Ria stood in front of them with a look of shock on her face.

## Chapter 6

# The Circle is Formed

Ria was utterly speechless, in the truest sense of the word. The old man and the boy were standing outside her door, together.

For a long moment, both her visitors were silent. Finally, the old man cleared his throat and asked, "May I come in?"

She nodded like an automaton as they stepped inside her house.

"I just wanted to thank you, Ms Ria, for the other day," the boy said hurriedly as though he had been battling with those words, trying to find the best way to say them, but when the moment came, he just blurted them out.

"And you have a nice house. Very clean and tidy. And very airy and bright too," he continued.

She saw the old man look at the boy with an extremely irritated expression, as though he could've done without him underfoot.

His name was Aryan. Right. *All the best.*

"I am Aryan, by the way, if you have forgotten my name," he said to her and then looked at the old man, "Aryan Khosla. I study in Sacred Hearts' School. Class Seven, section B."

An awkward silence settled for a few moments, after the boy had finished speaking.

"I am making coffee; would you two like to have some?" she asked, just to break the silence.

"Sure! Though I generally drink hot chocolate," the boy said and looked at her guiltily. The last time she had seen him, he hadn't spoken more than a few words. Now, it seemed he couldn't stop himself.

"I don't have any," she said.

Perhaps the boy sensed something in her voice. The old man, too. She turned around and walked quickly to the kitchen, hiding her eyes from them.

"Do sit down, please," she requested, with her back to them.

The kitchen of her flat, unlike all other flats in the society building, had a little window into the living room. When they had bought it, Raj had said it made the flat unique, as if it was designed just for them. That's the way he was, someone who could look at mundane things and find deeper meaning in them. Where he had found uniqueness in the window, she had found impracticality and inconvenience. Everyone would see me doing things in the kitchen, she had said. You move like a danseuse in the kitchen, Raj had said.

She knew the old man and the boy were looking at her, and wished a millionth time that the window wasn't there.

They patiently sat through her ritual of making coffee. Three cupfuls of milk, three spoons coffee, six spoons sugar, three minutes of heating, thirty seconds of stirring, no water. She wondered if they were observing each move. What were they thinking? And why did she give a damn? She decided to give them the coffee and nicely ask them to leave and then never step out of the house again.

The larger coffee tray was tucked in the back of a cabinet. It wasn't intended to be used ever. Now, she had to pull it out. It hadn't gathered dust, of course. She had cleaned it every third day of the week, when she cleaned the kitchen. The first day, she cleaned the living room and on the second, the bedrooms.

When she knew she couldn't hide inside the kitchen forever, she poured the coffee into three mugs and placed them equidistant from each other. She picked up the tray and walked out.

The old man and the boy hadn't spoken to each other, but she thought there was an obvious hostility between them. It was as if each had made some plans and now those plans were messed up because of the other's presence. She had no idea what those plans were and had no wish to learn more.

She mutely handed them a coffee mug each and they started sipping in silence. As she sipped at her coffee, she began planning how to politely ask them to leave as she had other things to do, like planning her suicide.

"I am sorry to barge in like this," the old man said and put the mug on the coffee table, "but I need to talk to you about something very important."

He looked pointedly at the boy, as though he wanted him to leave. The boy didn't bother even to look at him. Ria felt a headache coming on. She didn't want to be in her own house. Her favourite drink tasted bitter.

"I met your sister," the boy said, "She is nice. But why does she smoke so much? It is not good for her health, you know."

Anju had started smoking? When? It was bizarre considering that one of the biggest reasons of her second divorce (the way Anju said the words, it was as if she was planning to have several more) was her husband's non-stop smoking. She made a mental note to confront her elder sister. Perhaps Anju's legendary double standards had kicked in. But confronting her would mean things would get ugly and noisy. Anju would throw a tantrum, deny it and make horrified sounds. Or worse, she would swoop into her flat, throwing everything into disarray. Ria's headache was becoming unbearable with every passing moment.

The old man cleared his throat loudly. The boy followed suit, making more noise as he did so, as though he understood what the man wanted him to do and wasn't going to give in. The old man gave an exasperated sigh and looked at her.

"I just wanted to talk to you. It wouldn't take long, I promise," he said, "It is a matter of life and death."

She wanted to laugh. Of course, it had to be a matter of life and death. That was the current theme wasn't it? Like the countless soap episodes she had written for the telly. Every ten episodes or so, there was a common theme.

"I am an author, Ms Ria," the man said. Ria sensed a practiced smugness when he said it. "I have written twenty-nine novels. You can Google me. Rana Rathod. You will get countless hits. I also have a very thriving fan base. The reason I am saying all this to you is that I don't want you to think I am some . . . someone unpleasant."

The boy was looking at him as though he didn't believe a word of what the old man had said. Ria had to admit she was a little surprised herself. She had never heard words like 'Google me' and 'countless hits' being uttered by a man as old as he was. The writer used these words with an air of adolescent pride.

The boy giggled.

"Did you just laugh?" the old man asked him indignantly.

The boy was horrified at what he had done. His face was a kaleidoscope of shifting emotion. One moment he knew he had made a mistake and the next, he couldn't stop himself from chuckling again.

"That is very disrespectful. And what is there to laugh about?" the old man demanded to know, squaring his shoulders.

"Sorry," the boy said, a helpless smile still on his lips.

The old man looked at her as though he wanted her to step in and scold the boy. She didn't really know the boy well enough to admonish him, and she admitted to herself, all of it was funny. She was sure Raj would've found it hilarious and would've spun it into one of his scripts.

"Mr Rathod, Aryan. I am sorry, but you will have to leave. I am in the middle of something," she said. It came out brusquely. She almost told them that she had intended it to be a lot nicer.

The old man looked at the boy, his teeth clenched, as though the boy had ruined everything. She thought Aryan was actually feeling a little contrite, as he had never wanted to spoil anything.

"Will you teach me how to make that coffee?" Aryan asked her, "I loved it. I can then, maybe, show it to my mom. She is a big chef, you know. She also has a television programme of her own; *Sheila Khosla, the Commander-in-Chef*, every Thursday at nine. Don't miss it. I never miss it myself. I don't even miss the repeat telecast. She could, maybe, talk about your coffee on the show? Maybe not make it as good as yours, but she will surely make it famous."

Ria rubbed her temples. The two hadn't moved an inch from where they were sitting. She had never learnt how to be nasty. All the stocks of meanness in the family had been hijacked by her sister. She had never been able to tell people off, except, for the woman the other day, of course.

Both started talking together, and then both stopped and looked at each other; the old man angrily, the boy cheekily, and both again spoke at the same time.

"Okay, please stop," she said. The headache was about to split her head open."I will meet you tomorrow evening, Mr Rathod. There is a Barista down the street. Six o'clock. Aryan, I will email you the recipe of the coffee."

"Why can't I come over to learn?" Aryan said in a tone that implied, *He gets to meet you and I don't?*

"Because you have to go to school and your parents would worry about you. You shouldn't even be here right now," she said.

The boy looked as if he was about to cry. She steeled herself from falling for it.

"That's final," she said.

The boy got up sulkily. The old man rose, too, with a little look of triumph on his face.

She saw them to the door. They stepped out. She shut the door behind them.

The three mugs on the coffee table looked a little forlorn.

Rana stood in front of the elevator shaft, waiting for the lift. The boy stood next to him. Rana had to summon every ounce of his willpower to stop himself from smacking the child. He had always disliked children. They were clingy, needy and moody. And now this idiot had almost ruined everything.

"I had thought you would be a scientist or a professor," the boy said to him as though he was disappointed.

"Is that so?" Rana said.

"You look like one. I wouldn't have guessed you were a writer," he said.

"I would prefer it if you keep your mouth shut and your thoughts to yourself."

"What do you write?"

Rana said nothing.

"I haven't told anyone this, but I am a writer too."

"Boy, didn't you hear what I just said? Shut. Your. Mouth!"

"Sorry," the boy said and was quiet till the lift made its reluctant, creaky journey to the sixth floor.

The boy opened the double door and they entered the lift.

"You shouldn't leave school and wander around like this," Rana said.

"The school day was over," the boy said a little defensively, "And my parents wouldn't worry."

"You aren't back home, after what, two hours? And they wouldn't worry? What kind of parents are they?" he said and the moment he said it, he realized it sounded terrible.

"That is disrespectful since you don't know them," the boy said.

Rana didn't reply.

Rana didn't want to listen to the boy any more. He hoped he never met him again. He seemed a little slow, a bit of a dimwit. The way he was rambling on in Ria's house proved it. The lift reached the ground floor. He opened the door and started walking away briskly.

"If I Google you, I will find you, wouldn't I?" the boy called after him.

Rana stopped and turned.

"Yes. Spell my name correctly, though. R-A-N-A space R-A-T-H-O-D," he said and hesitated. But it had become a habit of repeating what he said next, "You can also find me on Facebook, MySpace and Twitter."

"I don't use any of those," the boy said.

"Why?" Rana asked.

The kid shrugged. Rana nodded and raised his hand as a form of goodbye, praying he would never see him again. The boy raised his hand too.

As Rana drove back, he hoped Ria would come to meet him. It was absolutely essential for his thirtieth novel. He had never written a love story before. Dev Chakravarthy did have many affairs in his novels, but that was different. In the early part of his career, he had modelled Dev on Raymond Chandler's Philip Marlowe, but somehow, Dev had outgrown Marlowe very soon, and become a womanizer who had a few conquests in every novel. And by the twenty-ninth novel, was as twisted and pathetic as the antagonists. It had proved to be a successful formula. But somewhere along the way, Dev Chakravarthy had started to look like a caricature rather than a character. Perhaps the readers had sensed it and had drifted away from his books.

Much to his annoyance, Rana couldn't stop thinking about the boy. He had said he didn't use Facebook. What school kid didn't use Facebook? Even his hair was dopey. As if he had stood in front of a mirror and cut it himself. Bloody wierdo. Bloody kids.

When he reached home, Vinny was waiting for him at the door.

"Yo," she said.

"Hey," he said and opened the door.

"I need to show you something," she said, "I think you are going to be thrilled about it."

"Okay," he said. He wanted to tell her that he had had his quota of dealing with kids for the day, but many times Rana got a feeling that Vinny was actually as old as him and not a fourteen-year-old girl.

She switched on his computer. She was more comfortable with each gizmo in his house than Rana was. He had bought many of them after she had told him to do so. Well, 'told him' was putting it nicely. Ordered him was more accurate.

"There is a way to connect all your apps now," she said with a grin.

"As in?"

"You can connect everything—Facebook, Twitter and MySpace on your mobile now!"

That sounded incredible.

"You mean I can update all three via my mobile?"

"Your website too," she said.

When she showed him, he was, as she had said, completely thrilled.

"Isn't that cool?" she said.

"Totally," he said.

"So," she said and got up from his cosy PC chair, pointed at it with her palms, as though she was asking him to sit on his throne, and said, "Enjoy!"

"Thanks," he said sitting on the chair.

"I'll see you later, then," she said and turned.

"Vinny, do you know any kid who doesn't use Facebook?" he asked.

She stopped and turned.

"Yes, a few," she said, "I have so much fun harassing them at school!"

And she was gone.

Harassing them at school. Rana thought about that for a while. The kid had a wound on his chin. Was it because he was being harassed in school? Poor dimwit—what could he do, if he looked like a walking bully target? Maybe his parents ought to change his appearance. It was surprising to know he was the son of Sheila Khosla, the celebrity chef. She looked hot on TV and cooked some stunning food–every man's wild dream.

He knew something terrible had happened to Ria very recently. And she was bottling it all up. It was not very obvious but it showed in subtle ways. The unconscious fidgeting, the dark circles around her eyes, the total disregard she seemed to have for what she wore and the way she wore it. She looked so heartbreakingly beautiful in spite of all that, though. Her house had been cleaned and scrubbed, like a high intensity germ lab. And the way she made her coffee was excruciatingly structured.

Something had gone horribly wrong in her life.

Aryan looked at Rana Rathod's website where he had proclaimed himself to be the greatest author of India. What a phony! He certainly wasn't the greatest author of India. Aryan would've heard of him. And besides, he knew who the greatest author of India was. It was Arundhati Roy. Nobody at school had read her book. He was sure his father hadn't read her book. His mother claimed she had read it, especially when she was asked on television. She had said, "I loved Arundhati's novel." She said it as though she and Arundhati Roy were close buddies and sipped cocktails every other day. But she had never said she had read it. There was a difference between read and loved. He knew it for a fact, because she had got it from a bookstore, put it on her bookshelf and never touched it again.

He had read it. Although he hadn't understood much of it, he had kind of liked it. It was about two kids who are twins. He had liked the scenes which showed the two talking in a funny way or doing fun things. It had made him wish he had a sibling, though there was no chance of that happening. He'd often heard his parents screaming at each other that the only reason they were together now was because they made the mistake of having a child together. Their voices came out muffled from the bedroom, but the walls weren't thick enough to subdue the hatred in their quarrels.

Aryan read through Rana Rathod's website and thought he was a braggart (he liked that word) for claiming that he was the greatest. Aryan had never heard Arundhati Roy call herself the greatest writer of India.

On the website, Rana had announced that he had started his thirtieth novel. Aryan wondered if he wanted to talk to Ms Ria about that. He also wondered how he had come to know Ms Ria. She hadn't seemed too pleased to meet him. She also seemed a little distracted—her manner was very similar to his mother's after a big fight with his father.

On a whim, he Googled Ria Marathe and was surprised to know that she was a scriptwriter. Apparently she had scripted some of the biggest television serials. Although he had never seen those serials, everyone in school had and they talked about the events in the episodes every day. He was never included in these discussions, but even if he had been, he wouldn't have contributed anything. Now, he could tell them that he knew who the writer of these serials was! That would surely make them talk to him. From what he had heard, all the girls in class, including the pretty ones, were big fans of these soaps.

He heard the rattle of the front door lock and knew his father was home. A few moments later, his father was standing at the entrance of his room. He hadn't shaved for days and looked wild and scary, like a drunk bear.

"Why didn't you tell me that you were hurt yesterday?" he said in his usual, slightly slurry drawl.

Aryan said nothing. That meant his mother had broken the bond and told his father about the wound on his chin. He had known she would do it to make his father miserable during their fights.

"Champ, that's not fair. You tell your mother everything and say nothing to me. Why?"

"It's not like that, Papa," he said.

His father stood at the entrance of his room, swaying gently on his feet. He held the door frame to steady himself a little, but didn't come inside the room. Aryan couldn't remember the last time he had stepped in his room.

"From today onwards, you tell me everything. That's the new rule of the Khosla house. Everyone tells Gagan Khosla everything!"

Aryan said nothing.

"Would you tell this to your mother?" he said.

Aryan's stomach churned with anxiety. What was he supposed to say? Didn't his father just tell him that he didn't like Aryan telling everything to his mother?

"No, Papa," he said in a whisper.

"Why not? You don't like the new rule?"

"No, I like the new rule. I will tell Mom too," Aryan said.

"Yeah, you do that. But don't tell her anything more, okay? Just tell her the new rule. Nothing more. Anything else you want to tell, you tell me."

Aryan thought he was going to lose his mind very soon if this didn't stop.

"You want to tell me something right now?" his father said in a way as though he had just remembered asking him that.

"No, Papa," Aryan said feeling wretched.

"That's okay. That's fine," his father said, as he stood there with his head down for several moments. Aryan thought he had dozed off when his father suddenly sneezed.

"Which class are you in now?" his father said.

"Seventh," Aryan said.

"Good. That's okay. That's fine. Study hard, okay, champ? Don't waste your time in the playground."

"Okay, Papa," Aryan said. He hadn't done anything in the playground in the last four years.

"See you tomorrow. Sleep now," his father said and walked away.

Aryan thought he hadn't breathed for a long time and took a deep breath.

He remembered he hadn't given his email ID to Ms Ria for her to send the recipe of the coffee. He knew when and where to meet her again.

Chapter 7

# A Table for Three

It was five by the clock and Ria still hadn't decided whether or not she would meet Rana Rathod in the Barista down the street. It would take her exactly seven minutes to walk the distance to the Barista. If she planned to step out of the house, she would need four minutes to check on every tap, switch and gas knob to ensure they were off. And if she was going out, she would need to wear something that didn't make her look as though she belonged in a hospital. Five minutes for that. In all sixteen minutes. So, she had to decide if she was going to meet Rana in another forty-four minutes or not.

Should she make him wait? What if she reached there by six-sixteen? That would give her one more hour to think through it. Or had she already decided to go and was acting strange just for the heck of it? She had hated people who weren't punctual. Actors, some of whom behaved like prima donnas and considered themselves beyond the norms of decency, did it all the time. They usually walked in for script reading sessions as though they were doing her a favour. She had made sure they got the message that she wasn't too pleased about it. She'd had the knack of getting her messages across without seeming too uptight. After which, they never did it again.

Thirty minutes to go, fourteen gone.

She looked at the room she had forever locked up, hoping she would get some signal, some direction. The door to the room stayed closed. It was shut so tight that not even an emotion would escape it.

She wondered, what was the worst that could happen if she met the old man? He had a kind and courteous look in his eyes, but she was sure he'd had more than his fair share of shenanigans in his younger days. Although he carried the photograph of a woman who was her mirror image, she knew it hadn't stopped him from chasing other women.

Aryan, that poor child, had looked so miserable when she had told him she would send the recipe via email. She couldn't fathom what prompted the boy to walk all the way to see her.

At five fifty-one she stepped out of the house. Wearing something half decent hadn't been that difficult. Her green salwar kameez, the one she had buried under a bunch of neatly washed, starched and ironed clothes, had peeked out of the pile, like an eager student in a class, wanting her to give it a chance. She had put it on in one minute and was reminded of the time when she could do it in forty seconds, a time when her life revolved around the unrelenting local train schedule of Mumbai.

She splashed some water on her face and looked at herself in the bathroom mirror. Nobody was going to haul her away in an ambulance. In a way she was glad about it. It was good that her grief remained invisible to the casual observer. There was to be no melodrama.

The old man had seemed a little too desperate. She was going to hear him out, say no to whatever he wanted, console him a little if he was disappointed and walk away with a final goodbye. There was a determined look in the man's eyes. He was someone who was generally used to getting his own way, so it was better to meet him and find out what he wanted, rather than appear unapproachable and encourage his needless drastic measures.

It took her seven minutes to walk the distance to the Barista down the street. She thought she should have chosen a different place. The bright orange décor of the coffee shop and the soft but cheerful music made her feel wretched. Her watch said two minutes to six. She hoped she wouldn't see the old author. Perhaps he would get over the impulsive request he had made her the day before, and it would just end there.

No such luck. The man was sitting on one of the two high-backed chairs around a table with a glass top. She wondered if the choice of the tiny two-seater table was a planned move, to make them sit a little too close. His face lit up when he saw her and he stood up. She sighed inwardly and walked up to the table. There was an exquisite mesh of lines around his eyes, which crinkled whenever he smiled.

"Glad that you could come," he said, offering his hand.

She took it a little too lifelessly. There was a time she had disliked people who did that. Some of her colleagues had once moaned that she shook hands a little too hard. But now, she could summon no power in her wrist and fingers. It felt like a mistake to have agreed to meet him. The man didn't hold her hand a moment longer than was necessary. His hand was warm and graceful. He motioned her to the empty chair. Ria was thankful that he didn't pull it out for her. He obviously knew which of his actions would fall on the wrong side of the fine line between suave and spurious.

"What can I get you?" he asked in a voice that was dripping with charm.

It was an act and Ria knew why a certain kind of woman must've swooned over him once. It wasn't offensive though, at least not yet. In the quasi-romantic setting of the coffee shop, he was coming into his element and showing her what kind of a man he had been, or still was—the kind that she had generally stayed away from.

"No, thanks, Mr Rathod," she said leaning back on her chair, avoiding the intimacy of the space around the table. "What can I do for you, sir?"

She had thought the use of word 'sir' and her overtly formal way of saying it would put some distance between them, and dissuade him from putting on his unnecessary performance. No luck, again.

"Well, that's too bad," he said, "this Barista here is known for its café grande."

She looked at him without any reaction.

"Can I get one for myself?" he countered.

"Okay," she said in a tone that she hoped made it clear that she would rather he didn't.

The old man rose, bowed a little as though acknowledging her discomfort but also encouraging her to be patient, and walked up to the order counter. She took a deep breath and braced herself to deliver the talk she had structured a couple of hours back and hoped this would end quickly and nicely.

That was when she saw Aryan. He stood outside the glass walls of the coffee shop and a smile lit up his face when she caught his eye. He waved at her. She sighed deeply, again.

The boy walked all along the glass wall, pushed the glass door open and walked up to her. By that time, the old man, too, had been served his order and carried it to the table.

The two looked at each other.

"Oh, well," the old man said through clenched teeth, "I would be damned."

"Hello, Mr Rathod. Hello, Ms Ria," Aryan said brightly, "How are you doing today?"

"I was doing fine till you showed up," the old man said and almost banged his cup on the table. He sat down in a huff.

"I Googled you, Ranasahab. Just like you had told me to. I found out that you prefer being called Ranasahab," the boy said.

Ria looked at the old man. He shrugged as if to say "What can you do?"

"You have written twenty-nine novels! That's incredible. Can I have your autograph please?" Aryan pulled out a little autograph book. Each page had sections for name, profession and autograph. She looked at Rana Rathod or Ranasahab as Aryan had addressed him and wondered why she had never come across any of his books. She tried to recall any reference to his name as an author, which made her temples ache.

"I am not going to sign that," Ranasahab declared, looking at Aryan's autograph book and shaking his head stubbornly.

"Why not?" Aryan's tone was so hurt it was as if he had been physically hit.

The old writer looked at the boy and said, "Oh, hell. Give it to me."

He snatched the little square book from Aryan, pulled out a very expensive and showy looking pen from his coat pocket and savagely scrawled something illegible on the page.

"Thank you," the kid said with a smile so heart-warming and genuine that it gave Ria the incredible urge to hug him tightly. She fought that impulse by biting her lip.

"Could I get a chair, too?" Aryan asked.

"No," Ranasahab said.

"I am a little thirsty after walking for so long," Aryan said, touching his throat.

The old writer looked at her and when he got no response, said, "Oh, hell."

Ranasahab rose and accompanied Aryan to the ordering counter.

"I will have a large cold coffee," the boy said to the clerk, "And a chocolate cake with ice-cream."

Ria couldn't believe she was sitting there. She looked at the glass door, which looked so inviting. For a crazy moment she thought she should just bolt from the table, while the two had their backs to her. Just then, Ranasahab looked at her and shook his head exasperatedly, and the moment passed. Ranasahab pulled out his wallet and gave the clerk some notes. He then waited with Aryan, all the time fretting and fuming, while the Barista prepared the boy's cold coffee. After a full five minutes, they walked back to the table and realized it was a too small for a café grande, a large cold coffee and a big slice of chocolate cake with a double scoop of chocolate ice cream melting on top of it. So they had to move to a larger table, something for which Ria was grateful.

"I forgot to give you my email ID," the boy said taking a large piece of the cake on the spoon. He dunked it in the milky ice-cream, loaded his spoon very carefully and put it in his mouth. "Delicious," he said.

"Can you please give her your email ID now?" Ranasahab said, rubbing his forehead with his fore finger and thumb.

"Sure. Can I finish my ice cream and cake first? It's melting away," the kid said.

"Unbelievable," Ranasahab said and leaned back on the chair.

"Why are you travelling this far, Aryan?" Ria said to the

boy, "I will have to call up your mother or father and tell them about this."

"My father is always in meetings and never takes calls on his mobile before nine at night," the boy said, taking a large sip of the cold coffee from the straw, "and my mother has disallowed mobile phones in the kitchen till twelve at night. So you won't be able to reach them."

She looked at the old man who ceased clenching his teeth after hearing what Aryan had said.

"So you don't meet either them before late night?" she said, hoping she didn't sound surprised.

He nodded with a sip of cold coffee in his mouth. Ria thought about it for a moment. There were two people who believed something was more important than the child they had. The old man, too, seemed to have given up on the prospect of Aryan leaving them in a hurry. The only noise for the next few minutes was Aryan munching the cake and sipping the coffee.

"Ria . . . may I call you, Ria?" the old man asked.

Ria thought that, for the first time since she had met him, he spoke without pretences.

"Yes, sir. You may," she said, still maintaining her act. She had experienced too many incidents where sounding genuine was an act too.

"Please call me Ranasahab," he said in a slightly tired voice, as though he understood what she was trying to do with her act.

"Okay," she said leaning back on the chair.

"I would've preferred to make this request of you when nobody was around," he said glancing at the boy, who had stopped gobbling the sludgy brown mix on his plate and was looking at the old author in an enraptured manner, "but I don't think I will get another chance to do this. You certainly wouldn't want to meet me again for a cup of coffee."

She nodded for him to go on.

"I am writing my thirtieth novel. And this is my last shot at finding something more valuable than my life—my dignity," he said and paused as if to give her a moment to process what he had said, "This novel is going to be a complete shift from the novels I have written in the past. It will be a love story.

And it will be based on events in my life—something that defined my life in a way."

She stared at him without saying a word. She knew what had defined his life—the woman in his wallet and in his heart. And the woman looked like her long-lost twin.

"There is..." he said, hesitated, rubbed his face with his palms, "There is one more thing. I am dying. The doctors have given me six months, maybe a year. I have pancreatic cancer"

She closed her eyes.

"Look, Ria, all I want is an hour of your time every three days or so. I will bring whatever I am writing and read it to you. I believe I could do something brilliant with that novel if I see your reaction when I read it to you. And that is the legacy I would want to leave."

His voice broke by the end of it. He shook for a while and then rubbed his eyes with his forefinger and thumb.

"If you say no," he said taking a deep breath, "I will die without completing my novel."

She didn't want to open her eyes. Perhaps a higher power that determines what happens with everyone in this world had decided that she would indeed face some melodrama in her last days. It was an unbelievable request. She wanted to tell the man that she didn't believe him at all. But what if it turned out to be true? What if the man was really going to be dead in a year's time? He was going to live longer than she; that was for certain, though it felt that he didn't want to die. He seemed like a man who would want to live forever. There would always be something interesting for men like him to do in this world. Life was a cruel game really. She didn't want it so she was going to destroy what was a perfectly healthy body. He so badly wanted it, but a disease was eating him up from inside.

What was she going to do? Every single instinct told her not to get involved. She opened her eyes and looked into the earnest, misty eyes of the old man.

"All I have to do is listen to what you have written?"

"That's all," he said.

"Okay," she said, "Fine."

"Thank you," he said in a choked voice.

The boy resumed eating as if nothing had happened.

When they stepped out of the restaurant, Rana said to her, "We meet on Saturday, then? If that's convenient for you. Same place? Would ten in the morning suit you? I don't want to spoil your evening."

She nodded distractedly and walked away. Rana wondered if she would come.

"What's the exact duration the doctors have given you?" the boy asked him.

The gall of him! To walk in and almost spoil everything. Again! What was he going to do with the boy?

"Look, what's your name?" Rana asked.

"Aryan Khosla. I told you yesterday. Does the cancer affect memory too?"

"Now, you listen to me, Aryan. Stop asking too many questions, okay? There is a bloody limit. You can't be disturbing people like this."

"You mean Ms Ria? She didn't seem too disturbed when I walked in," he said.

"But *I* am disturbed. Very disturbed," Rana said.

"But why? What have I done?" For a moment Rana thought the dim-witted kid really didn't know how annoying he was.

"Again, just too many questions," Rana said shrugging the thought away, "Let me say this to you in a plain and simple way. Please concentrate on your school and stop wandering around, disturbing people."

The boy suddenly had a hundred yard stare in his eyes as though he was feeling terrible about the discomfort he had caused.

"I am saying this for your own good, Aryan," Rana said, softening his voice a little, but not by much. This boy's intrusions were becoming unbearable.

"I think you are right," the boy said in a hollow voice.

"Good. Now I will leave and hope not to see you again,"

Rana said and was about to turn around to walk up to his car.

"Will you drop me home?" the bloody kid said.

"What? No! Outrageous," Rana said.

"It's dark and my house is too far away. I don't think I should be walking. There is a very dangerous street I will have to cross on my own at this late hour."

Rana looked at him and said, "Oh, hell."

The boy smiled. Rana hated to admit that when the boy smiled, it was the most charming sight. He had a no-holds-barred toothy smile, which was so hard to ignore. Rana couldn't help but smile back.

"I like your car," the boy said as Rana drove.

Rana grunted his acknowledgment, hoping he wouldn't have to talk much.

"What is this novel that you are writing?" the boy asked as Rana drove.

"Just a novel," Rana said.

"Crime fiction? Like all of your other novels?"

"No," Rana said.

"Oh yes, it's a love story, I remember. That's what you told Ms Ria."

"Uh-huh."

"Your own?"

"Well. . ."

"Well what?"

"Well, you are the most irritating child I have ever come across," Rana said. Somehow, the boy found this funny and he chuckled. Rana clenched his teeth.

"Do you have children? They must be all grown up now," the boy said turning towards him.

Rana clutched the steering wheel tightly and said nothing.

"Well?" the boy asked.

"Yes they are all grown up now," Rana said.

The boy sensed something in his tone and leaned back in his seat. Rana was glad that he said nothing more for the remainder of the journey. The boy lived in one of the swankiest building societies of Mumbai. Rana didn't want to ask the boy what his father did, but he was sure he was some big-shot in the corporate world. The 'fake rich', as some of his family would say.

When they stopped in front of the building society, the boy said, "I could've invited you to our house, but there is no one home right now."

"How will you get in?" Rana asked.

"I have a key," the boy said and got out of the car. "Goodnight, Ranasahab."

Rana thought that entrusting the keys of the house to a thirteen-year-old boy was giving the child a bit too much responsibility.

"Goodnight," he said and drove away. He looked in the rear-view mirror. The boy stood in front of the gate looking at his car as it sped away from him. Sad little bugger.

Rana wondered what kind of boy he, himself, had been. The memories of his childhood were a little hazy, since he grew up in a house full of people. No, it wasn't a house, it was a palace. The enduring image of his childhood was of numerous people floating around in the countless rooms of his palatial ancestral home. He had never shared it online with anyone that he was a scion of the former rulers of western India. The kingdom was snatched away from the family a long time ago, first by the British and then by the Indian Government, but that didn't stop them from parading around the world like royalty. The family now owned one of the biggest industrial conglomerates in the country. He wasn't a Rathod. He was *the* Rathod and was ashamed of it.

They are all grown up now.

He couldn't remember the last time he had seen his son and daughter. Was it two years ago or three? He hadn't met them after the terrible incident during his daughter's wedding, an incident that still burdened his heart with unbearable shame and regret. And when did his daughter's wedding take place? He felt a sudden pain in his chest. Cold sweat broke out all over his body. He couldn't stop shivering. Somehow, he managed to get the car close to the curb of the road. He hugged himself and rubbed his palms on his shoulders to calm himself down.

They were all ungrateful people. Every single one of them! And he hated them all. Yes, he hated his own children.

He wondered why he was doing this to Ria. What did he hope to achieve by telling her all those lies? Write a novel? Or relive the past? She wasn't Nina. Nina had died long ago. So why was he playing that dirty game with Ria? The answer was simple, really. After he had seen her, there was no way in the world he could avoid being with her. Nina was the reason he had started writing. Perhaps Ria would be the reason he would start writing again. And writing was all he had ever learned to do well.

When he reached home, he couldn't wait to start entering the words that were swirling in his mind like a cloud of buzzing bees. He lost track of time and when he leaned back, a little breathless, he was stunned to see that he had typed ten pages. He read it all back hungrily, and was astonished to see how well it read. It had been the most he had ever written in the last fifteen years.

By Sunday evening, he was spent. He had written dozens of pages. It was time to celebrate the return of India's greatest author! He posted the news on his website that the new novel was motoring along at breakneck speed. As Vinny had shown him, the status flowed everywhere. By eight in the evening, he was convinced it was time to celebrate by visiting his club. He wondered if he would be able to get the attention of the women. The strange confidence coursing through him was making him dizzy.

Everything was spoiled when he stepped out of the building. He saw the boy, who had been standing at a distance as if he had been waiting for him to show up. The boy saw him, tried to appear nonchalant and started walking towards him.

Rana took big strides and caught up with him.

"What in the name of God are you doing here?" he asked the boy.

"Hello, Ranasahab!" the boy said with his trademark smile. Rana suspected that it was a practiced art. Like a little kitten, the boy knew how to appear cute and get his way. Although his heart told him it wasn't so.

"You are stalking me now," Rana said.

"Stalking you? No. I was just taking you up on your invitation," the boy said.

"My invitation?"

"Yes. On your website you have said that fans can drop in any time to meet you. You have also given your address and phone number there."

Rana rubbed his forehead. He had posted his address and forgotten all about it as nobody had ever come visiting his house.

"Oh, hell," he said.

"So can I come to your house?"

"Not for more than five minutes, though," Rana said, turned back towards his building and started walking. The boy broke into a trot beside him.

"For a man who is on the verge of dying, you walk very fast, Ranasahab," he said.

Rana said nothing.

When they were climbing the stairs, Vinny bumped into them.

"Yo, Rana," she said and looked at the boy with narrowed eyes. "Who is this? Your grandson?"

"He is a nobody," Rana said.

The boy had turned crimson and wasn't even looking at Vinny.

"He sure looks funny for a nobody," Vinny said. Grown-up men lost their nerve around her. Aryan had no chance of surviving an introduction.

"How did you get that wound?" she asked.

The boy couldn't utter a word.

"Is he dumb?" she asked, looking at Rana.

"Leave him alone, Vinny," he said, motioned the boy to follow him and resumed climbing the stairs.

The boy trailed after him with his head down, his face flushed. Rana looked back at Vinny and shook his head tiredly. Vinny raised her eyebrow with a little shrug and bounded down the stairs. The boy stole a glance behind with utter dread on his face as Vinny disappeared down the curving staircase.

"Are you thirsty?" Rana asked him when they entered his flat.

The boy shook his head, indicating a no, still recovering from the Vinny ambush.

When Rana switched on the lights, he got the expected reaction from the boy.

"Wow, cool!" he said. Rana couldn't not like the wonder that spread on the boy's face. It was as if he had entered Ali Baba's cave.

"How come you have so many gizmos?" he asked.

Rana shrugged.

"My mom, too, has a lot of them, but they are all cooking-related. She hates electronic stuff," he said.

He gingerly touched the sixty-inch wall-mounted television. There was the latest XBOX with all the best games. He made excited sounds as he stood in front of the massive home theatre system, with its speakers as tall as he was.

"That's an incredible computer!" the boy exclaimed.

Rana knew it was. He had bought the most advanced configuration, the sleekest looking speakers and a thirty-two inch HD monitor. The boy was the first to admire his computer after Vinny. Rana hated to admit to himself that the boy was perhaps the only person, apart from Vinny, to enter his house who wasn't an inebriated woman.

"What is this?"

It was one of the world's most expensive espresso machines that Rana had ordered from a company, which specialised in making exclusive, custom-built espresso machines. It actually looked like a big time machine when Rana had seen it the first time after it was delivered by a team of six people from the company based in Sweden.

"It makes coffee," Rana said.

"That's all it does?" the boy asked because he thought Rana was pulling his leg.

"Yes."

"Amazing. Just amazing. My mom has a little coffee pot she makes coffee in. How does it taste, the coffee from this machine?"

"Just like normal coffee!"

The boy looked at him with narrowed eyes for a moment.

"Then why did you buy this massive machine if it tastes like normal coffee?"

"Aryan, look, I was going to step out of the house for some important work when you showed up," Rana said wanting to end it quickly, "I can't delay it anymore."

"I read your novel, *The Merchants of Death,*" the boy said as though he hadn't even heard him.

Rana wondered if anyone had said that to him in a long time.

"It's not meant for children," he said.

"I don't like whatever is meant for children, anyway. I can't read Hardy Boys or Famous Five. Stupid and boring," he said.

"So what do you read?" Rana asked. The kid *was* a little strange.

"I just finished *The God of Small Things* by Arundhati Roy," he said.

"Did you?"

"Yes," the boy said, sounding somewhat offended. "You don't believe me?"

"I just realized I don't care what you read, Aryan," Rana said, regretting he had asked.

"It is a great book. I liked it," the boy said, ignoring what Rana had said.

"Okay," Rana said looking pointedly at his watch, "I need to go out now. So, can you leave?"

"Where are you going?"

"None of your business."

"Have you taken your medicines?"

"Medicines?"

"For the cancer," the boy said, spreading his hands as though he thought Rana was a little slow not to get the obvious question.

"Oh, that. It is incurable now," Rana said and wondered why he was avoiding the boy's eyes.

"Okay," the boy said looking outside the window, "It is again late in the night."

"Oh, hell."

Rana locked the flat as Aryan stepped out. They walked

down in silence to the basement where his car was parked.

"Who is that girl?" the boy asked, without looking at him as Rana drove.

"Vinny. Her name is Vinita," Rana said.

"She is a little scary," he said.

"You were scared of her?" Rana said.

"A little, yes," the boy said with a grimace, "Don't tell her that, though."

Rana smiled and asked, "Are you scared of all the girls?"

"No!"

"Okay, you don't have to shout," Rana said.

"Sorry."

The previous evening's scene was repeated. The boy said he would've loved to invite him, but his parents weren't home, Rana nodded and drove away, looking at Aryan's forlorn expression in his rear-view mirror.

Aryan was fairly certain Ranasahab didn't have cancer. Nothing in his house suggested that a sick man lived there. Sakhu-mai had cancer and she looked so terrible lying on her little bed. He hadn't visited Sakhu-mai for four days now. It was the first time he had broken the routine in the last six months of meeting her every other day. He promised himself that he would do so the next day. He wished Sakhu-mai's niece had a mobile phone so that he could call her up on the days he couldn't visit her.

If anything, Ranasahab seemed to be enjoying his life a little too much. He had never seen a house so loaded with all kinds of gizmos. That monstrous-looking espresso machine was really strange, especially after Ranasahab admitted that it made coffee as ordinary as his mom's coffee pot. Aryan didn't think Ranasahab used many of those gadgets.

Why wasn't Ranasahab living with his children? He had said they were all adults now. Maybe, like they show in those movies, he was abandoned by his ungrateful children. Aryan wondered what he would do when he grew up. Would he abandon his parents? He surely wouldn't banish his mother. And what about his father? He didn't think his father would notice that he had been abandoned.

The girl, Vinny, was extremely scary. Her huge eyes had strange coloured kohl in them. She wore clothes meant for aggressive boys. And her hair was truly wild. Like the sparkles of a firecracker. He liked that—sparkles of a firecracker. He wondered if it was the best way to describe her hair. Maybe not, but he still liked it and made a note of it. He had learned very recently that using similes and metaphors was a very sophisticated way of writing. *The God of Small Things* had so many beautiful similes. Each one was apt.

The phone in the house rang. It startled him a little. It wasn't his mobile phone, so he was sure it wouldn't be his mother (his father rarely called him anyway). He rushed to the living room and picked up the phone.

"Aryan?" a voice said on the phone.

"Yes?" he asked, a deep foreboding rising in the pit of his stomach.

"Your mother collapsed in the kitchen a while back. She has been rushed to the Sardar Patel Memorial hospital. We are not able to reach your father. If he is at home, can you please inform him?"

Aryan couldn't say a word. He didn't recognize the voice, and for a terrible moment, thought that it was a prank. Maybe Samar was behind this. Though the hollowness in his stomach told him it wasn't so. The caller was perhaps one of his mother's colleagues—a junior chef.

"Aryan? You there?"

"Yes," he whispered.

"Do you know where your father is?"

"No," he said.

The voice was silent for a moment.

"I work with your mother in the restaurant. You wait for your father and try to reach him if you can," he said.

He put the phone down. He knew his father was not going to come home that night. His parents had a major fight the night before and his father had stormed out, screaming he was going away for a few days. His mother had told him never to come back. To which his father had said it was his house, too, and he would come back whenever he wanted to do so.

The few times he had accompanied his mother to the restaurant gave him a feeling that most of her juniors didn't seem to like her. They made exasperated gestures, mocked her and even bared their teeth when they thought she wasn't watching. But he had watched it all as he had sat in the corner of the hot and noisy kitchen. And now his mother was in the hospital at the mercy of her juniors.

Aryan dialled his father's mobile several times. It went into his voicemail each time. He didn't leave a message.

He dialled another number.

"Hello?" he heard Ranasahab's voice.

"My mother is in the hospital. They say she collapsed. And I can't reach my father," he said suppressing a sob, "Can you please come and take me to the Sardar Patel Memorial?"

He didn't hear Ranasahab's voice for a few moments

"Hello?" Aryan asked.

"Meet me where I dropped you in fifteen minutes," Ranasahab said and disconnected

He tried not to cry while they drove to the hospital.

"Aryan, did they tell you what happened to her?" Ranasahab asked him softly.

He shook his head. Ranasahab said nothing.

"I will not abandon my parents when I grow up," he said.

"What?"

"I will not abandon them. I hope they notice that I won't leave them when I have my own home and family."

It had just felt like the right thing to say. Aryan was shocked to know he had started crying.

"She is going to be alright," one of his mother's colleagues said to him when they reached the hospital, "I told you not to come, Aryan."

Aryan said nothing.

"What is wrong with her?" Ranasahab asked.

"The doctor says she has had a spike in her BP. It was a massive one, and she collapsed. She will be under observation for a couple of days."

"Can he meet her?"

"Don't know," the colleague said, "And you are?"

Aryan thought Rana was at a loss for words. He left him to fend for himself and walked to the room in which his mother slept. The door was shut but he could see her through the glass wall. Her mouth was covered with an oxygen mask. Her eyes were tightly closed and every few moments her hands shook as though in some kind of a shock. The images of the terrible pain Sakhu-mai had lived through flashed in front of his eyes. He didn't want his mother to go through that kind of suffering. Watching one of the two women who loved him go through hell was enough for a lifetime. He wanted to open the door and sit with his mom holding her hand and tell her that he was there, that he wasn't ever going to leave her.

Aryan sat on the chair, leaned back and closed his eyes, fighting back the tears. He shouldn't be crying. He had to be strong for his mother and for Sakhu-mai.

"Aryan, are you alright?" he heard Ranasahab's voice.

He nodded a yes.

Ranasahab sat next to him, put a tentative but very comforting hand across his shoulders and didn't leave his side for the rest of the night.

Next day, very early in the morning, the doctors told him to meet his mother, but not for too long, as she was still having the spikes.

Ranasahab looked at him and nodded. He walked into the room alone.

"Aryan," his mother said in a voice so feeble and wheezy that he didn't understand what she had said. Her mouth was still covered with the oxygen mask.

"Don't speak, Mom," he said holding her hand.

"Who is looking after you?" she asked.

He said nothing. He didn't understand what "looking after him" meant.

"Did your father return in the night?"

Aryan shook his head.

"Would you call up Geeta aunty and Mahesh uncle? They

will take care of you."

They were her friends. He had never liked them. They drank too much. Mahesh uncle couldn't keep his hands away from his mother. He had once heard Mahesh uncle and Geeta aunty fight. She was accusing him of trying to flirt with his mother. He particularly didn't like Geeta aunty. She pinched his cheeks viciously, laughed like a horse neighed and always said she couldn't believe Aryan was Gagan Khosla's son.

"Yes, Mom," he said.

"Will you go and tell Mata that I am sick and she needs to pray for me?"

"Okay," he said.

"Ask her to tell everyone to pray for me," she said.

"Okay."

"You will do this for your mom?"

"I will," he said.

"I am so tired. . ." she said and trailed off. A moment later, he heard her rhythmic but shallow breathing.

He stepped out of the room.

"Is she okay?" Ranasahab asked him.

"Yes," he said, "she asked me to pray for her."

Ranasahab looked at him.

"Could you please drop me to her guru's place?"

"Okay," Ranasahab said rubbing his bleary and tired eyes with his palms. At that moment, Aryan desperately hoped his suspicion that Ranasahab didn't have cancer was true.

When they reached Jaya's place, Aryan said to Ranasahab, "Do you want to come in? It is a meditation centre."

"Okay," Ranasahab said with a little grimace.

There was a bigger crowd than normal. They sat on the floor, waiting for their turn to meet Jaya. Aryan thought Ranasahab had the same reaction he'd had when he saw Jaya the first time—disbelief and awe. She was so huge and so funny, actually. And the way she kissed everyone and said cheerful things, it was a miracle that people weren't bursting out with laughter all the time. Everyone had said that she had conjured up some miracles, like walking on water or levitating. Aryan thought nothing compared to what he thought was her greatest miracle—suppressing so many laughs at the same time.

"She has done some miracles," he whispered to Ranasahab.

"Is that so?" Ranasahab asked sceptically.

"Including curing people with cancer."

"Okay," Ranasahab said looking at him with a furrowed brow.

After a few minutes, Aryan thought Ranasahab's initial surprise wore off and he was fidgeting, just as he had done the first time.

When their turn came, Jaya screamed his name and called him a prince. When he told her about his mother, she made horrified sounds. He told her his mother's wish, and she fulfilled it.

"Who are you, my son?" she asked Ranasahab.

"Uh . . . Rana Rathod," Ranasahab said.

"And how do you know my queen and prince?"

"Well, we are friends," Ranasahab said and looked at Aryan.

She grabbed him hard. An involuntary little yelp escaped Ranasahab's throat. And then she kissed him hard on the lips.

Aryan couldn't stop laughing when they were out of the *sthan*.

Chapter 8

# The Three Bond Reluctantly

Ria looked at the traffic outside the coffee shop as she waited for Ranasahab. The noise of the vehicles and their irritated owners was muffled by the glass walls and the conversations of people in the coffee shop. The world had become a much noisier place in the past eighteen months. She had managed to submerge herself in the silence of her flat. Now, the sounds of life beyond the walls of her house seemed too shrill and cacophonous.

The old man was fifteen minutes late and Ria felt a familiar disappointment. She wondered if the delay was because of the man's illness but she didn't think so. She had never quite understood the lack of social niceties in artistes and writers. Most of the film stars and directors she had worked with were so obsessed with the talent they had got from the almighty that, in their hearts, nothing else mattered apart from the self-obsession and self-importance. She had been told repeatedly that she was crazy to be punctual and demand punctuality from others while being a screenwriter in India. Many people had said laughingly both behind her back and to her face that she must suffer from Obsessive Compulsive Disorder (OCD).

Ria decided she would give Ranasahab five more minutes and then she would leave the coffee shop. And she would never meet him again. So, she was stunned when she saw Ranasahab and Aryan walk into the coffee shop together. They looked tired and dishevelled, but also at peace with each other.

"What has happened in just a couple of days?" she said,

unable to hide the wonder in her voice as they sat on the chairs.

"Nothing," the old writer said sullenly. The bleariness in his eyes was pronounced, as though he had stayed awake the whole night. Ria wondered if she had been unnecessarily harsh on the old man as she thought of him a little while ago.

Aryan was silent for a few moments and then burst out laughing. He proceeded to tell her about his mother's illness, which was terrible to hear. She was relieved to know that the poor boy's mother was stable and was going to be fine in a couple of days. She met the old author's eyes when Aryan told her he had called Ranasahab to take him to the hospital. Ranasahab shrugged. She couldn't help but smile when the boy told her how the "big fat whale" called Jaya Mata had planted a full-blown kiss on Ranasahab's lips. The old man squirmed like a little boy.

"Well, that's enough, Aryan," he said.

"You should've been there Ms Ria, you would've laughed. . ."

"I said enough! When are you going to stop talking about that? In fact, when are you going to stop talking?" Ranasahab demanded. He was blushing with embarrassment.

"Is your mother alright now? And where is your father?" she asked Aryan.

The boy's manner became sombre as he said, "The doctors think she has been under a lot of physical and emotional pressure of late. My father and mother fought long into the night yesterday. They were both drunk and called each other terrible names. I think they are terrible things ... don't know for sure. What is a cunt? And a dickhead?"

Now it was her turn to squirm along with the old man. Aryan told them about it in the forthright manner only children have. He waited for a moment as though actually expecting them to tell the meaning of those words.

"My father was so angry that he stepped out of the house in his pyjamas," Aryan continued in a voice filled with shame, perhaps sensing their discomfort, "I thought he would return a while later. I mean, he has left us like that in the middle of the night after their quarrels many times, but never in his pyjamas. I hoped he would find it silly to walk around in those clothes. But he hasn't returned."

"There is no one at home with you, Aryan?" Ria asked, hoping there was someone with him to look after him.

"No," he said without looking at either of them, "Sakhu-mai can't be with us anymore because of her illness."

"Who is Sakhu-mai?" Ria asked.

"She . . . is like my grandmother," he said uncertainly. Ria wondered what he meant by that but didn't question him further about Sakhu-mai.

"Do you have any relatives in town? Any friends of your parents you can go to?" she implored.

The boy shook his head and stared at his lap.

"Where are your relatives?"

"None of them are in Mumbai. Anyway, we have never been close to them. And I tried calling the friends of my parents. None of them said anything—just that they were very sorry."

Ranasahab looked at her wearily. She thought the old writer was thinking the same thing when she met his eye.

The boy was truly alone.

It seemed she and Ranasahab were the only people he could call upon. And their lives had crossed just a few days ago. The loneliness Aryan must've endured all his life overwhelmed her. She wondered if there was some kind of bizarre design at work here. What would Aryan have done had he not met her and Ranasahab? Who would've helped him?

Ria had come that day prepared to tell the author that she was sorry for his illness and wished she could do something about it. She had thought about him reading his novel to her and had felt it was a ridiculous thing. Aryan's situation put everything into a tailspin. Was she going to let a thirteen-year-old battle a tragedy of his life on his own?

"You can come and stay with me, Aryan," Ranasahab said to Aryan but looked at her, as though he was reading the thoughts roiling in her heart.

She wanted to let out a sigh of deep relief. Aryan staying with her would've been a grotesque joke. And what if he opened the room she had forever shut? What would happen then? It was unthinkable. She looked at Ranasahab and said a silent thank you. He nodded ever so imperceptibly.

"Can I read what I have written now?" Ranasahab said pulling out a sheaf of pages.

She wanted him to, only if as a way of showing her gratitude.

After almost an hour, Ranasahab stopped reading.

She had been utterly spellbound, the writer in her recognizing a wonderful creation by the dying author.

## *Rana's memories of Nina*
## United Kingdom, Forty years ago...

When he was twenty-three, Rana was sure of two things—he was the black sheep of the Rathod family and he was never going to be good at the family business. He wasn't particularly bothered about either. All families have black sheep and it was just a twist of fate that he was a member of the Rathod family. Unlike his three elder brothers, he could not understand how you could use your money to make more money. His father, the ageing patriarch, wasn't enthused about his youngest son's overtly expressed ambition to be an artist. Rana had never made it explicit what art form was going to be his destiny. Vagueness was the signature of his life, something that would not be popular with people obsessed with cold facts and figures. His mother, who had been a closet poet, died when he was barely in his teens. She had handed him a sheaf of papers with those beautiful poems in her handwriting a few weeks before she died. She had told him he was the only one in the family who would understand.

So, when he had told his father that he would like to go to England to pursue a university degree in political science and literature, his father hadn't bothered to ask too many questions. Money was never a problem and within no time, Rana found himself at Portsmouth University. He was soon trying to juggle the various incompatible elements of his life—his huge course load; the pride and prestige associated with the Rathod name; sleeping with several women at the same time and trying out every intoxicant available. He wanted to be featured in glossy and arty magazines and hoped one day they would publish a retrospective on his body of work, though he wasn't sure what that "body of work" would be. He hoped that it would be something that was enduring or something that would change the world somehow.

He and Nina had met because they were the only two Indians in their religion class, and when study partners were being decided, the professor had conveniently bracketed them. When he first saw her, she had seemed aloof and almost irritable. It was as if she wasn't too happy to be associated with someone like him, although he wasn't sure what the exact nature of "someone" was. But over several weeks of grudgingly sharing notes and classes, an unlikely friendship had formed between them. Later, when Rana thought about it, he deemed it to be destiny. He had no hesitation in admitting to himself that he had fallen in love with her the moment he had seen her. It took her a long time to fall for him though.

On a sunny day, after they had finished an assignment together, they shared a small table for a meal in the overcrowded restaurant called Big Ben's. It was a little place near the university and a favourite with all the students. Fish and chips and piss-warm beer was the only food served. If you asked for anything else on the menu, the reaction of the staff ranged from indifference to admonishment.

"Why do you eat so fast, like a sodding pig?" Nina asked him and pointed her finger at the plate, "This plate is yours. The fish in that plate is yours. The watery beer is yours. Nobody here is going to snatch it from you, for fuck's sake. You are twenty-three. Act like a grown-up. You are, aren't you?"

She started laughing. It was a beautiful sound, even amidst the din of the watering hole.

He smiled at her but slowed down.

"For a so-called member of a royal family, you sometimes behave like us ordinary peasants," she said.

She never missed an opportunity to have a dig at his "blue blood", as she called it.

"I am not one of them," he said still stinging from the "sodding pig" comment.

"It is in your blood, Rana," she said.

"I will go through a transfusion to take it all out," he said.

"That's a daft way of getting rid of it, but I like your intent," she said.

"Thank you," he said.

Nina had avoided even talking to him for most of the first year. He had never asked her specifically, but he knew he must've seemed very "typical" to her—a fake Maharajah, stripped of his empire but still strutting around like an overgrown rooster, who had landed on the college campus. And he must've reminded her of the things that made her uncomfortable about her roots. Although she was born and raised in Britain, she was the daughter of a couple who lived in a single-room council house and worked as cargo loaders. This was a profession her parents had forever hidden from their people in India, for the fear of being called *vilayati* coolies.

She wasn't exactly a loner, but wasn't always surrounded by people either. She didn't make any obvious attempts to hide the colour of her skin, nor did she try to wear it on her sleeve.

"Sometimes I regret meeting you," she said, "You are what we all ran away from ages ago."

"I am not one of them," he repeated, putting a morsel of fish in his mouth and washing it down with a large swallow of substandard beer. He was a little surprised by a sudden change in her tone.

"And what am I to you, Rana Rathod?" she asked, folding her hands, "One more of your conquests?"

He chewed his food silently for a few moments. He knew one day he would regret that he had unabashedly exploited his "exoticism", as some girls in the university had called it. If the definition of exotic was a good-looking man who wasn't a real prince but was as rich, that is. Throwing all that money around hadn't been a problem for him—another reason the stories of his conquests were doing the rounds in the campus.

"The first one is a difficult question to answer. The second is a lot simpler. No, you are not one of my conquests," he said and regretted the hint of haughtiness in his tone.

"Well, I am thrilled," she said, with a twist to her lips.

"Look, Nina, why are we talking this rubbish? We are having a good time."

"So, I am a bloody good time for you now," she said.

"What do you want me to say? That I love the way you talk? The way your lips twist when you are angry? The way you smile when you remember something funny? The way you cry when you watch silly romantic movies? The way your eyes become a little misty when you talk about your parents? The way you sometimes puff up your cheeks with your tongue when you are in deep thought? What do you want me to say?"

For the next few moments they looked into each other's eyes and the only sound was the banging of cutlery, blokes laughing at crude jokes and the hassled waitresses shouting orders.

"You could take me to a better place and repeat what you just said," she said.

"Better restaurant?"

"I was thinking more like your palatial flat," she said.

When Rana showed Aryan how to play *Need for Speed* on the XBOX, he thought it was the first time the boy had looked genuinely happy. They had played for two hours and Rana had to get his glasses towards the end of it. Some things had changed from the days in Big Ben's.

"Aryan," he said, "Have you tried calling your father again?"

Rana hoped the boy's father would come to his senses and return home. His discomfort at the prospect of taking care of the boy as long as his mother remained in the hospital was growing by the minute. Rana had a nagging suspicion that the boy didn't think he had cancer. He didn't want the boy to spoil everything by blurting it out to Ria. She had agreed to meet him, despite the fact that she, herself, was going through a tough time in her life. His novel had taken off, and he didn't want to abandon it.

"Yes," the boy said without taking his eyes off the screen.

"And?"

"And nothing. He is not reachable."

"Do you at least know where he could be? We could call that place," he said.

The boy paused in the game and looked at him, "Are you trying to get rid of me?"

"If asking *your* father to take you to your home is getting rid of you, then yes, I am doing that," Rana said.

"I told you I don't know where he is," the boy said morosely.

"Okay, you don't have to start crying."

"I am not crying!"

"Okay, okay. Calm down, will you?" Rana said feeling like a jerk.

Rana thought he had unnecessarily jumped at the boy. He had just seen his mother in terrible shape. His father had abandoned him. None of his relatives wanted to have anything to do with him. And he seemed to be friendless. Rana had to admit to himself that the last two hours had been wonderful. The boy had smiled a lot, had even laughed when he won the game a few times. Now, the boy looked at the screen glumly. He didn't restart the game. Rana couldn't recall a time when he had spent two hours not feeling miserable.

"How did you get this wound on your chin?" Rana asked, just to divert his attention, feeling terrible about the sadness on the boy's face, wondering if he was just too used to being wretched, that happiness jarred his comfort zone, made him wreck it.

"At the railway station. I fell down. That's how I met Ms Ria. She took me to the hospital." Aryan answered in the clipped way sulking boys do.

"What were you doing at the train station?"

The boy didn't answer. He seemed a little embarrassed about it.

So that's how he met Ria.

"Why do you want to read your novel to Ms Ria?" Aryan asked.

"Well . . . I don't think you would understand," Rana said and got up. He walked up to the oversized refrigerator, which could actually hide an elephant, as the company that made it had advertised. He opened the door and stared at the empty shelves inside. There were a few boxes of leftover food and a couple of bottles half full with water. Rana wondered why it hadn't struck him till then that the massive cooling machine, an engineering marvel, was so bare inside. He picked a bottle and gulped icy cold water that numbed his throat.

"She is a well-known screenwriter, you know," the boy said, "She has written for so many best soaps on the TV. I Googled it. Though in the last year or so she hasn't done any writing it seems."

Rana felt a spike of shame. "So typical of you blue-blooded bastards," as Nina would've said. He had wanted Ria to be his audience, but he hadn't even bothered to do a simple Google search to find out who she was and what she did. Even the boy had done it.

"Is that so?" he asked, not looking at the boy.

"You don't believe me?"

"When did I say that?"

"You say 'Is that so' only when you don't believe something," the boy said.

"Is that so?"

They both laughed. Rana felt a little better.

"Why do you think she hasn't written any scripts in the last year?" Aryan asked.

Rana shrugged and wondered about it for a moment. Something had gone terribly wrong in Ria's life, and he promised himself he would find out about it. He wouldn't have to listen about it from the boy. He did not like this curiosity, this desire to pry into Ria's life. Why did he want to know about it? Was it the primitive desire to pry upon the grief and misfortune of others? Perhaps. Or perhaps she had the same misty-eyed look of Nina when she was sad. He hadn't been there for Nina, for which he could never forgive himself. Perhaps he could be there for Ria and atone for it? Perhaps.

Aryan hadn't been able to sleep the whole night. The bedroom in Ranasahab's house was full of its own little noises and smells. Not that it wasn't nice, but it was different from his own room. It was more than nice, actually. The mattress on the bed was so soft that Aryan thought he had sunk into a cloud of cotton as he tried to sleep. The bed sheets were pristine white and it seemed they had never been used. The place smelled faintly of a lemony room-freshener. When Ranasahab had shown him the guest bedroom, Aryan had asked him if his children stayed there when they visited him. Ranasahab had said nothing. Aryan suspected that the guest room was very rarely used.

In the morning, Ranasahab had knocked on the guest bedroom door. He was all sweaty and huffing like a train engine. He said it was his routine to run eight kilometres every day. Ranasahab had looked at him in a funny manner, as though trying to gauge his reaction. Aryan had almost told him that he didn't think a terminal cancer patient could run so much. Sakhu-mai hadn't even moved from the bed in the last three months.

They ate a breakfast of cereals and cold milk in absolute silence. Aryan never liked muesli. His favourite mix was Chocos and Fruit Loops with warm milk. Sometimes, when his mother was home in the mornings, she would make him something that looked more like a painting or decorative object and less like food. He had never told her about his favourite mix and he didn't reveal it to Ranasahab either.

Despite his protests, Ranasahab had dropped Aryan to school after they had visited his mother. The doctors had said she still needed to be under observation as her blood pressure was quite choppy. She was sedated and he couldn't talk to her. They sat in the waiting room of the hospital for some time, but she was in a deep slumber. Ranasahab had asked the doctors repeatedly about her release. To which the doctors had patiently answered every time by saying that she would be let go when they thought she wouldn't be having a recurrence of the spikes. Ranasahab hadn't liked the answer at all and Aryan thought the self-proclaimed "greatest writer of India" was going to lose his temper. He had smiled at that thought and Ranasahab had spotted it and asked him in his trademark miffed manner "What's so funny?"

Aryan had wanted to stay with his mother in the hospital, but Ranasahab insisted that he had to go to school. Either that, or not bother coming to his place again. Aryan didn't want to stay in his parents' big flat alone, not knowing when the phone would ring because the doctors had even worse news about his mother and he had to rush to the hospital, but he told Ranasahab that it was fine by him. He would sleep in the hospital till his mother recovered. After that, Ranasahab had muttered a curse under his breath and spoken to the doctor some distance away from Aryan. The doctor walked up to him and told him to go to school as they couldn't allow boys to roam around in the hospital.

He had refused to talk to Ranasahab as they drove. After a few half-hearted attempts to get him talking, Ranasahab had given up. Aryan thought Ranasahab was actually happy that he wasn't talking. He had mutely stepped out of the car when they reached the school and hadn't even thanked Ranasahab.

Aryan was regretting his rude behaviour and wondering how to apologize to Ranasahab for not thanking him when he heard Samar's voice in his ear.

"Tick Tock Tick Tock!"

He had walked with his head down, again!

Samar held his shirt collar and yanked him. Samar had failed two or three years and was a big boy. He had started shaving a couple of years ago and missed no opportunity to parade his obscene muscles bared in his tight half sleeved shirts. Aryan had always wanted to tell Samar that the girls laughed at him behind his back.

"Ponchu," Samar said, "I was scolded by that fat Mathur bitch. Do you know why?"

Everyone knew why Samar had been scolded by class

teacher Ms Mathur—the assignment wasn't done. For the first time in his life, Aryan felt a blinding anger against Samar. It was as if all the bad things he had been through in the last couple of days were Samar's fault. His parents' hatred for each other was the bully's fault. The fact that he did not have any friends was because of Samar. His becoming a burden on Ranasahab was entirely this fool Samar's doing.

"Do you know why I was scolded?" Samar repeated.

"Because you are a moron and everyone hates you! Especially the girls. They laugh at you, you fool!" Aryan screamed. It was so sudden that Samar released his collar as if he was stunned by some kind of electric jolt.

The boys around them, who were till then watching all the familiar *tamasha* of Samar beating up some poor loser, were stunned into silence. Nobody in the combined memory of their class had ever dared to talk to Samar like that. Aryan couldn't believe he had done it, but he didn't regret it. In a way, it felt good, watching that oaf back off as though he had been hit. He wished he had done it earlier.

"You . . . you. . ." Samar couldn't utter a word. The script had gone completely off track. That wasn't what a meek, silent boy was ever supposed to say when Samar threatened him. Aryan knew this was going to end very badly for him, but he didn't care. What Samar couldn't do with his mouth, he did with his fist.

The first punch landed on his abdomen and Aryan let out a cry. The pain shot through his stomach as if there had been an explosion inside. The second punch hit him on the already raw wound on the chin. Blood spurted out as though Samar had punctured a balloon full of blood. Even Samar was shocked by the sight and took a step back.

Aryan looked at his shirt that was soaking up his blood. He let out a loud scream and pushed Samar with all the force he could summon. The bullying bastard landed on his muscled ass, painfully letting out a surprised cry. Aryan didn't wait to see what Samar and the Rebels would do next. He ran. He ran with all the strength he had in his wobbly legs. Surprisingly, the Rebels didn't follow him.

Aryan didn't stop. He kept on running when he knew he

couldn't see anything ahead of him because he was crying hard. He didn't stop even though he feared his heart would burst with exhaustion. He didn't stop when he reached the Chiraag Society buildings and the watchman tried to intercept him. He didn't stop for the lift to take him to flat 6B.

Ms Ria was shocked when she opened the door for him after he had banged hard on it.

"Your house was closest to the school," he said, sobbing.

Chapter 9

# The Three Get Involved

The sight of Aryan standing at her front door with blood on his shirt made Ria dizzy. She had helped him the other day, but the sheer amount of bleeding Aryan had suffered was terrifying. She banged the door behind her and rushed him to a nearby medical centre. A few people had looked on in surprise as she hurried down the stairs holding Aryan's hand. For a moment she had wondered if she should dress up his wound herself, but she didn't trust her shaking hands.

"What were you thinking?" she asked him when his wound was dressed.

Aryan said nothing. His eyes were red. She thought his tears had very little to do with the injury.

They walked back to her flat. He told her what had happened. She knew what needed to be done, but she wasn't the one to do it. The only two people who could go to the school and get the teachers to take action against these bullying boys were Aryan's parents or his relatives. She was a stranger; someone he had met just a few days ago. What was she going to tell the teachers when they asked who she was?

He sat on the couch staring vacantly into his lap. She had no idea what she was going to do with him. Calling Ranasahab was an option but it would seem totally impolite. He was as much a stranger to Aryan as she was. And what was she going to tell Ranasahab? Take away the boy from me because it is painful for me to see him? That it makes my resolve to die shaky?

He still wore the bloodstained school uniform. An image flashed in front of her eyes. A thirteen- year-old boy, lying on a metal stretcher, his eyes closed serenely as though he was sleeping, a small clot of blood on his shirt.

"You need to change your shirt," she said fighting back overwhelming tears.

Aryan said nothing.

She got up and stood in front of the room she had forever locked. There was no way to tell what would happen when she opened the door. She looked back at Aryan who hadn't changed his posture. She felt a sudden upsurge of grief when she saw how miserable and defeated he looked. The blood on his shirt was drying and turning brown.

She opened the door, not trusting her wildly shaking hands.

It was exactly the way she had closed it—the toys, the clothes, the memories—all that she had tried to enclose into the room.

She opened her son's cupboard and the familiar smell hit her. He had always smelled like a baby till the day he died. She held the cupboard frame to stop herself from collapsing. There was a poster of a smugly smiling Superman on the back wall of the cupboard. His favourite superhero—the invincible Superman. Her son hadn't been invincible. He was long gone. All that was left of him were his old clothes and posters.

She picked up a green and white checked shirt. It had been his favourite.

His name, VARUN, was embroidered on its pocket.

Varun—the wind. He used to say: "One day I will fly away like Superman, Mom!"

She put the shirt back and picked up a shirt which wasn't his favourite, but he had liked it nonetheless. It was blue.

She closed the cupboard and stepped out of the room. Aryan hadn't moved from the couch.

She walked up to him and gave him the shirt. He mutely removed his blood-soaked shirt and wore it.

"I am very tired," he said in a whisper.

She took him to Varun's room.

Vaun's bed was made. He had been a sloppy boy, never

caring about picking up after himself. But he loved making his bed.

"Sleep," she said to Aryan and tucked him into the bed.

Rana had decided to apologize to the boy when he picked him up in the evening from school. He had no idea how to deal with Aryan while the boy's entire world was collapsing around him. He should be focussing on his novel instead of worrying about a problem he couldn't solve, although, he couldn't understand the anger he felt at Aryan's father. He hoped he would never meet the selfish bastard; their meeting would not be pleasant. Rana thought about it for a long time as he worked at his novel on his computer. Was there any difference between the boy's father and himself? For he, too, had abandoned his family, hadn't he? He tried to defend himself, thinking there was a big difference. His children had abandoned him and not the other way round. When he recalled his behaviour since Aryan had come to stay with him, he couldn't write a word any more. He angrily switched off the computer without ascertaining if he had saved the file or not.

Ever since he had met Aryan, he had been trying to get rid of him.

Rana wondered what the boy thought about him; his house, the things he owned, his books. Then he shook his head in frustration, wondering why he cared about what the boy thought. Who gave a damn about Aryan's views anyway?

That was when he got the call from Ria. His initial delight that she had cared to find his number wore off the instant she told him what had happened to the boy.

Oh damn, Aryan. What the hell are you getting me mixed up with?

After half an hour of an angry, road-rage-filled drive to Ria's house, Rana watched Aryan as he sipped Ria's coffee in her living room. The boy refused to meet Rana's eyes. They had their coffee in complete silence and placed their cups on Ria's circular centre table. Rana thought Ria, too, looked as if she had been crying. Her eyes were red and her voice sounded raw—it seemed as though she had wept suddenly and violently. Strangely, she also looked at peace. Gone was the shiftiness and fidgeting he had seen in her just last evening.

"Who are these boys who beat you?" Rana asked after waiting for Aryan to say something.

"Just some boys," Aryan said without looking at him as though it was an irrelevant question.

"Aryan, please look at me," Rana said, feeling tired.

Aryan looked at him with hooded, hurt eyes.

"What do they beat you up for?"

"They beat up everyone," Aryan said.

"I don't think so. I think they pick on you," Rana said. He didn't want to say that Aryan was a walking bully target.

The boy said nothing.

"Have your parents met the teachers about this?" Rana demanded.

The boy looked away.

"Aryan, look at me! Have you even told your parents about this bullying?"

The boy said nothing.

"Well? Say something for God's sake!"

"Yes, I have," Aryan said in a burst.

"What happened then?"

The moment Rana said it, he knew it was a pointless question. Obviously, the boy's parents had done nothing to stop his bullying.

"My parents have been a bit busy," Aryan said quietly.

Rana tried to sense a hint of sarcasm in his voice, but found none.

"Okay," he said, making a decision, "We will go to meet your teachers tomorrow."

"We?" Aryan looked at him and Ria.

"I meant you and me, not me and Ria," he said.

This was a bit bizarre. Three days ago, if someone had told him that he would meet a woman who looked exactly like Nina and he would get involved with an unknown boy to the extent that he would become his surrogate parent, he would've thought that person was barking mad.

They left Ria's house together. She smiled at them—Rana thought that this was a genuine smile—for the first time since they had met her. It was so heartbreakingly like Nina's.

Rana drove the boy to the hospital, hoping his mother would be fine. Secretly, he was hoping to meet the woman and tell her off a bit. To stop prancing around on that stupid television show and start looking after her only son. It was outrageous, the way she made references to her 'beautiful' family all the while whipping a bunch of wannabe chefs into a cooking frenzy on her show. It was a big gimmick, in Rana's view. The show pitted its contestants against each other. There were six men versus six women. He was sure the people were chosen not for their culinary skills but for their stupidity and vulgarity quotient. Sheila Khosla terrorized them by screaming orders as though they were in a bloody army and not a kitchen. She made them go through multiple 'challenges' that basically involved cooking some rather ordinary dishes, and every week, one contestant was eliminated. There was a heavy dose of emotion, with grown-up men and women bitching about each other on camera as if they were in kindergarten. But they all revered Sheila Khosla, the bloody *Commander-in-Chef*, as the show was called.

The doctor told them a little wearily, since they had met him just a few hours ago, that the woman was still under observation. She was fading in and out of sleep. The boy couldn't meet her even after waiting a couple of hours. Rana sat with him patiently, atoning for the brusqueness he had shown in the morning.

"You can leave if you want to. I am sorry to behave badly with you, Ranasahab. Thank you for all your help," Aryan said.

"Shut up, kid," Rana said and smiled. The boy smiled back.

"You want to come home with me?" Rana asked

The boy nodded a yes.

When they entered Rana's house, Aryan said he wanted to sleep as he didn't feel all that well. Rana shrugged and was about to show him to the bedroom when the bell rang. It could be only one person.

"Yo, Rana," Vinny greeted him as she entered the house.

"It seems someone punched you at the same place again," she said after looking at Aryan.

"Stop picking on him," Rana said.

"Is he ultra-sensitive or something? That he starts bleeding if someone says a nasty word to him? Are you, dumbo?" she asked Aryan.

"No," Aryan said, in a tiny voice.

"Oh, you can speak! Wonderful," Vinny said, "I have got the latest *Need for Speed*. It is yet to be released in India but my dad got it from the US today."

Vinny was the only daughter of two doctors who were involved in research and development. From what Rana knew about them, they were the most respected team in the world on stem cell research and they were on the verge of a major breakthrough. Their work was the medical equivalent of walking on the moon. Rana knew Vinny's parents were absolutely crazy about her and doted on her to a fault. They had once allowed her to pierce her navel. When Rana had made suitably appalled sounds after they had told him, thinking they were equally aghast at their daughter's weird demand, they had said there was nothing wrong with it. As long as it made Vinny happy. Her mother, shockingly, had accompanied Vinny for the piercing. Rana didn't bother to ask if she had really done it.

Aryan looked at the NFS CD in Vinny's hand and smiled. The two children started playing. Within minutes, Aryan was smiling and no longer morose. Feeling light-headed and relieved, Rana joined them and they played till their eyes watered.

The next day, while Rana was getting ready to take Aryan to the school and meet the Principal, his mobile phone started to ring. He didn't know what to expect when he saw Ria's number flashing on the little screen.

"We might be making a mistake here by talking to Aryan's principal," she said after they had quickly exchanged greetings. Rana liked her use of 'we'. It was as if she had implicitly accepted joint responsibility for the boy.

"Why do you think so?" Rana asked feeling slightly irritated that the boy's problems were occupying all their conversations.

She said nothing for a few moments. Rana waited, wondering what she was going to reveal about herself.

"Ranasahab, when I was a couple of years younger than Aryan is today, my sister was the biggest bully in school. When I look back now, I feel she was like that because you had to choose. Either be a bully or get bullied. She chose the first," she said.

Rana took a deep breath. This was the first time she was letting him into her world, her past. A life that Rana had guessed would be quite different from Nina's.

"I remember a boy who was in my sister's class. She was two years ahead of me. This boy had asthma, so everyone called him a broken bamboo. One day, he had had enough of people picking on him. So he complained to his parents. When the school asked him to name the bullies, he blurted out my sister's name but didn't name anyone else. I have no idea why he singled her out. My sister was one of the dozens of children who harassed him. The next day all the teachers, every single one of them, either thrashed my sister or berated her for being such a cruel girl. And they didn't stop for a week."

She sighed deeply, as though relieving an unpleasant memory.

"The teachers forgot that my sister, too, was a child. When they called her cruel and other terrible things, they perhaps forgot that they, themselves, were being cruel to her. She needed to be told to stop her bullying; there is no doubt about that. But not in that way, not by bullying her, by beating her. There had to be another way; there always is. You know, instead of making my sister stop, it made her more defiant and she vented all her anger on that miserable boy. I know my sister didn't enjoy harassing that boy. She wasn't evil, Ranasahab. But that was the way she dealt with people. The boy left the school after six months."

She paused for a moment before saying, "My sister still cries when she remembers him. She has never forgiven herself for what she did to that boy. Her bullying stopped abruptly the day that boy left school, but had it been dealt with in a different way, maybe she would've stopped earlier and that boy would've been spared. The school created two victims that day."

Rana mulled over what she had said for a long moment. There had to be another way; there always is.

"Ria," Rana said softly, "We need to do something about it. We can't have Aryan go through it anymore."

She said nothing.

"I know we are strangers here, but we are all he has got right now. And I don't know what else we can do," he said.

"Okay, Ranasahab. I hope it doesn't get any more complicated for Aryan," she said and disconnected. Rana hoped she would make it to the Barista the next day.

Rana had expected Aryan to make a fuss when they drove to the school, but the boy sat still staring straight ahead silently.

"This is a great honour!" the Principal chimed when they entered his chambers.

He rose from his chair and walked around to greet Rana. "I can't believe my eyes that you, of all the people would walk into my office today."

"Uh, thanks," Rana said.

Aryan thought Ranasahab was totally flustered. Apparently, the Principal was his fan. He didn't think Ranasahab was too happy about it.

Aryan hadn't wanted to meet the Principal, Dr Ahuja, but he hadn't told Ranasahab that. Ranasahab wouldn't have agreed. Aryan knew Samar and the Rebels laughed about the Principal and called him a sack full of potatoes. Everyone in the school called him *Pahadi Aloo* (Giant potato) which over the years got morphed into *Padaloo*. The one man they were least scared of in the entire school was the Principal. All this complaining would do was end up riling Samar and the Rebels even more. His stomach churned with the prospect of stepping out of the Pahadi Aloo's chambers and facing his classmates. He would always be called the cry-baby who had moaned and complained. If, God forbid, the Padaloo did something about it, like rounding up Samar and the Rebels, then he might as well find a new school for himself. But there was little possibility of the Principal actually doing anything about it. There were many complaints in the past and the school had done nothing.

Padaloo being a fan of Ranasahab made everything terribly complicated. Now, there was a serious possibility of the Principal doing something about it. Aryan couldn't believe his bad luck. Ranasahab, till now, seemed like the only author in the whole world who had no fans and now Aryan was going to suffer a lot because Ranasahab had finally found his first fan. Aryan wanted to dash out of the chamber and never return to school again.

"What can I get you? Tea? Coffee?" Padaloo asked.

"No, nothing," Ranasahab said.

"Oh come on, sir. You are the greatest author I have ever read! And how can I let you go without a cup of tea, at least?" the Principal said and asked someone on his phone to get a couple of cups of tea.

These were all very bad signs.

"So what can I do for you?" Padaloo said.

"I . . . uh, I have Aryan here, who is getting harassed by a bunch of wild boys," Ranasahab said.

Aryan wanted to dissolve. Just cease to exist. Harassed by a bunch of wild boys? If this got out of the Principal's room, he was as good as dead. Surely, the Rebels had a very high opinion of themselves and wouldn't be too happy about the 'wild boys' tag. Just then, Dattu the peon entered Padaloo's chambers with a tray.

"Harassed by a bunch of wild boys, you say," the Principal leaned back on his chair.

Dattu heard it, looked at Aryan, and smiled. The peon, who looked like a skeleton, had a nasty reputation of being the school tattler. For the right price, he was known to reveal all the secrets of the teachers and the Principal to the students. That included leaking question papers, too. And the Rebels were his biggest customers. When Dattu went out of the chambers, Aryan had a vision that he was going to run around telling everyone, *Aryan Khosla is getting harassed by a bunch of wild boys! Aryan Khosla looks like a boy but is actually a girl because he complains!*

Aryan closed his eyes and wished he could close his ears too. He didn't want to hear any more of the conversation.

"This boy? Are you alright, son?" the Principal said.

Aryan opened his eyes and saw them looking at him. He nodded back.

"Is that the wound those boys caused?"

Aryan said no. Ranasahab said yes. They looked at him again.

"Well, they hit me on a pre-existing wound," he said miserably.

He was shocked he had said it. Now he had almost agreed that a he was being harassed by a bunch of wild boys.

"Uh-huh," Padaloo said and summoned the peon back in.

"I will not let this happen to my favourite author's. . .?"

"Grandson," Ranasahab said with a little frown.

"Yes, grandson," the principal said, "Although you don't look that old, sir! You look barely fifty five."

The peon, Dattu, was inside the chambers and was staring at Aryan, as though damning him for doing this. For being the traitor. For getting the people outside the school involved.

Aryan wanted to scream that this was all a big mistake. He had been lying all along. That he actually fell down again and hurt himself and no wild bunch of boys was responsible for it.

It was too late.

"Get these boys here. What are their names?" the Principal asked and looked at him.

He couldn't utter a word.

"Aryan? What are their names?" Ranasahab repeated.

He told them about the Rebels in a toneless voice. The deed was done. The die was cast. His death was sure.

The peon stepped out. The wait began.

Padaloo and Ranasahab began chatting about the state of literature in India. Aryan couldn't make any sense of what they were talking. It was all gibberish to his ears.

After a while, Dattu returned. Alone.

"They are not in class, sir," he said and looked at Aryan. Aryan could've sworn that the skeletal man had winked at him.

"Not in class, you say," the principal said, "Okay. Please

don't worry Mr Rathod. I will personally ensure that these errant children are seen to. I won't let his suffering continue."

Aryan wanted to tell him that he had no idea. His suffering had just begun.

They stepped out of the Principal's chambers.

"That went well, didn't it, Aryan?" Ranasahab said.

Aryan said nothing. He knew there was no way Ranasahab would understand.

He walked away from Ranasahab.

## Chapter 10

# Three Tentative Hopes

Rana had no idea what was wrong with the boy as he watched Aryan trudge away with his head down. The Principal, although incredibly annoying, was so supportive. Rana admitted to himself that it felt good to meet someone who knew so much about his books. Dr Ahuja had even promised to take care of the bloody boys who were harassing Aryan. And the boy had just walked away as if he was going to his own execution.

Later, as he sat in front of the computer, cudgelling his brains for words, the image of Aryan looking crushed refused to fade from his memory. Had he unnecessarily complicated the life of the poor boy even more? He had virtually no experience of raising his own children. Then why did he have to take the unilateral decision of meeting the Principal? Hadn't Ria warned him about it?

At five in the evening, Rana stepped out of the house to get Aryan from the school. While he was climbing down the stairs, on an impulse he rang the doorbell to Vinny's house, hoping she was at home. She opened it, wearing a T-shirt that read "What the hell are you looking at?"

"Where is the dumbo?" she asked in the form of a greeting, then pulled out a handkerchief and sneezed loudly into it.

"Stop calling him that," Rana said.

"He likes it. Didn't you see how he turns red when I call him Dumbo or Dumbster?" Vinny said with a little chuckle and coughed towards the end of it.

"Is that so?" Rana said. It was as if the two children already had a secret to which he was not privy.

"What's wrong with you?" he asked as she sniffled into the little cloth.

"I have a fever and a cold. Do you think you would find me at home at this time otherwise?"

Most of the people in the neighbourhood stayed away from Vinny, especially the boys her age. She moved around with older boys who had weird hair and wore strange clothes full of metal and chains. The only person she spoke to, apart from her parents, was Rana. And now it was Rana and Aryan. Rana had no clue what made Vinny warm up to the boy when he was her complete opposite.

"Anyway, we met his Principal today and complained about the harassment he is suffering in school," Rana said, hoping to get a pat on his back from a fourteen-year-old girl. He had no idea why the opinions of children were becoming so important suddenly in his life.

"What harassment?" Vinny asked with a frown.

"He is getting beaten up by the school bullies."

"One minute. Just roll back, okay? The dumbo is getting it in the school ... well, no surprise there. So you have complained it to the Principal? Are you out of your mind?"

"What do you mean?" Rana asked with a faint realization that it was the kind of reaction he had actually expected from Vinny.

"You can't be serious, Rana! You actually did that? Hell, the dumbo is dead now. Congratulations. You have just screwed up his life even more than it already was."

"You can't be serious," Rana argued feebly.

"What do you think is going to happen now? The Principal is going to say a few things to those boys, maybe make some comical threats like expulsion and stuff. And then what? The dumbo is still at those boys' mercy, Rana. They are not going to leave him. That's what happens with guys like him. It never stops."

Rana thought about it for a moment.

"How can it stop then?" This was a question as much to himself as to Vinny.

She shrugged and said, "I don't know."

When she closed the door, Rana knew he had made a stupid and unnecessary mistake by intervening. The boy's life was going on before he got involved. It was perhaps miserable but it was going on. Now, he had made it even more wretched. The frustrating thing was he had never wanted to get involved!

Rana began to worry when Aryan didn't turn up at the school gate. He had told Aryan that he would take him to meet his mother (he hoped she was better and could go home) and they would come back to his home from the hospital if she wasn't discharged today. The boy was nowhere to be seen. He waited till the stream of chattering and excited school boys came down to a trickle. He stepped into the deserted school and spotted the peon he had met in the Principal's chamber. When he asked him about Aryan Khosla, the peon just shrugged. The idiot acted as if he didn't even recall the boy.

Rana sat in the car and thought through. There were only two places the boy could go. It was either his house or the hospital. Somehow, he thought Aryan would be at his own home. He drove a lot faster than the speed limits on the maddeningly overcrowded streets of Mumbai would permit, to reach Aryan's Housing Society. The society was home to film stars and politicians. Rana thought Aryan's parents fitted in perfectly with the stupid crowd living there.

He rang the bell of the flat with Gagan and Sheila Khosla's nameplate on it.

After the fifth ring, Aryan opened the front door.

"What are you doing here? I waited for you outside your school." Rana exclaimed angrily, even though he tried to rein himself in.

"I am sorry, Ranasahab," the boy said in a hollow voice, "I have troubled you enough, already. And I won't bother you anymore."

"Stop talking all this nonsense," Rana said and tried to push the door so that he could get in. The boy held firm. Rana wondered if he should force his way inside the house, but stopped. As Ria had said, there had to be another way; there always is.

"You think I have made a mistake by complaining to the Principal?" Rana asked, stepping back a little from the door.

Aryan nodded.

"Then why didn't you stop me?"

"I had misbehaved with you yesterday, Ranasahab. I didn't want you to think that I am rude," Aryan said.

Rana rubbed his face with his palms before saying, "Tell me more about this Samar guy."

"Well. . ." the boy trailed off.

"It would be better if you let me come in," Rana said.

"Okay. . ." the boy said and relented.

The semi-darkness in the house was a little unnerving. The house was steeped in shadow and silence. It was high-class as high-class houses generally are, but it was devoid of any vitality, as if the air there was still, dead. It was the saddest looking posh house he had ever seen. Rana thought he understood what the boy went through every day and night. The silence and the darkness were his companions. It was depressing. Was it any different from his own life? Rana didn't want to answer that question.

"So tell me about this Samar," Rana asked, "What is he like?"

"He is, well . . . he is the biggest boy in the class, and knows how to use his size. He has terrorized all of us for as long as we can remember," Aryan said.

"Okay."

"For the last year or so, it feels as if I am his only target," Aryan said and was quiet for a while.

*There has to be another way; there always is.*

"What is he good at?" Rana asked, a thought, seemingly ridiculous, forming in his mind.

"What do you mean by that, Ranasahab?"

"He must be good at something, right? There is no way you can overpower him physically. But is he good at something at which you can try and beat him?"

"Well, he is good at body-building. He has muscles that are as hard as stone. That's what he claims."

Rana looked at the boy. Aryan was out of shape and

uncoordinated. It would take him years to get any muscles.

"Anything else?"

"He is popular with girls. I mean, the girls are afraid of him in a way, but they hover around him. I have seen them laugh at him behind his back, but they all go googly-eyed when he is around," Aryan said.

Rana was losing hope. Aryan carried so many layers of dopeyness that it would be impossible for the boy to become an overnight child version of Brad Pitt. Perhaps under those huge layers, there was a cute boy, but he wouldn't be coming out any time soon.

Perhaps the boy sensed what he was thinking and said, "I don't think I stand a chance with the girls, do I?"

Rana shrugged noncommittally.

"Is there anything else that this great specimen of humanity is good at?" Rana asked.

"He is the school champion in track and field—he's one of our fastest runners in the hundred meters race," Aryan said, his voice full of doubt.

Amongst the three options available, Rana thought this one was the least unpalatable. He knew the boy would not beat anyone, let alone the school champion in running. But this was something with which he could help the boy. It might bring Aryan out of his depression. Maybe distract him with something to do, something to look forward to.

"That's it!" Rana said smacking his hands together and hoping he sounded adequately enthusiastic, when actually he felt quite ridiculous.

"What?"

"You compete against him in running," Rana said, disbelieving the words he was saying, "And when you beat him, he will respect you and will stop bothering you."

"Running? Me?" The boy asked with a little snort.

"Why not, Aryan?"

"I don't know, Ranasahab," Aryan said, "I have never been good at anything physical."

"You just look ahead and run as fast as possible in one direction. How difficult can that be?"

Aryan said nothing.

"Or you will have to live with this torment for the rest of your life. Just think for a minute, okay? Imagine ten years from now, when you will be in college and some people ask you in a party full of girls, what your greatest achievement has been. Wouldn't it sound totally great that you beat the school champion in running?"

"It will, I guess," Aryan said with a smile. It was the kind of smile that made everyone smile back.

"You bet it will," Rana said hoping his voice didn't have the usual sarcastic tone. "When is the next track and field event?"

"A month from now, after the Diwali vacations" Aryan said.

"Brilliant," Rana said, "we have enough time to practise."

"We?"

"Yes, we. I am going to pick you up every morning and we are going to run together," Rana said.

"For a month?"

"Yes, for a month," Rana said and smiled.

Aryan could not understand why he had agreed to go ahead with Ranasahab's plan of competing against Samar. There was no way in the world he was going to beat the "fastest runner who ever lived" (in Samar's own words), even if he practised for several years, let alone a month. But as usual, he felt it had been the right thing to say at that time. He had loved the enthusiastic look on Ranasahab's face and didn't want to throw cold water on his plan.

After he had agreed to work hard at his running, Ranasahab drove him to the hospital to meet his mother. Aryan was thrilled to learn from the doctors that she was recovering fast and didn't need sedatives anymore. Ranasahab smiled from ear to ear for the first time in two days, as though he had heard good news after a long time.

When he entered her room, she was sitting up in bed—they had winched up the upper part of her bed, and she leant back against the pillows. She looked terrible and he hoped she wouldn't ask to look into a mirror. There were deep, dark circles under her eyes. Her lips looked parched and cracked. She had a sheen of sweat on her forehead and nose despite the room being air-conditioned. He had never seen her step out of the house looking tired or ill or without her make-up. *You need to look good while cooking*—that's what she used to say.

"Hello, Mom," he said, after staring at her for a few minutes, hoping she would acknowledge his presence.

She was a little startled, as if she had just realized he was in the room.

"Oh, hello, Aryan. How are you today?" she said as though they were meeting in their kitchen on a regular morning.

Aryan nodded his head to indicate he was fine.

"The doctors have said they will let you go tomorrow morning," he said.

"Let me go to what?" she said with a smile. It made her look ugly.

"Home," he said.

She snorted as she laughed, shaking her head.

"Oh yes, home," she said.

Aryan felt the same foreboding in the pit of his stomach like the one he had felt when her colleague had told him about her collapsing.

"Your father told me he is never coming home," she said and stared ahead.

Aryan said nothing. He didn't want to know the reasons. He hoped he never knew the reasons.

"What do you think? Will he come back?" she asked, without looking at him.

He wasn't thinking anything. He wasn't supposed to think anything. She was expecting too much from him.

"Well?" she said.

"I will never abandon you, Mom. And I will never abandon Dad either, when I grow up," he said.

His mother asked him to come closer and hugged him fiercely.

"Your father has abandoned you, Aryan," she said.

"But I haven't," he said. She smelled of hospital soap. She

held him for a few moments.

"You called Mahesh uncle and Geeta aunty, didn't you? The doctors aren't allowing me phone calls. I need to thank them. Will you thank them for me?" she said.

"Yes," he said and didn't elaborate any more.

"Are they waiting outside? You came with them right?" she asked.

"Well. . ." Aryan began. Just then, the doctor and a nurse entered the room carrying her food and change of clothes.

"So how is my favourite TV star doing today?" The doctor asked. The nurse made the kind of gushing sounds he had heard many people make around his mother.

"I have never been better," his mother said with a smile that only Aryan knew wasn't genuine, "Aryan, have you met Dr Gupta?"

"Yes, Ms Khosla. He visits here every day with the man sitting outside," the doctor said.

"Is Mahesh outside? Why don't you ask him to come in?" his mother asked Aryan.

"Well. . ." Aryan began again.

"Not now, Ms Khosla," the doctor interrupted, "You need to eat and sleep well. I can't keep you away from the TV too long, can I? My wife will kill me!"

"Thank you, doctor," his mother said.

"I will see you tomorrow morning, Mom," Aryan said and before she could ask more questions, he gave her a quick kiss on her cheek and hurried outside.

Aryan said nothing all the way to Ranasahab's house and Ranasahab, too, didn't ask him anything. He thought Ranasahab looked quite relieved now that his mother was going to get released soon.

"Can we ask Vinny to come over?" Aryan said as they climbed the stairs to Ranasahab's flat.

"Aren't you scared of her anymore?"

"No!" he said, "I mean I've never been scared of her."

Ranasahab had a smile on his face. He knocked on Vinny's door. She opened it. Her hair like the sparkles of a firecracker. She looked as if she had a cold.

"Aryan, here, wants you to come over to my place," he said.

"No no!" Aryan said, "I mean yes! You should come over. But it was his idea."

Ranasahab and Vinny looked at him for a moment before bursting into laughter. Aryan felt the heat in his cheeks.

"Dumbster, you look so damn cute when you blush," Vinny said as she accompanied them to Ranasahab's flat.

Ranasahab said he wanted to write his novel, so if it was fine by them, they would have to excuse him.

It was the first time he was playing with just Vinny. She beat him in every game and he didn't mind one bit.

"Have you never played video games earlier?" she asked.

"No," he said.

"Why?"

"I never knew they were so cool," he said, hoping it didn't make him sound uncool.

"So what do you do when you are back from school? Play with the boys in your society?"

"Umm, no."

"Now don't tell me you don't play because you didn't know that was cool," she said rolling her eyes.

"No, nothing like that," he said miserably, "it is just that they don't let me play."

He thought she looked at him as though seeing him for the first time.

"Well, you look a bit like a weirdo, for sure. Why do you dress like this?"

"Dress like what?"

"My God, dumbo, you are just so out of tune."

"What do you mean?"

"Who cuts your hair? Who allows you to wear these stupid clothes? Who bought you this horrible school bag?"

"Well, the barber cuts my hair. I wear my own clothes. And my mother bought me this bag and it isn't horrible," he said defensively.

"Like I said, out of tune," she said.

The truth was, although his mother accompanied him to

buy clothes, she generally got busy on her phone, just asked him to pick up whatever he liked and please hurry up, if possible. He had been going to the barber's alone for the last three years and the barber knew only one way to cut his hair. He didn't remember who had bought the school bag as it was two years old. It was a bit funny looking, admittedly, so he was sure he had chosen it himself.

"How old are you?"

"Thirteen," he said.

She laughed a little as though she didn't believe it and said, "You behave like an old man of fifty-three. And look at Rana. He behaves like he is twenty-three."

Ranasahab turned from his computer and said, "I heard that, young lady."

"Don't young lady me just to show that you are sixty-three, Rana."

Aryan was surprised that Ranasahab was that old.

"Rana tells me you are being harassed by some boys in school," she said a little enigmatically.

Aryan hadn't wanted her to know that. This news was spreading like wild fire. Everyone seemed to be talking about his misery.

He nodded without looking at her. He didn't want her to pity him.

"Okay," she said, twisting her lips with a firm shake of her head, as though she had decided on something.

"I write," he said.

"What?" she asked, a little bewildered by his abruptness.

"I write stories. I have written thirty thousand words of my novel already," he said.

"Write? Novel? Man, and here I thought you couldn't surprise me any more with your weirdness. What the hell is this novel about?" she said.

"Well, it is about this thirteen-year-old boy," he said and looked at her.

"Of course," she said rolling her eyes.

"He comes to know that his parents aren't his real parents. And that he was adopted. So he begins his search," he said.

Vinny looked at him as though he had said something terrible. Her lips trembled, and for a moment, he though she was going to cry. She quickly regained her composure and looked at him with narrowed eyes.

"Did I say something wrong?" he said.

She shook her head and said she would meet him tomorrow if he was still around and dialled a number on her mobile phone while walking out of Ranasahab's house.

"You are really writing that novel you told me about?" Ranasahab looked at him with narrowed eyes.

He nodded, regretting he had told Vinny about it.

"Did you tell her just to impress her?" Ranasahab said turning towards him.

"No," he said.

Aryan thought it was the first time he had ever mentioned the novel to anyone apart from Ranasahab. And depressingly, it sounded stupid.

"Hmm…interesting," Ranasahab said.

Aryan searched for a note of mockery in his voice, but Ranasahab sounded noncommittal.

"So are you going to finish it?"

"Yes," he said.

Ranasahab didn't ask him anything more.

The next day he thought he was quite calm when he walked into the school campus after Ranasahab had dropped him off at the gate. He knew what was going to happen after yesterday. He had had the whole night to prepare himself for the thrashing from the Rebels.

So, it was no surprise when the Rebels swooped on him from all directions.

"You are dead Ponchu Khosla! Dead!" Samar screamed as he virtually lifted Aryan off the ground. Samar's spittle flew at his face. His biceps were straining against the sheer fabric of his white shirt. Aryan had already resigned himself to a slow painful death. A crowd had already gathered around them. Everyone was deathly silent.

Samar raised his hand high in the air when Aryan heard Vinny's voice from behind him.

"You do that and you are dead."

In the silence on the school ground, her angry voice was the most beautiful and the most embarrassing sound Aryan had ever heard. This was the day when a girl, albeit a scary one like Vinny, was going to rescue him. In the fairytales, it was generally the other way round, wasn't it?

Samar let go of his shirt collar, his mouth open in a gasp of surprise. Aryan looked back to see Vinny standing in the middle of a bunch of mean-looking older boys wearing a red T-Shirt with the face of a monster on it. They were definitely not from his school. Samar's mouth stayed open. The Rebels were staring at Vinny's gang with scared eyes. The crowd suddenly came alive. A buzz went through as though they were witnessing something electrifying.

Vinny walked up to Samar slowly, chewing her gum in a deliberate and nasty way, and put a finger on his chest.

"Listen, snot-face. You stay away from him, okay? You promise to stay away from him and I won't harm you, ever."

For the first time since he had met her, Aryan realized how tall and scary she was. It was almost as if Samar had shrunk by a foot or two in front of her.

Samar stared at the older boys. They all wore black clothes and had black headbands. Samar looked like a scared little dog being admonished by his master. The crowd actually laughed. Some of them whooped. Samar looked at the Rebels, who in turn looked at the ground.

"Okay," he said in a whisper.

"Okay what, pimple-face?" Vinny said in a low growl.

"Okay, I will never bother him again," Samar said in a whisper.

"Good," Vinny said. She took out the chewing gum from her mouth and struck it on Samar's chest. The crowd laughed even harder.

"Just a reminder for you," she said and turned around.

"You let me know if something happens, Aryan," she said, motioned the boys away and began walking.

"I challenge you for this year's race, Samar!" Aryan screamed.

Vinny stopped in her tracks. The crowd guffawed and then cheered.

"What?" Samar asked, incredulously.

"I will beat you in running this year," Aryan repeated, slowly as though explaining to a toddler.

"Are you sure of what you said?" Vinny asked, her voice full of disbelief

He wasn't sure at all. He was shocked he had even said it. But it just felt right.

Samar laughed as though he had heard a great joke and said, "I will see you on the track, Ponc . . . Aryan."

The Rebels suddenly found their voices and started laughing.

"Stop laughing you eunuchs," Samar screamed at them and walked away. The Rebels followed him with their heads down.

"Dumbo, I think you are totally nuts," Vinny said with a shake of her head.

"I will beat him," Aryan said limply.

"You are an idiot. I don't know why I even bothered," she said and walked away with her boys. The crowd dispersed.

Aryan stood there, and after a while, he knew he had made a big mistake.

Ria was surprised to know she was actually looking forward to Ranasahab's reading as she sat at her study table on her reclining chair. She had spent all of yesterday thinking about Ranasahab's novel. He was a brilliant writer and she suspected that many elements of the story he was telling were autobiographical in nature. She had even made a list of a few tentative recommendations she would make. Writing had seemed so alien, so contrived and pointless just two days ago. She looked hard at the date she had marked on the calendar, hoping to get an answer to explain the sudden urge to write something, anything. Maybe just a meaningless poem. A Haiku of unrelated words. She had never shown her poems to anyone, believing they weren't great. Now, she felt like writing a really bad Haiku, to get the feel of words as they appeared on paper. She opened the writing pad as though her hands were on auto-pilot. The first page was the list she had made. The three not so small things. She closed the pad and leaned her head against it.

When she stepped into the coffee shop, Ranasahab and Aryan were already seated at their usual table for three with the circular glass top. She paused at the door watching the two. Aryan was saying something animatedly and the old writer listened with rapt attention. After a few moments he shook his head and laughed hard. A few people even stared at them. Although, it seemed, Aryan looked quite sheepish. The smile was back on his face. She wondered what she could do to make him smile like that forever.

That was when Ranasahab spotted her and waved a welcome.

When she joined them at the table, Ranasahab said to Aryan with a smile playing on the corners of his mouth, "Why don't you tell Ria what happened?"

Aryan blushed and proceeded to tell her what happened at school. She didn't feel the kind of shock she had a few days ago when she heard herself actually laughing at the way Aryan described the stunned reaction of the bully, Samar, when he was intimidated by a girl called Vinny. Ria thought Aryan held this girl Vinny in awe. As she had suspected, Ranasahab had complained to the Principal.

Ranasahab looked at her and said, "I agree that I was a bit hasty in talking to his school authorities. But I told Aryan, that there had to be another way; there always is."

She nodded at him.

That was when Anju made a noisy entry right to their table.

"Well, I am so happy for you!" she said as Ranasahab and Aryan looked at her. She was a sight that day. She wore an orange-coloured flowing dress—prescribed by her guru. Her hair, which was streaked with gold, was as messy as a bird's nest and she wore a large red *tilak* on her forehead which was shaped like an eye.

"I tried finding you at home, but your security guard told me you went to the coffee shop. I thought it was great; it's been some time since you have stepped out of the house! Who are these people? Hey, aren't you the boy at Mata's? Sheila Khosla's son? How is your mother? I saw on TV that she had been hospitalized? I bet all that stress and lack of family time caused it," she said.

"Anju!" Ria said. She had never learned how not to get embarrassed by her elder sister.

"What? I am speaking the truth, Chimni," Anju said and looked at Ranasahab.

Ria hated it when she used her nickname in public. She had told Anju several times not to do it, but to no avail.

"I am Anju," Anju said giving her hand to Ranasahab and batting her fake eyelashes, "Her sister."

Ranasahab shook it. Ria thought the old flirt inside him was trying hard to come to the surface, but he suppressed it well.

"How are you, ma'am?" he said

"I am fine and don't you ma'am me," she said with a phony laugh, "Call me Anju."

Ria decided to apologize to them later for her sister's behaviour, something she had learned to do since she was seven.

"I am so glad, Chimni, that you have stepped out of the house. I thought you never would after Varun and Raj's deaths."

Ria looked at Ranasahab and Aryan. They looked stunned. It was shocking. Her sister had crossed all the limits. Ria did what she had done since she was seven.

"I need to leave," she said getting up and almost pushing her wobbly legs to run to the exit.

Ranasahab and Aryan rose together.

"Ria, wait. . ." Ranasahab said in a shaky voice.

"No. I can't," she said, "I need to go now. Please don't follow me."

They sensed something in her voice and backed off. Anju had a terrified expression on her face. Ria decided she would never talk to her sister again.

She walked back to the house, feeling numb.

They were childhood sweethearts, Raj and Ria. He had been her first friend, the son of a couple who were Ria's family's neighbours for more than thirty years. They were each other's friends even when they were too young to understand the meaning of friendship. She could never recall how they had met. There were various stories. Her parents had insisted that they met on her second birthday, when a four-year-old Raj had planted a big kiss on her cheek, calling her an angel. Ria always thought it was just too cheesy. But many people claimed to have witnessed the incident. Raj had always embraced this story despite the relentless humiliation he was subjected to because of it, and she had never done so. He said it was a great story and he didn't care if it was true or just someone's imagination. Ria had always believed it was her mother's overtly romantic mind at its best, which Anju had inherited.

Ria always believed that the way she and Raj had accepted this fanciful story was what defined them. He was a dreamer. Reality was a concept just beyond him, even when they were growing up, aware of each other in a way only eternal lovers are aware of. She had never quite understood his passion for those romantic movies and books like *Qayamat Se Qayamat Tak* and *Devdas*. She thought of them as the emotional manipulation of gullible audiences.

Like all childhood sweethearts, they married early, immediately after she finished her degree in journalism. And within the year, they were the hottest scriptwriting couple on the television circuit. They weren't making much money—they were barely able to have two square meals, and an occasional bottle of wine—but they were happy. Happy in a way that doomed couples generally are.

His romanticism and her realism, instead of cancelling each other out, had complemented each other. Writing was their life and as long as it was flourishing, they never bothered to introspect on the inherent dichotomy of it all.

But Raj, who had seemed so endearing with his fantastical ideas and dreamy takes on life, had started his slow but inalterable journey to becoming a lazy escapist and irresponsible spouse in her heart. And she knew she had become a cynical, heartless old hag in his heart. It hadn't helped that sex, beautiful and wondrous till then, was becoming a drag and infrequent.

Exactly thirteen months after their wedding, she was told by a gynaecologist that she was pregnant. She had thought it was just too soon. They were barely able to feed two on their minute incomes, and having a baby would make everything so very difficult. Raj had called her a self-centred bitch when she had told him her feelings. He hadn't stopped smiling and laughing and generally fussing over her till they had that discussion. She knew something had died between them the day she had raised her doubts about the baby. She had told Raj his dreams weren't solid enough to feed three people and that he was going to starve them to death. He had told her that by the time the baby was born, he would be a man everyone talked about in the television industry and she would have to eat her words.

He had lived up to his promise. Well, almost, because they were both talked about in the industry within the year, she more than he.

It was Varun who had held them together. That tiny bundle of joy, when she had held him in her hands, with tears streaking down her cheeks, was responsible for sustaining the marriage of Raj and Ria. He had been an unbelievably calm baby, and had stared at everything with his brown eyes as though he was already aware of how the world looked and felt.

She had never admitted to him, but she had hated the memory of not wanting a baby, not wanting *Varun.* Perhaps it was the reason he was snatched away from her. As if the Almighty had waited till she had realized the horror of her thinking, allowed Varun to be the only thing she lived for, and then decided to punish her.

Chapter 12

# The Three Revelations

Rana smothered the instinct to follow Ria home from the coffee shop. He sat down on the chair, suddenly feeling very drained. He knew she had lost her only child and her husband. He guessed her son must have been twelve or thirteen years old when he died. He wanted to know why she was so unhappy and help her to overcome it, but this was beyond his meagre emotional depth to comprehend. How do you help someone who had lost everything they lived for? And what about his own children? Did he even know what state they were in? Had he always assumed that they would be fine?

"Oh my God, I have made such a terrible mistake again," Anju said to no one in particular.

She was an attractive woman. A little crazy perhaps, but attractive nevertheless. Rana thought, just a couple of days before he would've gone after her, telling her how great an author he was and how people were actually crazy about his novels with a couple of them in the pipeline to be adapted into movies, and finally just slip in the little fact that he was actually the scion of the Rathod family, just mention it off-handedly enough to make her grovel for more about that little bit. But now, he was surprised to know he didn't like her. She was a flaky, shallow woman. Rana couldn't believe he had actually had those thoughts. Flaky and shallow were his type, his speciality.

"I need to go apologize to her," she said.

"I don't think she wants anything to do with you right now, if you ask me," Rana said to the woman.

"Maybe you are right. Are you still having that coffee?"

The woman was impossible!

"Well, I need to be at some place urgently," he said looking at his watch and getting up, "Come on, Aryan."

She rubbed her forehead with her thumb and forefinger and said, "I am not a bad person, sir. She lost her husband and child in an accident. She is on the brink, Mr Rathod. I was just so happy that she was actually meeting new people. I had no clue you two didn't know about it."

They weren't supposed to know, Rana thought. They were strangers who had met her a few days ago. Strangers aren't supposed to know the manner in which your life has been devastated.

"I am sure you aren't a bad person, ma'am," he said and started walking. Aryan followed him. The woman stayed in the coffee shop.

Rana was silent as he drove to the hospital. He sensed Aryan, too, was deep in thought.

"There is a room in her flat. I slept in that room when Samar hit me the other day. I think it was her son's room. She has stored all his things in boxes. I wore her son's shirt that day," he said in a matter-of-fact way, as though everything made sense to him now.

Rana said nothing. The rest of the distance was covered in silence.

Rana stopped the car in front of the hospital entrance. The boy's mother was going to be released today, as they had already ascertained from the doctors.

"Why don't you come in, Ranasahab, and meet my mother?" Aryan asked, "I want her to know that you took care of me when she was here."

"It will be better if I don't," Rana said, "She is not going to like you staying with a man you met just a few days ago."

The boy nodded as though he understood. For a moment, Rana wondered if the Khosla woman could spend another night in the hospital. The boy had altered something in his house by entering it. Rana wasn't sure what had changed, nor was he certain whether he liked that change or not. He thought that, if Aryan were to stay with him one more day, he might understand how the atmosphere in his house had changed. Or maybe not. Maybe it took several years to decide whether you liked such changes or not.

"I will see you in the morning tomorrow. We will start our training then," he said to the boy, who looked a little downcast. Rana had expected him to be happy, at least relieved, now that his mother was finally going to be home.

He drove away slowly. In the rear-view mirror the boy looked lonely and despondent.

When Aryan entered the hospital, his mother had already packed her bag.

"Mahesh didn't come in again!" she cried, "I need to beat him up for being so busy."

Aryan had asked Jeevan, their driver, to report at the hospital. When they entered the car, the driver looked his usual morose and irritated self, and said nothing about Aryan not being at home for the last two days. His mother, as always, berated Jeevan a couple of times about his honking and rash manoeuvres while they drove home. She muttered loudly that it was becoming so impossible to get good maids, and that good drivers who don't drink and don't have body odour were even rarer. Aryan thought she was well and truly back.

When they entered the home, his mother said to Aryan, "I am a bit tired. I am going to take a bath and go to sleep, okay?"

"Okay, Mom," Aryan said.

"It feels like I have been gone forever, doesn't it? It's been just two and a half days," she said.

Aryan wanted to tell her that those were the longest two and a half days of his life.

"It does," he said.

He knew what she was stalling for.

"Papa didn't call," he said without looking at her.

"I didn't ask you that," she said sharply.

"I thought I would let you know," he said.

She sighed loudly, entered her bedroom and banged the door behind her. Aryan hoped she wouldn't call Mahesh uncle and Geeta aunty any time soon. She didn't. When he peeked inside the bedroom after ten minutes, she was in bed, snoring gently. She hadn't had a bath. Aryan covered her with a blanket. She curled up a little and opened her eyes.

"Sorry, Mom. Didn't want to wake you up," he said.

"Sit with me," she said and held his hand.

He sat with her and watched her drift back into sleep after a few minutes. He gently removed her hand, but sat with her on the bed for a long time.

The next day, he woke up at five thirty and checked his mother's room. It was empty. At first, he thought something terrible had happened to her and she was back in hospital. But then he saw her note. The notes had been her biggest form of communication. They would contain messages: *Dinner in the refrigerator, eat early kiddo.* Or...*Will be very late. Your mommy is on TV today!*

That day, however, the note was longer *'I can't stay home, kiddo. Need to work today if I want to get out of this. Going early as I know the kitchen will be in a mess. Only your mommy can take care of things, isn't that so?'* There was a big smiley on it.

He didn't think the kitchen would be in a mess and he didn't think she was the only one who could take care of it. Aryan sat on her empty bed for a few minutes, exactly where he had sat the last night for so long. He then walked to the kitchen, made a bowl of his favourite mix, poured warm milk on top of it and ate it slowly. It tasted bitter, but he finished it as he didn't like trashing food. Aryan wondered if it was time to try something new for breakfast tomorrow onwards because his favourite dish no longer tasted good.

When he met Ranasahab in front of the society's gate at six, he said nothing as he got into the car. Ranasahab, too, seemed lost in thought. Maybe he was thinking about his novel. The jogging park near the housing society was already teeming with people in their exercise gear. Some people were jogging with their dogs. Ranasahab gazed at the park. Aryan thought Ranasahab liked what he saw. There were several young women running in really tight and sweaty clothes.

Ranasahab looked at him a little disapprovingly and said, "Have you ever played any sports in school?"

"No," Aryan said with a shrug.

Ranasahab harrumphed a little and then proceeded to take him through a routine of stretches. Aryan liked the stretches, they made his body feel lose and limber.

After they had finished the warm-up, Ranasahab said it was time to start running.

"I want you to run to that tree there," Ranasahab said, pointing at a tree some fifty metres away. "Let's see how fast you can do that."

Aryan nodded and bent down on the ground in the runner's pose he had seen on the sports channels on TV.

"What are you doing?" Ranasahab barked.

"Uh," Aryan said looking at him from his kneeled position, "This isn't the right pose?"

"Oh, for God's sake, Aryan, this isn't a race! Just run to the tree now, will you?"

"Okay," Aryan said, got up and began running towards the tree. When he reached the tree, he touched it with his right hand, and turned back. Sweat had already erupted on his scalp and forehead. His heart was fluttering like a dying bird. Aryan ran towards Ranasahab with all the willpower he could summon. When he reached Ranasahab he bent over and breathed in large gulps. He thought he wouldn't be able to speak. His chest felt as if it would burst open. He had run for maybe a few minutes, but it felt as if he had been doing it forever.

"Are you okay? What happened?" Ranasahab asked in a disgusted tone.

"No . . . thing," he said huffing.

He felt a kind of shame he hadn't felt ever before.

"Disappointing, very disappointing," he heard Ranasahab say.

They sat down on the ground, Aryan sweating like he had

never sweated before and Ranasahab looking at him with a slightly angered expression.

"One month will not be enough," Ranasahab said.

It took him a long time to recover and he hated to admit to himself that one month was just too short. Anyway, he had never thought it was possible.

"It was your idea," Aryan said.

"And I am regretting it now," Ranasahab said.

He watched in awe as Ranasahab ran the whole expanse of the jogging park several times over. Ranasahab wasn't even breathing deeply when he finished eight rounds of the park. In that time Aryan almost completed two rounds before he collapsed on the ground, sweaty, humiliated and exhausted.

Later, when they drove back to his building society, Aryan thought he should ask Ranasahab something not related to running, just to divert him from the regret he was feeling.

"What are you doing for Diwali?"

"Diwali?" Ranasahab asked as though he had never heard of the word.

"The festival of lights. The day Lord Rama came home. . ."

"Yeah, smarty. I know what Diwali is," Ranasahab said as he changed gears and honked at a taxi that had veered dangerously close to the car.

"Right. So what are you doing?"

"Nothing."

"Everyone does something on Diwali," Aryan said.

"Is that so? What do you do?"

"I . . . uh . . . I set off crackers and eat a lot of mithai," Aryan said and trailed off.

"Well, that doesn't sound like much to me."

"Mom works overtime and Papa has always been. . ." Aryan paused before he said, "absent during Diwali. Mom says he and his friends gamble a lot and then drink a lot that night. What about your family?"

"What about them?"

"Don't they invite you for it?"

"I don't need anyone's invitation," Ranasahab said as they stopped in front of the society gate.

"Tomorrow same time?" Aryan asked before getting out of the car.

Ranasahab nodded vaguely, as though in severe doubt whether it was worth getting up to watch him struggle through his rounds of the park.

Ria had vowed not to take her sister's call, but Anju wouldn't stop ringing her number. She had switched off her mobile after dozens of missed calls from Anju. Her sister had rung up on her landline instead. Ria didn't want to disengage that phone too. Was it because she thought either Ranasahab or Aryan would call her? She needed to apologize to them for Anju's appalling behaviour, and she was surprised to admit that she hoped they wouldn't run away from her tragedy like everyone else had—everyone except her elder sister. That thought finally made Ria take Anju's call.

"Will you at least allow me to say sorry to you properly?" Anju demanded on the phone as soon as Ria took her call. She made it sound as if Ria had made a mistake and not she.

"Okay," Ria said resignedly.

"I am so sorry, Chimni. Can't even tell you how sorry I am," Anju said.

"You just did," Ria said.

"I hate it when you are so cold to me," Anju said with a series of practised sobs.

"Okay, don't cry, please," Ria said.

"I miss them so much, Chimni. Especially Varun. He was such a darling. You think I am a heartless bitch, but I am not," Anju said.

Ria wanted to tell her she didn't think Anju was heartless. Tactless was more like it. But she said nothing.

"Varun was such a pretty boy. I still remember how cuddly he was with all that baby fat," Anju said.

Ria closed her eyes. All this was unbearable.

"And you and Raj were. . ."

"Tai, it's enough. I forgive you. It won't matter anyway," Ria said and regretted it immediately.

"What do you mean? Are you trying to cut me off from your life? Don't do that! You are all I have now."

"No, I am not doing that," Ria said.

"Good. Thank you," Anju said, "You have to come to my house for Diwali though. I am going to make your favourite rawa laddoos."

Ria said, "Okay."

She had no intention of going to Anju's home. But Anju wouldn't let the topic drop if she said no. Worse, she would again start crying. Sometimes, Ria thought Anju had shed more tears for her dead son and husband than she had. She had no doubt that Anju's grief for Varun was genuine—they had shared a special relationship. At a very early age, he had been fascinated by the difference between his mother and her sister. Naturally, he had thought Anju was a much more fun person than his staid and dogged mother. Ria wasn't too sure about Anju's tears for Raj, though. They had disliked each other. It was quite strange, because temperamentally they were an exact match. Carefree, life-embracing, free spirited—people used the same adjectives to describe both of them. So it was strange that they hated each other with a passion. Funnily, they used to call each other 'shallow'. Ria had always laughed at their mutual derision of each other and had claimed that it was a case of the pot calling the kettle black.

"Good! I am shocked by how easily you have forgiven me this time. You haven't done your usual sulking-not-talking routine," Anju was saying.

Ria said nothing.

"Are you there or did I just remind you that you need to sulk?"

Despite herself, Ria couldn't help but smile.

"I also plan to invite your new friends," Anju said.

"New friends?"

"That old man and the boy. The man is dashing, isn't he? Reminds me of Amitabh Bachchan a lot. I wonder if he is married," Anju said.

"Oh, for God's sake, Anju," Ria said with a deep sigh.

"What? I am just wondering," Anju said, "On second thoughts, maybe I am doing more than wondering. Anyway, I have invited them over and they have accepted."

"Tai, now this is too much," Ria said and banged the phone down.

Diwali. She hadn't thought about it.

The lawyers had said it would take them at least two weeks more to set up the charity. It meant she had to endure Diwali. She had never liked the festival—the noise made by firecrackers exploding; the unnecessarily hyper people, the flood of sweets. Her mother and sister would go nuts during Diwali. They would pretend to clean the house for days and would panic when the festival was just a few days away. Ria had had to step in and clean the furniture, cook a lot of snacks and decorate the house to make it presentable. They would then exclaim at how beautiful it looked, conveniently forgetting to thank her, and would accept compliments from the guests as though it had been their handiwork. The two would frolic around like rabbits on steroids for the duration of festival, talking loudly, managing to say the wrong things all the time to the relatives, asking the wrong questions ("What are you eating nowadays? You have put on at least ten kilos, no?"), messing up whatever they tried to cook and generally getting on her nerves. It was exasperating. And now she had to endure it all one last time. There was no way Anju would let her be alone.

She wished she had been like Nina—ambitious, strong-willed, no-nonsense. Nina had been the only child of her parents, another thing she wished she had been although she hated herself for having that thought. She wanted to know more about Nina. She wanted to know what happened to her. Had she committed suicide too? She shook a little at the thought.

The woman was dead, and now Ranasahab was dying too. The old man was enduring a mortal disease and there can be no bigger horror than being aware of something destroying you from within. She had to help him write that novel, even if it meant it was his last hope. She wondered what her last wish would be. How could criminals responsible for heinous crimes get a last wish and not she? Perhaps her last wish would be just impossible for anyone to fulfil.

Get me back my son and my husband. And while you are at it, could you also make my husband faithful?

### *Rana's memories of Nina*

### United Kingdom, Forty years ago...

He had never understood when he actually knew he wanted to live the rest of his life with Nina, unlike the way it was shown in the movies (*Breakfast at Tiffany's*) or novels. He didn't tell her so immediately. She would've actually laughed at it. Not laughed in a nervous manner, leading to a similar declaration from her, but laughing in a mocking "Have you lost your marbles?" way.

There wasn't a moment he didn't think of her. Every morning after he got up, he had a feeling that his subconscious mind had never let her go, like a favourite song that keeps running in your head. He tormented himself for days and weeks about it—deciding to tell her every day and then chickening out. He even thought of not meeting her for a few days, just to get over his feelings for her, but felt wretched when he imagined the day without seeing her.

He had stopped sleeping around, stopped drinking too much, restricting himself to just a pint or so and stopped paying the tab for other people. The news had spread.

"What's wrong with you suddenly?" she asked him one day.

"What?"

"You have been generally sober for a record six days. The girls are saying you don't answer your door in the night. You seem a bit distracted around those blokes you call your mates."

"Well, as Hindus we are encouraged to practice abstinence

for certain periods of time. You wouldn't know, what with you being an atheist and all that," he said and knew it sounded lame.

"You think I am one of those wind up dolls you bang every night? The ones who have cabbage for brains?"

"No," he said hating the view she had of him.

"So?"

"Well, I don't know. It just doesn't feel right anymore," he said.

They were sitting on the steps of the university building with paper cups filled with coffee.

She said nothing for a while.

"Are you going to tell me you have fallen for me?" she said.

"What? No!" he said.

"Because that would be outrageous. Know why? Because I was going to tell you that I am falling for you."

He didn't think he heard her right.

"Are you messing around with me, Nina?"

"No," she said quietly.

He held her hand. It was warm because of the thin paper of the coffee cup. It was shaking because of what she had said. It was so soft and he never wanted to let it go.

That was the way he remembered her thereafter. A beautiful dimpled smile, eyes brimming with tears and shaking hands.

That was the last time he was truly happy.

# Part 2

## Chapter 12

# The Three Celebrate a Festival

Aryan looked at the calendar and realized that ten days had gone by since he started going to the jogger's park. Although he had embarrassed himself on the first day, time had flown as he carried on with his training. Ranasahab picked him up every morning religiously. They stretched and they ran, but they didn't speak much to each other. The first few days were the toughest, when Aryan thought he would have a heart attack with all that exertion. But over the last three or four days, he realised he could sprint without huffing and puffing. But that wasn't quite enough for Ranasahab, as he still had a disgruntled expression whenever they finished their morning run. Aryan was now absolutely certain Ranasahab was lying about his cancer.

Ranasahab and he met Ms Ria almost every day at the coffee shop, where Ranasahab read them instalments of his novel. It was an amazing story in Aryan's opinion. Ranasahab never asked him for his views, but he nonetheless told Ranasahab and Ms Ria what he thought about the story, the characters and the events. Although Ranasahab snapped at him from time to time for speaking his mind, he had started accepting his suggestions a little grudgingly. Whenever he said something about the writing or the story, Ms Ria looked at him somewhat amazed, as though she couldn't believe he could make those suggestions. She was even more surprised when he told her he had read *The God of Small Things* and *A Suitable Boy*. She had smiled when he told her that he didn't like children's books. Even she hadn't liked them when she was a young girl. He and Ranasahab had paused for a moment when she had said that. She never spoke about herself. Ms Ria told him often how wonderful it was that he knew so much about books and writing. Aryan had felt very embarrassed, but very good every time she paid him a compliment.

Aryan had resumed visiting Sakhu-mai's house on alternate days. When he went to meet her after his mother got back from hospital, he held her hand and told her everything that had happened in the previous week. He wasn't sure if she heard him. Her breathing was shallower since he had last met her, and it seemed she had shrunk even more, if that was even possible.

His father hadn't returned. He had asked his mother a few times about it. She had clammed up every time, refusing to tell him anything. Aryan wondered if he should go look for his father, but didn't know where to start. He suspected his mother knew where he was. Aryan was hopeful he would return in a few days or, at most, a week.

The Diwali vacations had started three days ago and Dhanteras, the festival of wealth, was to be celebrated in the next couple of days. Ria's sister had invited him and Ranasahab for a party she was throwing today. Aryan wasn't going because Ranasahab had refused to take him in the night.

Samar and the Rebels hadn't bothered him at all in school, at least not physically. But they heckled him all the time. They called him 'turtle' or 'seashell' and never stopped telling him how he would pee in his pants when he came last in the race. Aryan didn't really mind all that jeering as long as they didn't beat him up. He knew Samar wouldn't dare, what with the constant threat from Vinny and her gang. He missed playing XBOX games with Vinny. And he was embarrassed to admit to himself that he actually missed Vinny and not the XBOX.

On the eleventh day after he had started running, Aryan knew something was wrong when his mother came home at nine at night. He couldn't remember the last time she had been home that early. She called out his name from the living room.

"Mom, you are hurting me," Aryan cried out when his mother grabbed his shoulders in a painfully hard grip and demanded to know where he had been when she was in the hospital, because Mahesh and Geeta had told her they never got a call from Aryan about moving in with them, and Jeevan told her he never saw Aryan in the flat.

"Tell me the truth!" she demanded.

"I didn't go to their place, but they are lying too," he said, flinching; instead of releasing his shoulders, she squeezed them even harder.

"What do you mean, they are lying?"

"I called Mahesh uncle after you told me to. When I said I wanted to come over to stay with them, he laughed and said I must be joking. When I said my mother was in hospital and I was alone at home and it was no joke to be in this situation, he said it was still a joke to him. Then he told me he couldn't take me in because they had no place in their house and they were going to Mauritius for a holiday. He called Papa an irresponsible idiot. So I banged the phone down on him," he said.

"You are lying again! Mahesh is my friend and he would never say that to you," she exclaimed.

"I am sorry I lied to you that day, Mom," he said, the pain in his shoulders unbearable. He hadn't actually lied to her. He just hadn't had an opportunity to tell her properly. She was fading in and out of consciousness while she was in the hospital and telling her all these terrible things about her friends would have surely sent her BP up. And besides, he was surprised that it took her ten days to talk to Mahesh uncle about this. Knowing Mahesh uncle, he wouldn't have bothered to take her call when he was holidaying in Mauritius.

"You would've felt awful if I had told you the truth then. You were in pain and I didn't want you to get hurt anymore," Aryan said with a grimace as her fingers dug into the tender part of his shoulder.

She relaxed her hands. Her mouth opened in shock as though she had just realized how hard she had gripped him and how painful it must've been for him.

"Where were you, then?" she asked, folding her hands.

"I . . . I was with Ranasahab," he said, avoiding her eyes.

"Ranasahab who?"

"He is an author."

"A what?"

"An author, Mom," he said, "A very great author. Sadly, he doesn't have any fans, though. He has written twenty-nine novels and he is writing one right now. . ."

"Aryan," she said, making his name sound like a single expression of admonishment, "Listen to me. I have absolutely no idea what you are talking about. Who is this man? And how do you know him?"

"I met him at Ms Ria's place," he said.

"My God! Who is this Ria? Who are these people, Aryan? Have they done anything to you? Have they been hurting you?" she suddenly knelt down in front of him, moving her hands all over his face and head.

"No," he said, "Why would they hurt me? Although I think Ranasahab doesn't like me too much."

She looked at him as though she was seeing him for the first time.

"I want you to tell me everything. From the start," she said.

Her voice was ominously cold.

Aryan took a deep breath and told her everything: how he was almost crushed by a nasty crowd on the railway station platform; how Ms Ria had saved him; how she had taken him to the doctor; the real reason he had hassled that woman at Mata's; how he had gone to meet Ms Ria and thank her; how he had met Ranasahab there; how Ranasahab had helped him, albeit very reluctantly, when she was in the hospital; how he had come to know that Ms Ria had lost her son and husband very recently; how bullies had hit him on the chin; how he had met Vinny; how Vinny had saved him from bullies. . .

She listened without saying a word or blinking her eyes. She was clenching her teeth and frowning by the end of it.

Aryan knew these were bad signs.

"Where do they live?" she asked in an eerily calm voice.

"What are you going to say to them, Mom?" Aryan wanted to know.

"I asked you where do they live?" She enunciated each word

as if she was spitting them out.

"You can meet them at Ms Ria's sister's house tomorrow night. She has invited all of us for a Diwali dinner."

She looked at him as though he was a stranger to her. Someone, she had just realized, who was living in her house all this while completely unknown to her.

As Ria had expected, she received a call from Anju the day before the party to come to her house and help her with the cleaning. She tried every excuse that had already failed in the past, but Ria refused steadfastly. In the end, when Anju told her she would lock herself up in her bathroom and never come out, Ria finally agreed to go help her elder sister.

When she saw the state in which Anju's preparations for the gala dinner were, Ria had to bite her finger from screaming in frustration. Anju lived in a house she had clawed out, in her words, from her first husband Dr Juneja's stingy fingers. Her first husband was a mild-mannered man who was at least two decades her elder. Ria had stopped talking to her when Anju had told her about her "impending first marriage". Anju had confided in her that the man was moneyed—in her words, he was like a "low-hanging fruit ready to be plucked". It didn't matter if he was twenty years older than her and actually looked fifty years older. She said there were "advantages" to such a marriage. Ria told her that if she decided to marry the poor man, she could forget she ever had a sister. Anju had retorted by saying that she was a fool for not recognizing an opportunity in life.

Ria hadn't spoken to her for weeks after the wedding. She had actually liked the doctor. He was a lovely man—older, but so meticulous and obviously in love with her annoying sister, although how he could've fallen for her was a mystery. Ria wished she had straightened out Anju, maybe even begged her not to divorce the man. She knew Anju wouldn't have changed her mind, but she could've tried. The last time she had seen the doctor was when he was walking out of the court, humiliated, with tears in his eyes. Anju had told the court that she was divorcing her husband because he had never told her that he was impotent. Funny, considering he was a doctor.

Anju had taken the big house from the poor man and he dutifully paid her a handsome alimony every month. When Ria had accused her of being a heartless bitch, Anju had remarked that it had been truly the doctor's fault, as she had always wanted to have babies and he had never told her he couldn't give her the ultimate satisfaction of being a mother. Ria had hated her for breaking the man's heart. Bizarrely, over the years, Anju and the doctor had mended their relationship and were in a perfectly harmonious divorce. When, a year or so after their separation, she had told Ria that she and Dr Juneja were going on a holiday together, Ria had burst out laughing.

The doctor's house, as Anju called it, was a mess. It hadn't been cleaned for months. There were clothes lying all over like flung cadavers. A strange smell, reminiscent of unwashed utensils and rotten food, had settled in the house.

"This isn't a place fit for human habitation," Ria said when she entered the house.

"I have told you that frequently, baby sister," Anju moaned. "You have just abandoned me."

It had been Ria's job a year and a half ago to visit her sister every few weeks and goad and help her to take care of the doctor's house. Raj had neither understood nor reconciled to the reversal of roles between the two sisters. He had indulged Anju for a while, but then had rebuked her for exploiting her younger sister's niceness. He accused Anju of treating Ria like a doormat. Anju had called him a leech, for earning less money than Ria and not being a good role model for her nephew. Ria, for reasons unknown even to herself, had always found their fights comical and couldn't help but laugh whenever they were at each other's throats, trading insults like kindergarten children. They wanted Ria to choose between the two of them, something she had resolutely refused to do.

"How do you expect me to do so much in barely a day?" Ria wanted to know as she surveyed the disarray in the house.

"You are a miracle worker, Ria," Anju said, "Please!"

Ria didn't want to make the effort. A year and a half ago, she would've just jumped at it and wouldn't have left till the house smelled of room freshener and everything was clean and shining. It didn't matter now. The world would go on just fine without houses being cleaned. She need not worry about it.

"Ria," Anju said, "What's the matter? Are you alright?"

"I am fine," she said.

"I am so sorry, Chimni. It is so insensitive of me to do this to you."

Ria recalled that Anju, her elder sister, had been with her constantly for almost six months when her world had collapsed a year and a half ago. She had cried for her, she had lain awake with her, she had washed her and had tried to feed her. Ria knew there was no point to any of it, ultimately, but Anju had valiantly tried to save her sister from dying. All she had achieved was to prolong the misery by eighteen months, but she had done what she had thought was the right thing to do for her sister.

"No, Tai," Ria said, "Shut your melodrama shop for a while, will you?"

"What would I do without you?" Anju asked with a big smile.

Ria wanted to tell her that she should learn how to do things for herself now. But she said nothing, fought back her tears and smiled at her sister.

Rana didn't want to go for the Diwali party. What was the point? It would consist of a bunch of strangers getting together and chatting over vomit-inducing sweets and oily salty snacks. He hadn't celebrated Diwali for years, certainly not since the incident at his daughter's wedding. There was no point to the festival, which provided an occasion for everyone involved to pollute the environment while deafening their neighbours.

Anju had told him he had to come because he had

miraculously pulled her sister out of her self-imposed confinement in her home. He didn't think the reward for such an act was an invitation to a stupid dinner, but he had agreed. Ria's presence did something strange to him. It was as if his muse, who had deserted him decades ago, had suddenly deigned to bow down to his wishes.

She wasn't Nina, of course, he knew that. But she *was* Nina in so many ways. And he didn't want her to leave again.

The woman had lost her husband and son.

Just thinking of it made him sick to the stomach. How she coped with it was beyond his comprehension. Once, it seemed like hundreds of years ago, his son had climbed on the parapet wall of the terrace in the palatial Rathod mansion. His son was eight and had wanted to do it for a long time—walk along the parapet wall with his eyes closed. Rana had watched in horror as he had climbed the wall, but couldn't do anything about it. He was on the ground and the boy was on the fourth floor. A scream had died in Rana's throat because if he had screamed, the boy would've known he was being watched and would've lost his balance.

In those terrifying few seconds, every single scenario had run in his mind—would his son lose a limb, or would he become paralysed, or would he become brain dead, or would he die? He had imagined living with the knowledge of whatever happened to his son for the rest of his life and for a moment he had rationalized that if the boy lost his balance, it would be better if he died rather than become paralysed.

His son had completed the walk and whooped in joy. Rana had stifled a screaming expletive with herculean effort, smiled at him and told him to come down because a reward was waiting for him. The boy had taken the stairs and ran down, only to receive the severest spanking of his life and no food for one full day.

Rana had never forgiven himself for accepting the death of his son so easily over all the other possibilities. The boy had cried after receiving the beating, and had never known Rana was also punishing his own shame. He had hated his son for showing him what kind of a man he truly was.

Ria lived with a reality to which he had become so readily

reconciled. Rana wondered what he would've done had his son died that day. Would he have killed himself, too? Rana didn't want to answer that. His son, when he became an adult, hadn't even bothered to talk to him for years. All this while, Rana had blamed his son for betraying him, for abandoning him. Now, he wasn't sure how much of it had to do with himself.

He got ready. He wore a finely embroidered chikan kurta and an expensive but light stole.

When he reached Anju's house, he found a row of parked cars outside it. It seemed the entire neighbourhood had been invited by the crazy woman. When he couldn't find a place to park the car, Rana regretted accepting the woman's invitation even more. Diwali was an endless stupidity. The children were already on the streets, bursting crackers. The biggest festival day was a couple of days away, but the damned children were already very excited. He wished they would stay indoors and celebrate like civilized people should—quietly. But this was a festival of noise and there was no hiding from it.

He had made up his mind to turn around and head home when a car moved out of the parking slot. Wondering if the fates too wanted him to attend the party, he moved his car towards the slot. Just when he was about to slide the car into the slot, he saw a massive sedan come out of nowhere and stop literally inches away from his front bonnet. His heart hammering away, he stifled curses and peered through the windshield to look at the driver. The man in the black Mercedes had the same annoyed expression on his face. Rana indicated to him to move back so that he could park the car, but the man mimicked his action.

"Oh hell," Rana said loudly and opened the car door.

"Are you blind? Can't you see I am parking here?" he shouted.

The man stepped out of the car. He was a young man and was dressed like a Bollywood wannabe.

"I am sorry, but I was going to say the same thing to you. Although much more politely, considering your age," the man said.

Rana said, "Are you deaf too? Get your car out of here!"

"I am not sure why you are so worked up, sir. I saw this spot first," the man said with a smile.

Rana wanted to smash his teeth in.

"There is a. . ." Before the man could finish, a bunch of children lighted a big chain of firecrackers and the noise drowned out what he had to say. This is a goddamned joke, he thought.

Rana regarded the man closely for the time it took the firecrackers to die. He seemed like someone who went to men's parlours for a manicure and pedicure. Rana suspected the man was a lot older than he looked. It seemed he was in his late thirties rather than his early twenties. He was sure the baby fat that made him appear so gratingly cute when he smiled was surgically planted on him.

When the firecracker died, Rana said, "I am going to park in here, whether you like it or not."

Raising his arms in the air as though he was giving in but didn't care, the man said, "Fine."

They got into their cars, the man reversed his, and Rana took his rightful slot. Bloody pansies, he thought and started walking towards Anju's house. The man drove slowly ahead of him and when they were near Anju's house, he parked right next to it. Rana was miffed at missing such a convenient place to park.

The man stepped out of the car and waited till Rana caught up with him.

"All I wanted to say was there was a slot right next to Anju's house. But since you insisted. . ." the man said and shrugged.

Rana said nothing.

"By the way, my name is Abhi."

"Okay," Rana said without stopping.

The man smiled and followed him in.

When they entered Anju's house it was crammed with people. Children were running around the rooms like irritating wasps. Women were sitting in the living room chatting and laughing loudly. The men had glasses full of red sherbet. He was in a party where people were guzzling red sherbet, Rana thought. What next? The dinner would be served on the floor with people sitting in rows? Rana's first instinct was to turn around and run as fast as he could. He thought he would just have one look at Ria, if she was there and find his way out. Perhaps have a quiet word with her too, if she was okay with it. When he couldn't spot her, he turned around towards the door.

"Are you leaving already, sir?" he heard Anju's voice and flinched.

She had a fake smile on her face. She hadn't known him for more than a few days and she was smiling as though they were long lost childhood chums.

"Well. . ." he said but couldn't come up with anything.

"Oh, don't leave so soon. We have just started the party! Please have some sherbet. There is something harder in the kitchen if you want," she said, giving him a wink.

The woman was impossible.

"No, thanks," he said, "I am fine."

"Have you met Abhi?" she asked and called after the Bollywood wannabe.

"Abhi, meet Rana Rathod, the famous author!" she said famous author as though she had actually wanted to say big loser.

"Ranasahab, meet Abhi. He is an adman," she said, "And he has carried the torch for my sister for ages."

The man actually turned crimson. Anju was a tornado, destroying everything in her wake.

"Well," Rana said, "We have met."

Abhi raised his hand and Rana shook it. They had something in common now. They had both been humiliated by their host.

"Anju," Rana heard Ria say in a tone reserved for exasperating family members, "Leave them alone. Please."

"Oh well. Now that she is here, I can attend to my other guests," Anju said and walked away.

Harass other guests was more like it, thought Rana.

"Hello," he said to Ria.

She said hello back to him, but barely recognized the man called Abhi. He, too, seemed to have a sudden bout of squirms.

"I just thought I would drop in," Rana said and wondered

what that even meant. He thought he would drop in and then he did drop in, and then what? What was he going to do now that he had dropped in? Have a sherbet or something harder in the kitchen?

She, too, seemed at a loss for words. Ria wore a sari and had somehow managed to rein in her hair. He wasn't sure of their colour, as if they had never made up their mind whether they wanted to be black or brown. But there was a terrible sadness behind her hastily put together facade. She was someone who was once spectacularly beautiful, but now was withering away.

Rana thought it was the first time he was meeting her without the boy being around. And just when he thought of that, he saw the boy walk into Anju's house. There was a familiar looking woman with him, who was surely his mother. And she was fuming, much like the way Rana had watched her on TV.

Chapter 13

# The Three Are Involved in a Confrontation

When Aryan saw the number of people in Ms Anju's house, as he trailed behind his furiously marching mother, he knew his shame would be remembered by everyone. His mother had refused to talk to him all the way to Ms Ria's sister's house. He had pleaded with her to not say anything nasty to them, as they had done nothing to him. Ms Ria and Ranasahab had in fact helped him while she was in the hospital. He had no clue why his mother was so angry. She had refused to even look at him, only once telling him to shut up because she needed to drive and control her anger at the same time.

"Who is Anju Marathe?" she asked a woman as they entered the house. The woman pointed out Ms Ria's sister, who was unrecognizable from the woman she must've seen at Jaya's because of her sari and her neatly done hair.

His mother waded through the people and he followed in her wake, on the verge of tears, hoping some miracle would happen and his mother would not create a scene. No such luck.

His mother tapped Ms Anju on her shoulder while she was in the middle of her head-thrown-back-all-teeth-visible laugh and said, "Where is your sister and where is that old man?"

Ms Anju turned around and looked at his mother, then looked at him and said, "Hello Aryan! You are looking cute today. And you are here with your mother who has generally ignored you."

It had started. There was no stopping it now

"I don't ignore him! How dare you say that?" his mother shouted and then looked at him, "What have you been telling these people about me?"

He couldn't say a word. He didn't think he would be able to speak for a long time.

"Stop abusing your child!" Ms Anju shouted back.

Everyone at the party had suddenly become silent. They were all observing the drama and he was at the centre of it. He looked at the marbled floor of Anju's house and hoped there was a crack big enough to swallow him up.

"I am abusing my child? You people have some guts! You get involved with strangers, a thirteen-year-old boy, and then have the audacity to insult his mother?"

"Are you thirteen?" Ms Anju said looking at him, "You look more like ten to me."

"Stop talking! Where is your sister and where is that old man?" his mother demanded.

"How will I tell you where they are if you have asked me to stop talking in my own house?"

Ranasahab suddenly materialized out of nowhere and said, "Hold on, ladies. Can we please talk in civil tones?"

His mother regarded him from head to toe and said, "Is this the dirty old man who is trying to harm my son?"

The people guffawed. A few looked at Ranasahab as though he was a pervert. Aryan wondered if he should just run away from there. Ranasahab looked as though he was going to vomit.

"I am going to take you to the police, Mister! You will not go unpunished."

"Mom, please," Aryan said and was surprised he could still speak, "He has cancer. Please don't talk to him like that."

The people guffawed louder. Now, Ranasahab was a diseased dirty old man. Ranasahab looked at him in astonishment and Aryan knew he had made a big mistake.

"Well, what is this, Mister? What else do you have? AIDS?" she said and turned to Aryan, "What has he done to you? Has he touched you?"

"No," Aryan said. It came out like a sob.

"Well, can we please talk about this in lower voices, Mrs Khosla? I know you are very upset but I think you are way out of line here," Ranasahab said.

"You haven't seen my line yet, Mister," his mother said.

"Well, I have," Ranasahab said with clenched teeth, "Your line is just too short and your son is standing way out of it."

His mother looked at Ranasahab as though she had been slapped.

"Why are you looking so damn stunned, Mrs Khosla? When was the last time you visited his school? Three years ago? When was the last time you had a meal with him? You cook for strangers in your damned restaurant, but your only son eats food out of the refrigerator and cereal boxes. Do you even know who his friends are? Do you know whether or not he has any friends? Do you know that he gets beaten up by boys in the school?"

His mother looked as though she was going to cry.

"You bastard," she said softly.

"I think you need to swear at yourself rather than me," Ranasahab said and then turned around to the people, "I haven't touched this boy in any way. I never even wanted to meet him. And I would be just as happy if I never see him again."

Aryan looked at Ranasahab who refused to look back at him. Aryan wondered if it was true, that Ranasahab wouldn't want to meet him ever again. He knew it wasn't so.

There was a long and terrible pause. Aryan hoped he could just slip away. Nobody would notice. He couldn't move an inch.

"I think I am going to faint," his mother said holding her head and swayed as though she was going to fall.

Amazingly, Ranasahab held her and steadied her.

"Please have a seat," he said and pushed her gently towards a sofa. She flopped down on the sofa with a loud groan.

"Do you need water?" Anju said, "Or sherbet? There is something stronger in the kitchen, if you want."

Ranasahab looked at her and rolled his eyes.

Somebody gave his mother a glass of water and she drank

it in one big gulp.

"How are you now?" Ranasahab asked her in a soft, almost apologetic voice.

"You didn't touch him?" she asked in a whisper.

"Ma'am, I swear to God I didn't do anything," Ranasahab said in a surprisingly calm voice.

"And where is your sister?" she asked, looking at Ms Anju.

Ms Anju looked around as if to spot Ms Ria but couldn't find her.

"Where is my sister?"

They couldn't find Ms Ria anywhere.

When it seemed the woman was finally calming down, Rana rose and said, "I will take your leave now. And please get on with your lives."

"What do you mean?" the celebrity Commander-in-Chef asked.

"I mean please don't interfere with my life," Rana said, "It is already quite complicated as it is."

"How is it complicated? Tell me more," Anju demanded, rubbing her chin.

"I will leave now, Ms Anju, and I apologize to both of you. Everyone in fact," he said looking at the people who were still staring him like he was a vile molester.

"I have no clue why I am apologizing, but I am sorry," he said and looked at Anju, "Please tell your sister that she won't have to bother with me anymore."

He turned around and walked towards the exit. The boy held his hand and said, "Ranasahab, I am sorry too."

This was one big apology session. But the woman who should be apologizing was still glaring at him as though taking care of her only son while she was in hospital was a big crime.

"Aryan, get on with your life. You can beat that boy if you practice hard every day. You don't need me to tell you that,"

Rana said to Aryan and wondered why he felt a slight constriction in his throat.

The chef looked at him in surprise and then she looked at her son as though he was a stranger.

"What practice?" she asked.

"But I don't think I can beat Samar if you don't help me, Ranasahab," Aryan said.

"Who is Samar?" Sheila Khosla demanded to know.

"You can. And I don't know why am I still here and talking to you people," Rana said and finally walked out. He hated to admit to himself that he would miss the early morning jog with the boy. After this episode, he wondered if Ria would still want to meet him. Although he had never accepted it, their meetings in the coffee shop would somehow seem totally incomplete and hollow without the boy. It was as if Aryan was the glue that was binding them together. Without him, everything would be pointless.

When he reached his parked car, he was surprised to see Ria standing near it. There was a strange calmness on her face, as though she had made up her mind about something. Rana expected it would be to not meet him ever again.

"I am sorry," he said, "I shouldn't have bothered you all these days."

She stared at the ground and said nothing for a few moments.

"I want to know what happens in the story," she said.

"Okay," he said, relief and elation coursing through his body.

"Could we meet at the same place tomorrow?"

"Okay," he said, "Ria, did you know what just happened in your sister's house?"

She nodded a yes and said, "Don't worry, Ranasahab. Aryan will be at the coffee shop, too."

Rana couldn't hide his surprise. "You think so?"

"I know so," she said, "We will meet you tomorrow."

Rana said goodnight to her, got into his car and drove away thinking about what she had said.

Ria waited outside her sister's house after Ranasahab had left. She looked at the night sky as the beautiful fireworks lit up the darkness. She had always loved fire crackers that flew up into the sky. It gave her a sense of exultation, this need to brighten the darkness above, even if it was just for a few moments.

She saw Aryan and his mother walk out of Anju's house. Sheila Khosla looked as stunning as she looked on TV. Ria had rarely watched her show, but knew everyone associated with it. Most of the people who had worked with Sheila Khosla had used one word consistently—intimidating. Sheila Khosla was a tall woman and had sharp features, and she constantly scowled on TV. The audience loved her, which nullified what everyone else thought of her. At the moment, though, she looked spent and exhausted. Ria braced herself by taking a deep breath.

"You are Ria Marathe, aren't you?" Sheila Khosla said when she approached her.

Aryan looked totally mortified and on the verge of tears.

"Yes," Ria said.

The woman didn't respond for a few moments.

"I know you. The producer of my show also made a couple of serials for which you wrote episodes. He talks about you a lot. He says you were the best scriptwriter he ever worked with. His name is Rehan Khan."

She nodded a yes. Rehan Khan was one of the few people in the TV industry she had liked and respected.

Sheila Khosla looked at her son and said, "Aryan, would you mind walking up to the car?"

Aryan's lip trembled and it seemed he wanted to say something. Ria give him a reassuring nod. He walked away from them with his shoulders slumped.

Someone lit a firecracker on one of the nearby terraces. It rose high up in the sky and exploded in bright and beautiful sparkles. Ria and Sheila Khosla looked at the spectacle above.

When it was over, Sheila Khosla leaned on one of the cars for support.

"I need to thank you for helping Aryan at the railway station and taking care of him when I was in hospital," Sheila Khosla said.

Ria nodded an acceptance but said nothing.

"I don't think there is any point in hiding it as Aryan might've already told you. My husband left us a few weeks ago."

Ria waited.

"For a few days, it felt as if my life was pointless," Sheila Khosla said with a deep breath, "My husband has walked out on me many times before. But there was a finality this time. I collapsed, Ria. I never thought I would, but I did."

They waited for a few moments before Sheila Khosla said, "I can't imagine losing Aryan."

"He won't abandon you," Ria said.

Sheila Khosla stared at the ground as though trying to understand what Ria had said.

"But what if I end up abandoning him? Banishing him despite living under the same roof? Maybe what my husband did is better than what I would end up doing. He dropped the pretences and just ran," she said in a hollow voice, "The old man in your sister's house said things to me that made me feel inadequate, incompetent as a mother. And I had thought that you and he were snatching my son away from me."

She paused as a bunch of squealing children holding sparklers ran past them.

"You know, he writes stories," Sheila Khosla said with a wistful smile, "They are beautiful, but are full of pain and sadness."

Ria hadn't asked Aryan for his stories, but she had suspected they would be about pain and sadness.

"Sometimes, I feel as if I don't even know my son. All the things I have done, this head chef's career, this TV show, all of it, I believed it was for my son, for his future. Isn't that what parents are supposed to do?"

"Yes," Ria said.

Sheila Khosla looked at her before saying, "I can't really talk to you about my sense of loss, Ria. It is absurd and callous of me to do. But I can request you, beg you actually, to help me not lose my son."

Ria closed her eyes.

"Writing and books are what he loves," she said, "And I can't really help him there at all. Would you help my son discover himself?"

When Ria opened her eyes, she realized that Sheila Khosla was now standing right next to her. She held Ria's hand in a warm but gentle grip and said, "Please?"

Ria nodded a mute yes.

"Thank you," Sheila Khosla said, her eyes brimming with tears of gratitude.

Chapter 14

# The First of the Three Promises

Aryan didn't go that morning for his run with Ranasahab. He wondered if Ranasahab had decided to not visit the jogger's park that was near Aryan's house. He missed running, missed the burst of adrenaline he felt when he started the sprint.

Aryan had never seen his mother so subdued when they returned home after the fracas at Anju's place. He didn't know what she said to Ms Ria, but after their talk she seemed lost in deep thought.

So, it was a surprise when she walked into the kitchen while he was having his cup of milk and said excitedly, "I have taken a day off today!"

Aryan didn't want her to take a day off, because it meant trying to find peace in a meditation session at Jaya's. He said nothing.

"Aryan, did you hear what I just said?"

He nodded a yes.

"We are going to cook together at home, you and me. And we are going to talk while we do that."

There was hope. He smiled at her. She was actually going to spend an entire day with him.

"But first, let's have a quick stopover at Jaya's. What say?"

His smile froze. The disappointment couldn't be so quick.

"I won't do it, Mom. I am sorry but I don't like going to Jaya's," he said.

She chewed her lips for a few moments and said, "All I want is a little co-operation from my only son. I have strangers in my life telling me how to raise my own child, but they don't know how stubborn he is."

Aryan didn't think refusing to go to Jaya's was being stubborn. No rational person would want to be kissed by a fat, smelly whale.

"You don't have to do this, Mom. I am fine," he said.

"No you are not fine, Aryan. You are a difficult person to be with. This is something you have learned from your father," she snapped.

Aryan wanted to tell her he had no idea how difficult his father was. And that he had learned absolutely nothing from his father, except for the word *chutiya,* which he had annoyingly used for a long time while talking to Sanjay in school.

"So what do you want me to do?" she said.

"Go to work and go to Jaya's if you want to. Stop worrying about me," he said.

"I can't go to work now. I have told them I won't be coming in today. It would look weird if I walk in now," she said.

Aryan thought it wasn't such a big deal. His mother sometimes thought too much about what people in her kitchen would think about her. He had been with her in the kitchen a few times and he had seen her team. They were generally so hassled and busy that they had no time to think. Besides, they were very scared of her.

"You don't want to go to Jaya's and I can't go to work. So what can we do?"

"We were going to cook together, weren't we?"

She sighed as if it wasn't what she had looked forward to actually. Jaya's was her first preference, her work second and cooking with him was third. When, after several moments she said nothing, he walked back to his room. He checked Ranasahab's Facebook page and website. Ranasahab still had just seven followers and there were no new updates on the website. Aryan had thought of asking his mother if he could go to the coffee shop at least, but knew what her answer was going to be.

"What are you checking?", he heard his mother's voice.

"Ranasahab's status," he said, hoping she wouldn't ban him from doing that too.

She looked at the screen for a few moments and said, "What did he say to you about me?"

"Mom, for the last time, I haven't said anyone anything about you or Papa," he said.

She rubbed her face with her palms and said, "We will meet him tomorrow at his house."

"Why?"

"What do you mean why? I want to meet him; that is all."

"I thought he said he never wanted to meet any of us."

"He can't decide that now, can he? He can't alter things and then just walk away as if nothing has happened."

These were, again, very bad signs.

"I won't come with you if you are going to do what you did the last time," he said.

"I'm your mother and I will decide what to do, okay?"

He said nothing.

"Well say something for God's sake," she said throwing up her hands.

"Okay, Mom," he said.

Rana missed the jogger's park near Aryan's house. It was a much livelier place than the little garbage dump he jogged in near his own home. He wondered if it was because of Aryan. So, maybe, he missed the boy more than the park, he thought. It was already ten and Rana hadn't stepped out of the house for the run that morning. He hadn't spent his daily fifteen minutes to trim his beard. He had listlessly stared at the things in his house – the espresso machine, the giant refrigerator, the wall-hung television, the XBOX and all the gadgets the boy marvelled at when he was in the house. They suddenly looked like meaningless expenditures. He wondered if he could sell all those things, or maybe donate them. He laughed at that thought. Donating the stupid espresso machine would be a cruel joke. The doorbell rang.

When Rana opened the door and saw the boy and his mother, he couldn't help but groan.

"Did I not make myself very clear at the freak show the other day?" Rana demanded angrily, looking at the chef.

"Can we please come in?" the woman asked. There was an unspoken apology in her voice.

"To do what?"

"Maybe apologize properly," she said as though he was a fool to not even understand something so obvious.

"Okay," he said and moved away from the door.

They walked in but didn't sit on the sofa. The woman surveyed his house as though she was looking at a museum room full of hideous artefacts. She gave a little nod of her head and moved her lips, as though saying, "So, this is it".

"What did you say?" he said.

"So this is where my son was staying when I was in hospital," she said as though she couldn't believe it.

"Against the wishes of the owner, I must add," he said, looking at the boy.

The boy had a goofy smile on his face.

"Aryan writes too, you know? He has written thirty thousand words of his novel," she said.

The boy was shaken to hear his mother say this. He looked at his mother open-mouthed.

"It is very easy for you to pass judgment, Mr Rathod. I have raised my son. I know him, even if he doesn't tell me everything," she said with a pensive smile, "It's just that I am at a strange crossroads right now. I don't know what direction I need to take, but I know I will not go somewhere if it takes me away from my only son."

He said nothing.

"Right now, I don't know how to reach him, how to break this barrier that we both have built up. My husband has decided to leave us," she said and looked at the boy, "I am sorry to be saying this, Aryan, but it is true. Your father has left us and he isn't coming back. You and I have to deal with it."

The boy looked at her with no emotion, as if he hadn't expected anything else.

"It's just that I don't know how to deal with both things together," she said looking at Rana, "If you have any humanity in you, Ranasahab, I would request you to please help me and my son to deal with this. He loves being with you and Ria Marathe. I have seen how miserable he has been all of last night and I have hated myself for doing this to him. That's the way he wants to cope up with it right now. To be with strangers rather than his mother, and believe me, I am fine with it. I know we will figure out how to deal with it together some time. You have gotten involved, Ranasahab. Whether you wanted to or not doesn't matter anymore. You will have to play your role in this now."

They were silent for a long time.

The woman still hadn't apologized. He thought of reminding her, but then thought it would seem very churlish.

"Would you two like to have a cup of coffee?" Rana asked her finally.

"Sure!" the boy chirped, "Mom, you should see his coffee machine in action. It makes a great coffee too."

Rana and Sheila Khosla looked at the boy in wonder. He knew the woman, too, wished she had the ability to accept life and its strangeness the way children do. Rana couldn't help but smile.

The next week Rana had a strangely comfortable routine. He woke up every morning at half past five, met the boy in front of his housing society and they proceeded to run at the jogger's park. Astonishingly, Aryan was becoming better at it. There was no way he was ever going to be called a sprinter, but Aryan ran without complaining, and towards the end of the week, as long as Rana wanted him to. At the end of the run he always collapsed on the ground, holding his stomach, his cheeks all red and puffed, but the boy never said he didn't want to run. Rana didn't believe he was ever going to beat the school champion, not by practicing for a few weeks during the Diwali vacation, but that was never a real possibility.

"You think I can beat him?" Aryan asked him one day while he was recovering from a sprint.

"Sure," Rana said without looking at him.

"You don't believe that, do you?"

"Of course, I do," Rana said.

"Your eyes say otherwise."

"What are you now? A bloody face reader?" Rana asked, irritated.

"I will beat him," the boy said in a determined tone of voice Rana had never heard him use.

Almost every evening, the three of them, Rana, Ria and Aryan met at the same circular table for three in the coffee shop where Rana read what he had written that day. Ria didn't comment much. She listened without looking at him, very rarely showing any reaction. Aryan, though, had so many inputs to give. He didn't like the name of the protagonists. He didn't like the way they met. He didn't like the way the man's character behaved.

"What do you mean?" Rana had asked him the day when he had said he didn't like the writing because there aren't too many similes in it.

"Have you read Arundhati Roy's *The God of Small Things*?" Aryan had asked him.

"No," Rana admitted. It was a little embarrassing.

"She is one of India's greatest authors," the boy said, pointedly looking at him.

"So?"

"So, you can read her book and adopt some of the great things there," the boy had said.

The gall of him!

"I don't read such stuff," Rana said.

"Such stuff?"

"Well, I don't like such highbrow books," Rana said.

"What's highbrow?"

"Oh, hell! Why do you have to know everything, Aryan?"

"No, tell me, what's highbrow?"

"Something that appeals only to people who are intellectual snobs," Rana said.

Aryan looked at him as though he thought Rana was trying to make a fool of him.

"I don't think so," Aryan said with narrowed eyes.

"Nobody gives a damn about what you think," Rana had said and hated the little petulant sounding note in his voice. He was being cornered by a thirteen-year-old boy who had read *The God of Small Things*.

"So what have you read?" the boy asked without a hint of sarcasm, as if he genuinely wanted to know what kind of books Rana liked.

Rana hadn't answered him.

Despite that, he looked forward to their evenings together. The last time they had met, Ria had looked as though she had slept a little better. Her eyes were calm, something he had rarely seen before. He wondered if it was because of his novel, but thought that it would be laughable to make such an assumption. She had lost everything in life. There was little that words, written or spoken, could do to fill the void. He wondered about the Bollywood wannabe he had met at her crazy sister's house. Rana couldn't recall his name. Her sister had said the man had always carried a torch for her.

Ria wasn't fragile. If anything, Rana had sensed a strange determination in her. It was as though she had made up her mind about something and wasn't going to deviate from it no matter what happened. He knew it had to be the way she had decided to live her life without her son and husband. He didn't think there was place for another man in her life anymore.

He was most surprised to realize that he hadn't thought of visiting a bar or a night club for the last week. He could now hardly believe that he used to make a fool of himself in a night club that was meant for hormonal teenagers.

Aryan wandered in his house every day in the afternoon. They didn't talk much. There were hours when they didn't say a word. The boy sometimes watched his giant TV, drank fruit juices from his refrigerator or tinkered around with the coffee machine and other gadgets while Rana wrote on his computer. Aryan really came into his own in the evenings when they played *Need for Speed* on the XBOX. It was partly because the boy loved video games, but mostly because of Vinny.

Rana thought it was a miracle to see Vinny stay home in

the evenings. She was treating the boy as though he was her little makeover project. She had bullied him into changing his hairstyle. Gone was the shaggy hairstyle he'd had earlier. His hair was brushed back, revealing his forehead. Rana thought the boy looked so much better now that his hair was set properly. Vinny endlessly corrected him, telling him not to speak like an old man, not to walk as though he needed a walking stick, not to move his mouth as if he wanted to say something but wasn't sure. She had even goaded him to wear clothes that didn't look like rags.

The boy was changing. He smiled a lot, as if a weight had been taken off his chest.

One day, he took Aryan to the bowling alley. The boy told him he had never been to a bowling alley. His parents had never even asked him if he wanted to go.

Rana introduced Aryan to the boys in the alley and they took him under their wing, as though he was a long lost friend.

"How do you get your hair like that?" Aryan asked the boys.

"Simple. You spit on your hand and rub your head with it," they said. "Why don't you try it?"

Aryan had done it and the boys had laughed till their eyes had watered. And Aryan had laughed with them too. Rana had thought Aryan knew they were pulling his leg, but he was happy about it. Nobody had ever pulled the poor boy's leg. The boys had whooped, perhaps realizing Aryan was playing along. They had taught him their secret handshake, the strange language they spoke in, given him a couple of T-shirts with 'LICK ME' and 'HATE THE WORLD' printed on them. The boy had smiled as though he had found a treasure trove.

"Aryan, you rock!" the boys had said when he came in last in a game.

Aryan didn't seem to mind it. It was a good sign, Rana had thought. The boy would be alright when he lost the race to that bully Samar. Perhaps the humiliation would last for some time, but Rana hoped the boy would overcome it. The boys in the alley were surprised when Rana lost every game badly. He didn't mind it much.

Rana had to admit to himself that he liked the new routine.

It all changed when he got the letter from his son. It wasn't just a letter. There was also an invitation card along with it. It was for his son's wedding.

"What's the matter? Has someone died?" Vinny asked him. Vinny and Aryan were hammering away on his video game console.

He said nothing.

"Are you going to tell us or do you want us to annoy you some more?" she asked, pausing the game.

"It's a letter from my son," he said.

"Oh God," she said.

"He is getting married," Rana said. It sounded strange saying it aloud, as though it were some unforeseen thing.

"So that's bad?" she asked.

"I don't know," he said

"Are you invited?"

"What do you mean?"

She said nothing. Perhaps she had sensed something frightening in his voice.

Rana read the letter. It couldn't be called a letter really as it consisted of a few angrily scrawled lines.

*I am getting married. I never wanted to write to you, but Divya, who by the way is your daughter if you have forgotten it already, wanted me to. I would be extremely happy if you didn't turn up. It would be much better not to have a repeat of what happened at Divya's wedding. If you do decide to show up, please don't do so drunk. I wouldn't hesitate in kicking you out of the place.*

The letter wasn't signed.

Rana remembered the little boy who had walked all along the parapet wall with his hands stretched out and with a victorious smile on his face. The little boy he had wished death upon.

The invitation card was very expensive, and it invited the recipient to the wedding of Rohan and Mitali. Rohan, it said, was the elder son of Late Leelawati Rathod and grandson of Late His Highness Mehrabsingh Rathod. Rana was not mentioned. It was as though striking him out of the invitation card meant they were wiping him out of their lives. It was almost as if his son and daughter were conjured up out of thin air by their mother. He felt a blinding anger rising deep in his heart. He wanted to trash the letter and the invitation card, but before he could do anything with it, it was snatched out of his hand by Aryan.

"Do you need some water, Ranasahab?" the boy asked.

"No," Rana said, "Can you two leave me alone for a while?"

"I don't think so," Vinny said, "You look as if you are going to have a stroke."

"Vinny, out of my house," he said and looked at Aryan, "You too, boy."

The two looked at each other. Vinny gave an indifferent shrug and dragged Aryan out of his house. Rana closed the door behind them and leaned on it for a few moments.

It took him a long time to recover. When he did, he realized the damned boy had taken the letter and the invitation card with him.

## *Rana's memories of Nina*
## United Kingdom, Forty years ago...

After their conversation on the stairs of the university building, Nina had disappeared. He had tried desperately to understand what had gone wrong. She had said she had fallen for him, hadn't she? She wasn't seen in the university or in the hostel. She had never given him her phone number at home. The people she generally socialized with were unaware of her whereabouts and had no idea how to contact her. Nothing made sense to him. It was as if his most beautiful dream was followed by the most terrifying nightmare. On the sixth day, he saw her walk into the campus.

"Where the hell have you been?" he pounced on her.

"Can we please talk later?" she asked as she walked the

campus street with her head down.

"No, we can't. You can't do this to me! You can't just disappear like this," he said.

"Stop whingeing. You know my views about it, don't you?"

"Fuck your views! I want the answers, right now," he shouted.

Later, when he thought about it, he had no idea how he could've missed the deep dark circles under her eyes. She had come back to the university looking ten years older. He had been so blinded by his anger.

"You want to know here? While we are being stared at by all these people? Okay, so be it. I disappeared because I think I made a stupid mistake and I had no clue how to correct it."

"What do you mean?"

"Think about it a little, Rana. You are the scion of a once-royal family that owns half of Indian industry and I am the daughter of two immigrants who are the sorts your family employs," she said.

He was too stunned to speak.

"What's your family going to think about it when you tell them you want to live your life with me?" she asked with a chuckle, "I so hated those rich boy-poor girl sob stories and now I am living it."

"I have told you many times. It doesn't matter to me," he said.

"It will, Rana. You can't cut them off, can you? And think about it, what would your folks think about me? A gold-digger; that's what they'll call me, isn't that so? I don't have the emotional depth to go through all that."

"And what about us, Nina?"

"What about us? I am sure you will forget me soon, like you have forgotten many before me."

"Now you are insulting me. How do I prove it to you?" he demanded with desperation creeping up his throat.

"You don't have to. This isn't some test for you," she said calmly.

"All I want to show you is that I have an identity outside my family."

"Do you?" she asked, with what he thought was a sarcastic smile, but was actually a sad one, "And what is that identity? What are you if you are not the son of the wealthiest man in India?"

"I am. . ." shockingly he was at loss for words.

She stood there, without looking at him, sparing him the shame.

"I am yet to decide," he said in a defeated voice, even as he hated saying it. He had said the same thing to hundreds of people in the past. Every time he had been asked that question, it had seemed like a pointless, almost condescending one. Not today, not when the only woman he ever loved needed to know what kind of man he wanted to be, and he didn't have an answer.

"That's the difference between you and me. You are one in a hundred million people who don't have to decide what they want to become in their lives. But I can decide if I want to become a gold-digger or not."

"Stop using that word," he said. He wanted to hold her in a tight embrace and never let her go.

"The word is real, Rana. It will be uttered by everyone. Can't ignore it," she said and walked away.

That evening, Ria waited for Ranasahab and Aryan in the coffee shop for a long time. When they didn't turn up, she called Ranasahab's mobile a few times, but every time she reached his voicemail. For a few moments, she feared Ranasahab's cancer had reared its ugly head.

She was about to go look for Ranasahab when she saw Aryan enter the coffee shop. She had noticed there were very obvious changes in him. He looked quite different with his hair pulled back. Earlier when he walked, he did so as if he wished he was invisible. Now, it seemed he had acquired a little swagger. In the last seven days, he had asked her so many things about writing – how do you write a scene? How do you create characters? How do you build tension? How do you write a climax? She had explained to him at length and he had listened as though soaking in every word she uttered.

Aryan wore a T-Shirt that said HATE THE WORLD as he walked into the coffee shop that evening. It was several sizes big, but he looked happy in it.

"Ranasahab is a bit upset today. He isn't coming," he said.

"What happened?" she asked fearing the worst.

"He got a letter this morning from his son. There was an invitation card along with the letter. Apparently his son is getting married. He became very agitated after reading the letter."

She hadn't known the writer had a son. She hadn't even bothered to ask the old man about it. As if the sole reason for his existence was to tell her Nina's story.

Feeling miserable, she said, "Why would he get agitated?"

She thought 'agitated' was a little too grown-up a word to be used by a boy wearing a HATE THE WORLD T-shirt. But that was the way Aryan had always spoken. It will take him a long time before he changes other things apart from his clothes and hair, she thought.

"Don't know," Aryan said, "I have his letter though."

"Aryan, that's very impolite of you! You can't take people's things like this."

"He seemed about to collapse, so I took it from his hand. He asked me and Vinny to get out of his house and it stayed with me. I did think of going back to return the letter, but he was very angry when he shoved us out."

"Have you read the letter?" she asked.

"No," he said putting the letter and the invitation card on the coffee table, "it is his letter and I shouldn't be reading it."

The boy was amazing, she thought. Any other thirteen-year-old wouldn't have thought twice before reading it. She wished some things about Aryan would never change. She wondered what he would be like when he grew up? Would he turn out to be a bitter, resentful man who was bullied and ignored when he was a boy? Or would he turn out far better, having beaten the demons of his childhood? She didn't think Aryan was capable of nurturing a lifelong bitterness, but then she had never been a good judge of character.

"I hope it has nothing to do with his cancer," she said.

Aryan said noting.

"Does Ranasahab stay alone?" she asked and hated the fact that she didn't even know that much.

"Yes," Aryan said, "He has many gadgets in the house, though."

Aryan said it as though people and gadgets were interchangeable.

She and Aryan walked out of the coffee shop and hailed a taxi to take them to Ranasahab's house. When they reached the author's house, he wasn't there.

There was a girl who stood in front of another flat in the floor below. She and Aryan smiled at each other. There was an easy familiarity between them which only teens can develop. The girl couldn't be more different from Aryan. Ria knew she would grow up to be a beautiful maverick, someone who would do something great but unexpected.

"Vinny, meet Ms Ria," Aryan said.

"Oh, hello. I have heard the old man and the boy talk so much about you. Nice to meet you finally," she said.

Ria felt a little overwhelmed with what the girl said. What did Ranasahab and Aryan say about her? In her present condition, she wasn't anyone anybody would want to talk about. She wondered if they had guessed what she was going to do. Did she ever say anything that would be construed as suicidal? She didn't think so.

"He is in the hellhole nearby," Vinny said with her mouth twisting in distaste.

"What do you mean?" Ria said.

"The dank bar in which he drowns his sorrows," she said.

"Could you take us there?" she said.

Ria felt weird entering the bar, which was known to be rather shady. The lighting in the place made it appear even darker. There were figures floating around the bar like ghosts. The only sound in the clammy hall was of cutlery. When her eyes got used to it, she saw people, all men, hunched on the tables, not talking to each other, drinking without making a noise. She knew it must seem very odd to see a couple of children and a woman enter the bar. She sensed a few people turn around and look at them as though their arrival was interesting enough to break their reverie. It was a desperately forlorn place and Ria thought she understood something about Ranasahab.

"There he is," Vinny said as she pointed him out.

Ria walked up to the table and said, "I never thought you would come to a place like this."

"What are you doing here?" Ranasahab demanded. His voice was slurred. He looked at the girl and asked, "Why did you bring them here?"

"Simple. Because they asked," Vinny said angrily.

"Vinny, you are impossible," Ranasahab said and shook his head.

"I think you've had too many for the day, Ranasahab," Ria said, "We should leave. You shouldn't be here in this condition."

"What condition?" Ranasahab asked.

Ria didn't want to point out that he was battling a deadly disease and drinking would only make it worse.

"I think we should leave. I don't think the children should be in this place," she said.

Ranasahab nodded as though he was giving in for the sake of the children and rose unsteadily. He pulled out his wallet and threw some notes on the table. They walked out of the bar.

Chapter 15

# The Three Face a Dilemma

The lights on the busy street assaulted Rana's eyes with a vengeance when he tottered out of the dingy bar. The sounds of traffic were heightened and unbearable. He hadn't wanted Ria to see him like this—drunk and sloppy. How would he explain this to her? A cancer patient getting drunk would seem outright suspicious. In Rana's muddled mind, a clear thought emerged like a beacon - Ria would hate him for lying. The thought hit him with such force that he stumbled. Why did he have to lie to her? And why hadn't he told her the truth yet? Or was it that she unconsciously knew he was lying?

"Are you able to go home?" Ria asked, her eyes clouded with concern.

"I am fine," he said and realized it sounded slurred even to him.

He wasn't fine. The air outside the bar made him feel dizzy. It was going to be a struggle going home. He didn't want Aryan and Vinny watching him while he stumbled on the streets to find his way. But they would have none of it and refused to leave him alone. He tried to focus on the pavement and to walk as straight as he could.

"Don't hate me, Ria, okay?" he said to her.

He thought she looked at him with something akin to sympathy in her eyes. Or was it pity? He wasn't sure. His shame was increasing with every faltering step and every suppressed rise of vomit.

They reached his flat after what felt like an eternity. He

struggled to open the door with his unsteady hands.

"Ria, I think you ought to go home now. Aryan, Vinny, you too," he said and was surprised that he could still make sense with what he said.

Ria nodded and took a small step back, still watching him.

He was at the very end of his resistance before the sickness took its toll. He wanted Ria to leave immediately. But she hesitated. It was enough for him to collapse on the floor in front of his flat. He was vaguely aware that the three of them picked him up and dragged him inside his house. They removed his shoes and made him lie down on his bed.

He thought he said sorry to them before the darkness took over.

When he opened his eyes, he thought he shouldn't have. The little sunlight that had escaped through the drawn curtains hurt his eyes. He looked at the watch, and it said eight. His mouth felt as if it was full of little pointed metal pieces. He stood up and stepped out of the bedroom, only to see Ria dozing on the sofa.

Ria looked beautiful and was sleeping fitfully. Her eyes moved behind her eyelids while she slept, as though she was having a bad dream. Her brow was furrowed. Rana felt terrible for doing this to her. Why had she helped him? For a drunkard has-been writer who had failed in every aspect of his life? He didn't deserve the care she gave him, especially when she was trying so heroically to emerge from a tragedy that would've devastated almost everyone he knew.

She sensed he was in the room and woke up with a start.

"Sorry," she said.

"No. I need to apologize to you. I have never been more ashamed in my entire life, Ria. I don't know how to make this right," Rana said, with a nauseating bitterness in his mouth.

She went to the kitchen without a word and got busy making her coffee. He thought she struggled in an unknown place, her rhythm distorted, her measurements a little awry. She hadn't made too many things in others' kitchens, Rana presumed.

"My son is getting married," he said without looking at her

when she got two cups.

She said nothing. He was grateful for her silence and the absence of judgment in her eyes when he looked at her.

"It doesn't justify my behaviour last night. Nothing justifies it at my age and in my condition, I guess," he said, "I am actually very happy for my son. He has finally found someone to live his life with. But I have grown used to being miserable even when I am happy."

She sipped her coffee without saying anything.

## *Rana's memories of Nina*
## United Kingdom, Forty years ago...

He spent the days after Nina told him she would have nothing more to do with him in a boozy haze. He had no idea when he had started popping pills. Very soon, that was all he wanted to do—pop a pill, swallow it down with alcohol and wait for the numbness to wear off to repeat it. Nina hadn't come to see the state he was in while he wasted away. He had no idea of time, no recollection of how long he'd spent in the five-bedroom flat his father had got him near the university.

One morning, he felt someone slapping his cheeks and tried to open his eyes.

"Stop this drama, will you?" he heard Nina's voice.

Unknown to himself, he had smiled. She had cared enough. It meant she had everything to do with him. It meant all she had said earlier was a charade.

"If you think this act is going to change anything, you are the daftest man I know," she said and slapped him harder than she had earlier.

"You are a disgrace, Rana Singh Rathod, and I am so glad I didn't fall for it," she said leaning back now that his eyes were open. He peered at her, as though she was sitting far away instead of on the same bed. She looked beautiful; beautiful and very angry. She looked most beautiful when she was angry. He knew his thoughts were getting all messed up because of the drugs.

"What did you just say?" she asked, incredulous.

"What?"

"You just said I look beautiful when I am angry," she said with a chuckle.

Had he said that aloud?

"God, that's the cheesiest line I have ever heard in my life," she said.

"Sorry."

"No, you aren't sorry. Not yet. You will be when Professor Hinkle decides to keep you back for one more term. What are you going to tell your father then? That you failed?"

"I am going to be a writer, Nina," he said.

"What?" She asked, bewildered.

"A writer. You asked me what I was if not the son of a wealthy man. I am going to be a writer and I am going to write the greatest novel there ever was," he said, scarcely believing he had actually said that.

She started laughing.

"Don't laugh," he said, a little hurt by her mocking, but loving the sound of her laughter.

"You did all this drama just to come up with something that lame? All you had to do was ask me! I would've told you that you are a damn good writer and that would've been the end of it," she said and laughed again.

"Does that mean we are back together?" he asked, sounding desperate even to his own ears.

"No. It means you are making some sense of your pointless life," she said folding her arms, "Now get your arse in the bathroom or l will kick it so hard you will not be able to sit on it."

It had been a breeze after that. He had written the first draft of his novel in a matter of weeks, and she had been with him throughout. She had never said anything when he read it to her every day and had never given him any inputs. She had listened with an impassive look in her eyes and her lips drawn in an unimpressed line when he read the novel to her.

He struggled the most with the last chapter of the novel. He didn't know how the story would end—happy or sad? He couldn't decide for days. It was Nina who had helped him write it, imploring him, goading him, cajoling him and even telling him to write one word at a time. He had eventually finished it and had thought it was the most hauntingly beautiful end for his novel. When he read it to her, she had tears in her eyes.

He had asked her to write the last line in her own handwriting—"They stood holding hands, looking at the waves of the blue sea and the fading rays of the setting sun, knowing in their hearts that it was going to be alright, that they were going to be together."

She had said the line was a little corny, but she was okay with it. In fact, now that he had finished the novel, she was actually okay with it all. And she had smiled. The most beautiful smile ever, as though it was going to be his greatest reward. In a way, it was. He had never been so ecstatic after finishing any book. When he wrote anything after finishing this novel, it was with the hope of seeing her dimpled smile at the end of it.

After Rana and Ria had finished their coffee in the silence and stillness of his living room, he looked at the invitation card in his lap. He touched it with a kind of tenderness he didn't think he had in him. Rohan and Mitali.

He thought his hands were shaking after yesterday's shameful behaviour and the impending exposure of how he had deceived Ria. He handed the invitation card and the letter to her, unable to hold either in his hands anymore. She read the invitation but didn't read the letter.

"My son has invited me for the wedding but doesn't want me to show up," he said.

She stared at the invitation card for a few moments before saying, "Is that what he has said in the letter?"

He nodded and said, "You are going to hate me even more if I tell you why he wrote me that letter."

"I am a stranger here, Ranasahab. But since you have showed me this, all I can say is that it is your son's wedding and you should be there. Whatever may have happened between the two of you, the fact that he has sent you this letter means that he wants you to be at the wedding," she said and paused for a moment before asking him gently, "Have you told them about your condition?"

Rana avoided her eyes and said, "No."

He thought it was the truth. He hadn't told that lie to anyone except Ria and Aryan.

She nodded as though she understood why a father wouldn't want to tell his children about his impending death. The roiling acid in his stomach threatened to overcome his resistance. He couldn't summon the courage to tell her the truth.

"It says the wedding is in three days," she said.

He had been so cut-off from everyone that he hadn't bothered to check if his son and daughter were alive or not. They were alive, and doing very well. They didn't need him. They had never needed him.

"I can't go there alone," he said.

"I can't go with you, sir," she said.

He thought her use of the word "sir" was a reminder of what their relationship originally was – that of strangers helping each other out of a sense of compassion. And compassion had its limits.

"I know, Ria. I have already made your life a lot more complicated than it should be," he said.

She shook her head and said, "It's not that. It's just that I have no clue what I will do there. You are the father. What exactly am I?"

He wanted to tell her that she was all he had right now. She, and, he had to admit to himself, Aryan. Without them he would be the same lonely Facebook, Twitter and MySpace maniac. It had been so many days since he had visited those sites. It didn't matter anymore. Perhaps it never had.

"I can, maybe, introduce you to my family as my friend,"

he tried and regretted it immediately. His family had just one definition for his lady friends and he didn't want Ria to be given that label.

"No, sir. I am sorry," she said with a firm shake of her head.

"Forget I even mentioned it, okay?" he said.

Ria rose from the sofa and said, "Ranasahab, sometimes forgiving someone could alter everything. And if a father can't forgive his children, who can?"

She walked up to the door and looked back at him before walking out of his house. He thought her eyes were wet with tears.

Rana fidgeted over his thoughts for a long time. He tried to divert his attention by opening the file of his novel on his computer, but words had suddenly deserted him. Finally, giving in to the thought he had wrestled with, he called Aryan.

"Why didn't you come over today?" he asked as Aryan answered his call.

"I thought you would be sleeping the day off," Aryan said.

"And why did you think that?"

"That's what my father used to do to get rid of the hangover," the boy said in a "been-there-seen-that" tone. The boy spoke about his father in the past tense. It was astonishing how children accepted the realities of life, Rana thought. Rana wished he could swap ages with Aryan right now, have the ruthlessness of a child to accept what lay ahead for him.

"Would you like to come with me to my son's wedding?" Rana asked.

The boy said nothing for a few moments, while Rana prayed that he would say yes.

"Okay," Aryan said, "What gift should I get?"

Rana laughed from sheer relief. He realised that the boy had asked a very important question. What should he get his son as a gift for his wedding? It suddenly struck him that he had no idea what kind of a man his son had become. In Rana's heart, he was still the adamant eight-year-old boy who had wanted to walk on the parapet wall at any cost. What did his son want with the same intensity now? Was it a sports car or a chopper of his own? Maybe he already had all those things.

Perhaps he was the kind of man who wanted a nice big house to settle down with his bride. And who was his bride, Rana's daughter-in-law? There were just too many unanswered questions. Rana knew he wouldn't get the answers until he met his family. For them, he had been an infrequent visitor, who occasionally influenced the sphere of their existence and brought terrible destruction in his wake. Was he going to do that this time too? Would everything end in bitterness, as it always did? Again, too many unanswered questions. He decided not to get a gift for his son. He couldn't afford a sports car or a chopper or a house anyway.

When Rana picked up Aryan the following morning, the boy told him that he went running without him yesterday. Rana was surprised to know Aryan wasn't huffing and puffing while they ran.

"Can you actually sprint now?" Rana asked him after they had stopped.

"What have we been doing all this while?" Aryan asked.

"We have been jogging. You are not going to win that race by jogging."

"Okay," the boy said doubtfully.

"I will stand here. I want you to run these hundred meters as fast as you can, okay?" he said pointing at the track that was hundred meters long.

Aryan nodded.

"Go!" Rana said and the boy started running. Rana looked at his digital watch. The boy took fifty seven seconds to run hundred meters. Aryan stopped and bent down to catch his breath. Rana wanted to go back in the past and stop himself from advising the boy to participate in the race.

"How did I do?" Aryan asked after Rana jogged up to him.

"You did okay," Rana said.

"What kind of okay?"

"What do you mean?"

"Bad okay or good okay?" the boy asked as if he was slow not to understand something so obvious.

"There is nothing bad or good about okay. Okay is okay," Rana said.

"No there is. Have you watched the movies *The Hostel* and *The Grudge?*"

"No," Rana said.

"They are horror movies," the boy said, "*The Hostel* is a horror movie that has a lot of blood and gore. There are people cutting each other's limbs and plucking out eyes and things like that. It is an okay horror movie. But it is a bad okay movie. *The Grudge* has no blood or cutting of limbs. It has this creepy looking woman and scary music. It is an okay horror movie too. But it is a good okay movie."

"Hell, where do you children come up with such nonsensical definitions? And why are you watching such disgusting stuff?"

"Yes, *The Hostel* is disgusting," the boy said with a grimace, "Sanjay watched *Hostel 2* also. He says it is even more bloody and gory."

"Don't you have any friends who watch good movies?"

"No," the boy said.

"Everyone watches just the horror movies?"

"I mean, I don't have any friends," the boy said.

Rana chewed his tongue. He should have known not to say that.

"But I am sure I will have a lot of friends when I beat Samar," Aryan said with a smile.

"Why? What's going to change it?"

"They would know who I am. That I can run," he said with a shrug.

Rana said nothing.

"So? Good okay or bad?"

"Well, it is still okay. It isn't bad okay, for sure," Rana said.

"I like that!" the boy said, "You want me to run again?"

"No, that's enough for the day," Rana said, "I have to write."

"Yes, sorry. Do you mind if I run some more?"

"No," Rana said, "Don't get too tired, though."

But the boy hadn't listened. He was running with his head down, mouth twisted in a determined scowl. Rana had wanted to tell him that he would have a lot of friends now. The boy had changed. He looked a lot less dorky. Vinny had managed to instil some dress sense into him. Aryan was never going to be a lady-killer, but perhaps the bullies might not see the nerd in him anymore. Maybe Aryan could patch up with that boy Samar. Admit to Samar he had made a mistake by challenging him and stay out of his way for a while. Boys generally forget things, don't they? Perhaps the boys can become friends too.

Someone had to break the news gently to Aryan that there was no point in making a fool of himself in front of the entire school by running in the race and coming in last. Rana had no idea how he should say it to Aryan.

Ria looked at the list she had made such a long time ago. It still had the three items in it. The lawyers had virtually stopped taking her calls after telling her that procedures can't be speeded up, even if she called every hour instead of every day. The date on the calendar was four weeks away. She wondered if she should add some more things to the list. How about helping Aryan overcome his loneliness and alienation? Or helping Ranasahab achieve his dream of writing his last novel? Or help Aryan come out of his self-imposed inhibitions? Or help Ranasahab find some peace in his last days? Somehow those things didn't seem unimportant at all, like returning the library books. The books weren't overdue yet. Nothing had ever been overdue in her life. Was the suicide going to be the first?

Sometimes forgiving someone can alter everything. She felt like laughing at what she had said to Ranasahab. She was asking him to do something she hadn't even thought of doing herself. Forgive. The word felt powerful and liberating, but she didn't know what it truly meant. What act in her life would constitute forgiving and seeking forgiveness?

She decided to finish one of the things on the list. Clean the house once more. Perhaps some dust flecks had settled in the two hours after she had last scrubbed it and it was time to get rid of them. It took her an hour and a half, and all the time she was thinking about what she had told Ranasahab. The only room she hadn't cleaned was Varun's room. It was airtight anyway. Nothing can go in it, or out of it.

That was when she remembered. There was something inside the room that didn't belong. It was Aryan's shirt. Aryan hadn't come to her house since that day, and somehow she had blocked it out in her mind.

Ria did not recall when she opened Varun's room and found herself sitting on her son's bed with Aryan's blood soaked shirt in her hands. Varun hadn't bled apart from the tiny blot of crimson blood on his school uniform when he died in the car crash. The doctors had said he died of internal injuries. All the bleeding happened inside his beautiful head.

On that day, it had been Raj's turn to pick up Varun from school. She had insisted that he study in a school that was the best. It meant travelling a fair distance from their house and so the school bus wasn't an option. She had loved dropping Varun to school every other day. Just like when he was a little baby, her son looked at life with a kind of wondrous enthusiasm that filled her with hope and warmth. Sometimes she had wondered if he had learned more from her or was it the other way round. When they drove to his school, they talked as if they were close friends, equal in thought and wisdom. Varun's smile was a gift he had received from the almighty; he had also inherited her dimples. The magic of his smile came from his own goodness. Her son had been incapable of having an evil thought. She knew it the way a mother knows her child's heart.

That evening, she received a call from Varun telling her that he had been waiting for Dad for an hour and had even tried calling him. He asked her if he could take the city bus instead of waiting, as he enjoyed sitting on a window seat while the bus circumnavigated a longer route home. She told him not to do it as it was the duty of his careless father to pick him up. She told him to stay put in the school.

After trying to reach Raj several times, she finally managed to get through to him. She had screamed at him, called him a callous and shoddy father. He tried to give her a work-related reason to account for why he had not picked up Varun—it sounded like a ridiculously lame excuse to her. It had become a pattern in the last six months or so, this lateness of his. She learnt about the real reason much later, when everything had ceased to matter. Raj was with that woman every evening, perhaps saying the same charming things to her that he had once said to Ria. What if Ria had known about his infidelity? She wouldn't have been living with him and perhaps Varun would've grown up and changed the world as he was destined to.

Ria and Raj were working on different films at that time. Their scriptwriting partnership had died a few years ago, and all that was left was an uninspiring marriage held together by their only son. Ria told him in a voice she later believed was the coldest she had ever sounded, that he had to drop everything he was doing, pick up her son from the school and reach home before seven or he could forget he had a wife and a child. Raj said quietly that he would, perhaps accepting the pent-up despair in her heart.

It was the last thing she had said to the man who was once her childhood sweetheart.

Anju had verified the bodies. Ria had refused to go inside the morgue, all the time believing it was a mistake. The call she had received from the police asking her if her husband's name was Raj Marathe and her son's Varun had been a mistake. The police telling her that both of them had died in an accident was a mistake. Their asking her to come to the hospital morgue to verify the bodies had been a mistake. She had called Anju telling her about this horrible prank someone was playing on her, even suspecting Raj for doing this to her as she wasn't able to reach his or Varun's mobile. She had vowed never to forgive Raj, who had always been a practical joker, for this sickening joke. After half an hour, Anju had picked her up from her home.

Ria had told her sister that if she was acting along, she wouldn't speak to her after this madness was over, ever again.

At the morgue, the impatient police constable had told her she needed to move along fast as they had others in the queue. Anju walked into the morgue after Ria's refusal to be part of this horrible prank any more. A few minutes later, she came out and held Ria in her arms. Her sister had held her like that once, several years ago, when their father had died. Even then,

Ria had refused to be with him when the doctors had said all hope was lost.

Anju had told her that Varun and Raj were gone. Anju's face was brittle like stone, her eyes blood red and filled with tears, her voice raw.

Ria had said she had to see them. Anju had said no, as though the thought itself was grotesque.

Ria had left her and walked into the morgue.

They had covered Raj's face. It was his blood-soaked hand with the little star-shaped burn mark that she had felt with her fingers and her lips for twenty five years that told her he was forever gone. The man she had loved with all her heart; who not so long ago could still leave her dewy-eyed with love; whom she could no longer tell what she still felt for him . . . was reduced to an unrecognizable form of torn flesh and broken bones.

They hadn't covered Varun. He looked as if he was sleeping peacefully. There was no fluttering of his eyelids, none of the twisting and turning. Her son looked so serene, something she had always prayed he would become one day. And now he had. His right hand was resting on his chest, as if he was hugging something close to his heart.

She had held her little son's hand. It was warm and soft, as it had always been.

She thought that they would not take her away if she never let his hand go. She would somehow make herself so tiny she would occupy the little crest of Varun's hand. She would go with her son, wherever they decided to take him.

Anju, the constable and three or four more hospital staff had had to summon every ounce of their strength to pry her hand from Varun's. She knew he wasn't hurting because of her grip. He would've told her if she had hurt him. He always told her everything.

She hadn't cried then. She had screamed and screamed. She had screamed till her throat was hoarse and raw.

She held Aryan's blood-soaked shirt and she cried. She cried for her son and for her husband.

Aryan had washed the shirt Ms Ria had given him to wear such a long time ago. He packed it in his backpack and decided he would visit Sakhu-mai first and then go to Ms Ria's place to return the shirt.

When he reached Sakhu-mai's hut in the slums, he saw a doctor, who sometimes checked up on her, leaving. Aryan thought of asking him about her condition but dreaded what he would say. He heard Sakhu-mai's niece crying when he entered the house. She wiped her tears hastily when she saw Aryan.

"What has happened?" he asked, with his heart thudding away.

"The doctor says she has gone into coma now," the niece said, "Don't know how long she can hold on."

Aryan sat with Sakhu-mai for a long time. He told her how good he was becoming at running and how he was going to beat Samar. He told her about his new hairstyle and asked her what she thought about it, but got no response. Sakhu-mai continued to breathe shallowly when he told her about his new clothes and new shoes and how he liked them a lot more than his old clothes. She didn't respond even when he told her that he didn't like the mix of Chocos and Fruit-Loops, something she had always admonished him for eating too much.

When he left Sakhu-mai's house he felt anxious. To quell his anxiety, he started running and ran all the way home. Jeevan, the driver, looked at him as though he had gone mad. Aryan told him to drive to Ms Ria's house as he had to give something back to her. When the driver started to complain, Aryan told him his mother had instructed that he be allowed to go to Ms Ria's and Ranasahab's house any time he wanted to and if Jeevan had a problem, maybe he should speak to his mother. That got an instant reaction from the driver as he was suddenly very keen and alert.

Aryan thought Ms Ria looked as if she was very tired when she opened the door for him. Her eyes were red, but she had a smile on her face. He thought she should always smile because she looked so much better when she did that.

"I am sorry, Ms Ria, I totally forgot to return this shirt to you," he said taking out the blue shirt from his backpack.

She held it gently in her hands and said, "Thank you, Aryan. Come, I need to show you some things."

She opened the door of the room he had slept in a few weeks ago. There were several boxes on the floor. All of them were full of stuff, which he guessed were her son's things.

"These are some of the video games I thought you would love," she said fishing out a bunch of video game DVDs from a box.

"They were your son's?" he said

She said yes and smiled.

"There is his cricket bat too," she said "Do you play cricket?"

He didn't, but he said he would like to try his hand at it. She got him the cricket bat. He held the DVDs in one hand and the bat in the other.

"Actually, there is the complete cricket kit here. You want it?"

He nodded a yes.

She also asked him if he liked roller skating. He said he didn't, but he would love to try it. She put the skates in a bag and gave it to him.

"Do you want anything else from these boxes?" She asked pointing at the brown containers, "I'll donate whatever you don't want to charity."

There were lots of clothes, toys, figurines of Superman, Batman and Spiderman. There were also many other things like a little tricycle, which he was sure was used by her son when he was maybe three or four years old. All of it was neatly stacked in those cardboard boxes. All the boxes were marked with the stuff that was in them – toys, clothes, gadgets.

"All this was his?"

She said yes.

"Who are you giving this away to?"

"There is an orphanage my sister knows about."

He thought about it for a few moments.

"Some children are going to be very happy," he said, "I don't think I can take these. I would want those children to have them. I already have a lot of this stuff."

She said okay and that it was very nice of him.

"But I will keep this Superman figurine, if that's okay with you," he said pointing the little blue plastic Superman with his red cape fluttering and a smile on his face.

She pulled out the toy out of the box and said, "It was his when he was seven."

He said, "I had one myself, exactly the same. Don't know where it's gone. I could have it, a sort of replacement."

She looked at him and smiled, "It was his favourite amongst all the toys. Here, take it."

"Thank you," he said.

"And thank you," she said, although he didn't understand why she was thanking him.

She asked him if he would mind waiting in the living room while she tidied everything up one last time. Her voice shook when she said that. He told her she could take as much time as she wanted. He would wait outside.

Aryan sat at the study table in her living room. It was a nice chair and he knew she wouldn't mind if he sat on it for a while. One day, he thought, when he too wrote as well as Ranasahab and Ms Ria, he would have his own study table and chair. Maybe one room dedicated just for that, as they showed in the movies.

There was a pad open on the table. He didn't intend to read it. But it was open and he happened to look in its direction. Aryan wished he had never learned how to read when he saw what was written on the page.

He read: *Things to do before the day (13 December) I die*

There were three things on it, a sort of a list. He read it, unable to stop himself.

There was no sound from her son's room.

He walked without making a noise to the room's door, just wanting to make sure that she was alright. His heart was hammering away when he peeked inside.

She was closing the lids of the boxes. She had a smile on her face.

Aryan didn't know what to do.

Chapter 16

# The Three Learn to Forgive

Rana had sensed there was something wrong with the boy when he opened the door for him, but what Aryan told him shook him like nothing had before. Rana thought he understood his own selfishness in its stark ugliness when the boy told him what he had read on Ria's notepad. This was a woman who had vowed to die and he was using her to redeem himself in his own eyes. The lies he had told her now seemed like a perverted joke. She must have thought she was fulfilling the wishes of a dying man before she killed herself. He wanted to beat himself up for doing this to her.

Aryan was close to tears when he finished.

"Are you sure you read that?" Rana asked, hoping that the boy had perhaps misread.

"Yes," the boy said, wiping his eyes, his voice muffled by tears, "You think she is going to kill herself?"

Rana said nothing. They sat on his sofa for a long time. Rana had been watching a football match when the boy walked in. The commentator's voice, interspersed with the spectators loudly cheering and chanting for their teams was the only sound in the room while Rana struggled to think of a plan now that he knew Ria's actual state of mind. The signs had always been there—her constant fidgeting, the restlessness, the mania for cleanliness in her home and the lack of photos of her son or husband. It was all there in front of him. He had always fancied himself as a keen observer of people, hadn't he? He wondered why she wanted to hear his story so desperately. He thought about it for a long time before finally making a decision.

He muted the television and said to the boy, "Don't say a word about this to her, okay?"

Aryan had regressed into the state of moroseness he had been in when Rana first met him. The boy coming to know about it was a deeply disturbing situation.

He said in a surprised tone of voice, "Shouldn't we stop her from doing anything bad to herself?"

"We will do something. But she shouldn't know about it. If she knows, she will cut us off and then we wouldn't be able to do anything."

"Shouldn't we tell her sister about it?"

"I don't think it will be of any help," Rana said, "Anju is useless."

"But she is her sister," Aryan said as if Rana had suggested something outrageous.

"And she is also a little crazy," Rana insisted, "She will drive her to do it."

"How can you say that? Sisters don't do that!"

"I am approximately fifty years older than you, Aryan. I know what family can do to you. You have seen her sister, haven't you? Do you think she would help anyone?" Rana said, trying to be patient with the boy, something at which he knew he was not very good.

The boy said nothing but looked at him with narrowed, angry eyes.

"What did your family do to you?" Aryan asked.

"This has nothing to do with me," Rana said and hated his defensive tone. The boy was again cornering him.

"And what did you do to your family?"

Rana said nothing.

"I still think you are wrong about her sister. She will surely help if we tell her," Aryan said.

"Aryan, you are getting on my nerves now. For once, just listen to me, okay?"

Aryan was quiet for a long time.

It explained so much about her, such as the reason why she

had gone to Lakhani's office. It was terrible to think that, had she not thought of dying, he would've never met her. He had to tell that worm Lakhani to lay off creating the charity for a while. He knew there would be a big price to pay for it, but that was fine by him. For once, he would order the slimy lawyer to do something that was right, something that would actually help someone.

He wondered how to put Aryan at ease and said, "Okay, don't worry. I will ask her about it. I will also talk to her sister about it, when the time is right."

The boy looked at him as though he didn't trust him.

"Have you decided on what you will wear at my son's wedding?" Rana asked, trying to divert the boy from the desperation he was sinking into. The boy refused to answer him. They watched the football match on the muted television in sullen silence.

"He won't let her do it," Aryan said suddenly.

"What?" Rana asked, somewhat startled.

"Her son, Varun—he won't let Ms Ria kill herself," the boy said with a smile.

"What do you mean, boy?" Rana asked. He wanted to tell Aryan that her son was dead, but it would've sounded terrible.

"I know her son is gone, but he is still there in that house. I think she will remember all the good times she had with him and she won't do it," Aryan said.

Rana thought of telling him that it didn't work like that in real life. Guardian angels existed only in fantasy fiction, but not in real life. But Rana said nothing, not wanting to say something that sounded harsh to the boy.

"You don't believe me?" Aryan asked.

Rana shrugged.

The doorbell rang after they had exchanged annoyed grunts and harrumphs for a long time. Aryan opened the door and smiled. Vinny entered and demanded to know, "Are you taking him to the wedding and not me?"

"Of course," Rana said, "I don't want to scare people off."

"I don't bite," she said.

"Why take chances?" Rana asked, dismissively.

Rana decided to ask the boy about the smile later. Aryan was much more comfortable around Vinny now and even cracked jokes at her expense. She indulged him a lot, as though revelling in his attempts to break out of his shell. She reminded him of a gardener gloating and fussing over a sapling emerging from a seed. The boy and Vinny talked a lot about the novel Aryan was supposedly writing. Rana didn't believe his claims at all. How could a thirteen-year-old write thirty thousand words? Rana was sure the boy was fibbing just to impress Vinny. However, he was surprised at Vinny's keenness—the interest she took in the story of the orphaned boy Aryan was writing about.

"There was a time when I was your only friend, old man," she said with fake grumpiness, "Now, you have new friends, so you are ditching me!"

"Oh, hell," he said, "Vinny, your melodrama isn't going to work with me."

"Can she come?" Aryan asked. Rana looked at him as Aryan lowered his eyes, realizing he had said something extremely daring.

Rana laughed and said, "Of course she can. Everyone is welcome to see an old man getting humiliated by his own family."

Ria sat on Varun's bed, looking at all the boxes she had neatly taped and secured. All that had belonged to her son would soon leave the house in which he was supposed to grow to adulthood. She had heard of separation anxiety, suffered by mothers when their children left home. Ria had known she would suffer a much heightened version of it when Varun eventually grew old enough to leave her house. Now, she felt a calmness overcome her. Her son had left this world long ago for what she was sure was a far better place, and it was time for her memories of him and the things he had owned to become assimilated in this world.

Ria had asked Anju to come over to her house as she needed

some help. Her sister had, as expected, jumped into a long-winded explanation of how busy she was and how difficult it would be for her to come anytime that day.

"How long will you continue to do this?" Ria asked.

"Continue what?" Anju asked, feigning ignorance.

"Saying no to anything I ask you do, even before you know what it is?"

"Where have I said no? All I am saying is that I can't make it today," Anju said.

"You mean your sister is of little importance compared to a sudden manicure appointment with a beautician three hours' drive away?"

"You have taken the entire beauty quota in the family and left nothing for me! And now I have to take care of it, no?"

"It is for Varun's things, Tai. I want to donate all his possessions to the orphanage you told me about," Ria said. Six months after their deaths, Anju had suggested that maybe Ria should donate Varun's belongings. There were many children who deserved those beautiful toys, she had said. Ria had lashed out at her, calling her heartless and cruel, for wanting to destroy her memories of Varun. Anju had stoically endured Ria's outburst and had never mentioned it again.

Anju was silent for a few moments before she said, "I am coming right now."

After disconnecting, Ria thought for a long time before dialling Ranasahab's number.

"Could you help me take some stuff out of my house?"

Ranasahab said he would do so. She wondered about the irony of it. A few weeks ago, Aryan had called upon the old writer when he needed someone. She was doing the same. It was as if all her past relationships, apart from that with her sister, had faded into nothingness.

She waited for them in Varun's room with the boxes. They were seven in all and rather big. Varun was a little boy with big dreams. One day he wanted to be a pilot, the next day he wanted to be a spacemen. On one occasion, he had told her he would be a writer, just like her. Secretly she had wanted him to become a writer and carry forward the legacy of his parents.

She had been happy for a day—the next day, he wanted to become a cricketer. He was a normal boy in so many ways, frequently changing his dreams. He was a well-mannered boy who had learned to speak well before he had learned to walk. But he spoke far less than he ran. There was no sport he hadn't wanted to be good at. Two boxes were full of his sports gear—badminton racquets, squash racquets, tennis racquets, table tennis bats, roller skates, cricket kit, even a baseball bat. He had once sulked for a day because she and Raj had refused to get him a set of golf clubs. He was a normal, healthy boy, who was a little messy.

She wondered if the boys who inherited his things would wonder who had owned those racquets and bats. How would they treat those things? Would someone look after them? Would they love those things as much as Varun had?

It didn't really matter. Varun would've wanted her to give them away. He had a generous heart.

Ranasahab arrived before her sister could. She was sure if Anju was going to drive down to her home, she would cause a huge traffic jam. Her sister never acknowledged it, but Ria knew Anju had become a very cautious and slow driver after the accident that killed her beloved nephew.

"Thanks for coming. Are you alright?" she asked, looking at his flushed face.

"I am fine," he said softly, avoiding her eyes.

She heard a loud noise at the society gate, and knew Anju had come. Her sister routinely quarrelled with the security guards about the parking. They had never agreed upon where she should park. Sometimes Ria thought Anju deliberately parked in a place the guards didn't want her to.

"Men are bloody morons!" Anju said as a greeting when she entered the house.

"Present company excluded, of course," she said looking at Ranasahab.

Ranasahab sighed exasperatedly, as though he wasn't expecting anything else from her sister.

Ria thought Anju's eyes were like the day she had taken her to the morgue, red but dry. Her sister had cried secretly, not wanting Ria to know about it. And that was the reason for the delay.

Anju insisted that they load the boxes in two cars and that Ria should travel with her. Ranasahab agreed. When they were heading towards the orphanage, Ria wondered if these were truly the last rites for her son, and the beginning of her end. She had never believed in an afterlife, always believing that when you die, you are truly gone. She desperately wanted to start believing that she would see Varun soon.

What would she tell him if she met him? That she had followed him and his father? What would he say to her?

She couldn't breathe.

"Are you alright?" Anju asked.

Ria couldn't speak. What would Varun say if he saw her?

*What did you do, Mom? Why did you end your life?*

"Ria! Open your eyes!"

*Why did you do this, Mom?*

Anju shook her shoulder hard.

"I am fine," she said realizing that she had actually screamed Varun's name.

Anju had stopped the car in the middle of the road. The cars behind them were honking angrily.

"Should we turn back?" Anju asked, her voice shaky.

"No, I want to do this," Ria said and sat up straight.

She saw Ranasahab draw his car parallel with them. He gestured to ask what was wrong, his face full of concern. She gestured back to say she was alright.

They moved ahead.

Rana thought Ria handled the entire process of donating the mementoes of her son with grace and dignity. It was as if she was giving away little pieces of her soul. Apart from that moment on the road while they were driving down to the orphanage, she was composed, even smiling when she gave her son's things to the people at the orphanage. She had politely declined when they asked her if she would like to see the toys being distributed to the children.

Her hand lingered for a brief moment on the box that contained toys. Later, she walked up to her sister's car, thanked Rana for helping her, got into the car and didn't look back when Anju drove away. Rana stayed there for a few moments as he watched her sister manoeuvre the car clumsily through the traffic. The car took a turn and disappeared. She had lost her father, her husband and her son. Perhaps all the men she loved. All were gone forever. Then there was the thing Aryan had read in her diary. Rana wanted to go home and never trouble her again.

In the evening, he decided not to go to the coffee shop. The charade had gone on for far too long. He looked at the computer screen and thought he had written perhaps the best he ever had. Only the last chapter of the novel had yet to be written. But he would no longer use Ria's grief. He was certain he would spend more time staring at a blank screen than writing, but he accepted it—he would no longer practice deceit to carry on his self-centred pursuits.

When the doorbell rang, he didn't want to open his front door, thinking it would be Vinny, wanting to vent her pent-up frustration on him. She was at the age when she would begin to irrationally and intensely hate everything and everyone—her doting parents, her teachers, her friends, and her neighbours. That's what his children had done. He didn't want to witness her transformation into a snarling, feral mutant of herself.

The doorbell rang again.

He rose cursing and decided to tell Vinny off, to leave him alone for a while.

Ria and Aryan stood at the door, looking disappointed.

"You didn't come today to the coffee shop," Ria said, "We thought you were again at that dank bar."

Rana swallowed the lump he had in his throat when he heard her concerned voice. Even in her state, she was worried about his well-being, when actually there was nothing wrong with him, at least physically. It was his soul that was corrupted.

"I didn't want to disturb you after this morning, Ria," he said, wanting her to go away and never care for a man like him.

"But you have disturbed me. Disturbed us," she said glancing at Aryan, "By not turning up."

The boy had a Cheshire cat smile on his face, as if he was very excited about something.

"Please come in," Rana said, as he walked away from the door.

Ria and Aryan walked in and sat on the sofa. The smile on the boy's face had deepened.

"Okay, Aryan. Why are you smiling?" Rana asked raising his hands.

"Ms Ria and I were just discussing what we could wear at your son's wedding," Aryan said, raising his eyebrows.

"We?" Rana asked looking at Ria.

"Yes. I thought I would accept your invitation for the wedding," Ria said with a smile.

Rana thought he needed to sit.

"Ria," he said, feeling both grateful and anxious at the same time, "Thank you, but I hope it isn't a bother."

Ria shook her head and said, "No, Ranasahab. I am sorry for being rude when you asked me last time."

Rana wanted to tell her that she hadn't been rude, but thought of saying nothing. It would've sounded phony.

Rana and Ria looked on as Aryan started talking about how this was the first wedding he was attending in a long time. And how he was going to wear some really smart clothes his mother had bought for him.

Rana couldn't sleep the night before he went for his son's wedding. After hours of twisting and turning, he walked to the bar in his living room several times, only to return to the bed without a drink. He was determined not to disappoint Ria and Aryan any more. He gave up his attempt to sleep a few hours past midnight, sat on the reclining chair next to the window and stared vacantly at the night.

Rana hadn't told his son that he was going to grace his wedding. At least, the boy had sent him a letter. It was the most hateful letter ever, but it was a letter nevertheless. It meant he still remembered him. He hadn't faded from his son's memories.

Outside, the darkness was slowly nudged out first by hesitant rays and barking dogs, and then by the chirping of the birds and the rising sun.

It was time to get ready for the big event in his son's life.

He had decided to wear the best suit he had. Perhaps trim his increasingly greying beard a little. And wait for his people – Ria, Aryan and Vinny.

When they arrived at his doorsteps, he was ready—a simple *kurta* and an unattended wild beard.

He opened the door for them. Ria wore a sari and looked resplendent. He knew she had no make-up on her face. He suspected she had never needed it. The sadness was still there in her eyes, but somewhere, Rana thought, a hesitant hope was also taking root.

Aryan looked like a geek who had completed the makeover to being a cool dude as Vinny had wanted him to be. He wore an expensive suit and didn't look as if he was uncomfortable in it. The boy had got a new haircut and Rana knew it was Vinny's handiwork.

Vinny's transformation was the most surprising. He wouldn't have recognized her had he met her without Aryan and Ria. She looked lovely in a rich blue salwar suit. She had done something to her hair, made it more human, as she would say.

"Ready?" Ria asked, looking at him.

"Yes," he said feeling the uncertainty in his voice and stepped out.

"This is quite strange. The father of the groom is less decked up than his friends," Vinny said.

"Shut up Vinny," Rana said.

"Oh, seems as though you didn't even sleep, old man," she said.

Rana said nothing as they climbed down the stairs.

Nobody spoke for a long time after they got into his car. He thought that each of them was coming to terms with this strange situation, where they did not know what would happen in the next few hours. They had all urged him to attend this wedding, thinking it would be good for him, but perhaps they had second thoughts now. For a brief moment, he thought of turning back, telling them it was all a very bad idea, even scolding them a bit for making him fall for it. Hadn't they read the letter? His son had told him he would be actually happy if he didn't turn up. And now he was turning up and was bringing a young woman and two children along with him.

The faces of his entire family flashed in front of his eyes—their expressions of disappointment, anger and hurt.

## *Rana's memories of Nina*
## United Kingdom, Forty years ago...

Rana hadn't found a publisher. He had moved to London from Portsmouth after completing his graduation, but after months and months of struggle and dozens of soul destroying rejections from publishers, he hadn't found anyone willing to take on his novel. All those days he spent in London, away from Nina, had yielded nothing. He had refused to take any help from the family. It would've been much easier. All he had to do was call up his father and request him.

When he had once mentioned it to Nina, as if he was pulling off something heroic, she had laughed, a little mockingly, and had told him he wasn't doing himself or her any favours. He had written the damned novel without his father and he could get it published without his help too. So what was the big deal about it? Rana had had no comeback to that.

She hadn't changed her views about their being together.

Slowly the bitterness of failure started to consume him. He began to party, drink, do drugs and chase women as he used to earlier.

His conversations with Nina had degenerated into angry

and frustratingly repetitive arguments. He wanted her to relent and marry him. She didn't, telling him they were doomed if they went ahead with his half-baked ideas of marriage. She had also steadfastly refused to leave Portsmouth to be with him in London, telling him she was a small town girl and had no wish to disappear into the anonymity of a metropolis. After numerous telephonic fights, he had screamed at her that all the time he had spent with her was pointless, and he was never going to talk to her again. She had said, very calmly, that she was fine with it, as she had already fulfilled the role she was supposed to play in his life.

Rana hadn't called her for six months after that, and neither did he hear from her. Her reasons, as he came to know later, were tragic. His reasons were entirely attributable to his worthless ego.

His novel was dead. He had started to believe that it was a stupid love story. He hadn't liked the ending particularly. It was cheesy, with the man and the woman walking into a fucking sunset. Such endings never happened. The real endings were always dark, angry and unsatisfied.

His family hadn't asked him what he was doing in London after he had finished his degree some time ago. He wondered if he had even told them he had finished it. They hadn't bothered to ask so he hadn't bothered to tell.

He finally broke down and called Nina when he could no longer stop thinking of her almost every moment of his life. The phone was picked up by her roommate. She demanded to know where he had been all this while. Didn't he get her messages? He had rarely read his messages. None of them were from Nina anyways, so what was the point? The roommate started crying, and told him where Nina was.

He was numb when he was on the train back to Portsmouth. She had been suffering from severe headaches for the past several months. He hadn't bothered to ask. The headaches had become so unbearable that the doctors had asked her to undergo a series of tests. He hadn't bothered to find out more. The doctors had told her she had an incurable malignant brain tumour, like a little time bomb, waiting to explode any time it wished. Nina had gone back home to die. He hadn't bothered to get the details.

When he reached her house, he had had to knock several times before a middle-aged woman wearing a white salwar kameez and a brown shawl, with a striking resemblance to Nina, had opened the door. He had no idea how to introduce himself. Who was he really? The woman spared him the embarrassment. Perhaps she had been expecting him. She motioned him inside.

"She is sleeping," the woman said in a whisper.

He nodded.

"Have a seat. I will let you know when she is awake. She rarely gets to sleep. The pain is terrible," the woman said and showed him to the sofa.

He sat in the little living room for hours, motionless and wretched all the time.

Nina walked into the living room unsteadily. He felt like crying when he saw her. It was as if she had been stripped of her beautiful spirit. All that remained was a shell of her body, empty and withering.

"Hi," she said.

He held her hand while she sat next to him.

"Why didn't you tell me?" he asked.

"Is that all? Is that the question you came all the way to ask me? You can't be that lame, your highness."

"Stop calling me that," he said, desperately trying not to cry.

The six months of existence without hearing her voice, without touching her, without seeing her, suddenly felt like a lifetime spent in a void. How could he do it to himself? How could he do it to her? Rana had wanted to lash himself till he bled to death for all the time he had been away from her.

"Rana, will you promise me one thing?" She asked.

He had nodded mutely.

"Promise me that you will write. You have a gift. And you will spread that gift. Did I ever tell you that you are a wonderful writer? I didn't, I guess," she said, gripping his hand.

"I promise," he had said, his voice cracking like glass.

"I knew you would promise me that," she said tiredly. All the talking had made her exhausted. But she looked at peace, as if she had been waiting to tell him that for a long time.

"I love you, Nina," he said. It had felt the right thing to say.

She smiled tiredly at him, her eyes brimming with tears.

"I will always be grateful for that. As a little girl I had dreamt of a prince who would sweep me off my feet. How many girls can really claim they have experienced that?"

"I never got to sweep you off your feet," he said. He did not realise it then, but he was crying.

"You did. You did," she said and closed her eyes.

She died a few months later, painfully but heroically.

He was with her all the time.

Something died inside him along with her.

The wedding was in the biggest five star hotel of the city. Rana knew a lot of ceremonies would've taken place in the preceding days, where the two families must've tried to outdo each other on the show-off stakes. His daughter-in-law was from an equally rich clan.

There was a long queue of cars when they reached near the hotel.

"The entire city has been invited by the maharaja today," Rana said.

"Why didn't you become the maharaja?" Aryan asked, not getting the sarcasm in Rana's voice.

Rana said nothing.

"Good job, bucko," Vinny said to Aryan.

He wasn't the king, or the head of the Rathod business empire, as the media preferred to call their new kingdom. He was never supposed to be. It was his eldest brother Vijay Singh Rathod. How old would he be? He'd be over eighty years of age, certainly.

Rana stopped behind a car. His low-end sedan was an aberration in a road filled with Mercedes and Audis. The hotel was a fair distance from where they waited. Suddenly, out of nowhere, four moustachioed men wearing large turbans swooped on their car. They were security guards and opened all the doors at the same time. For a scary moment, Rana thought his brothers had sent men to beat him up.

"Good morning, sir! Welcome to the wedding. May I see the invitation, please?" one man asked Rana politely.

"You are speaking to the father of the groom!" Vinny retorted.

The man looked at her and smiled as though he thought she was cracking a very bad joke.

Rana gave the invitation to him and glared at Vinny. The man looked at it as though trying to find a reason to send them away. When he was satisfied that the invitation was indeed genuine, he reluctantly motioned to the other guards. As if out of thin air, two large palanquins, each carried by four muscled men, appeared next to their car.

"You will be taken to the wedding hall in these palkis, sir," the man said with clenched teeth, as though he didn't think people coming to the wedding in a low-end car deserved a ride on a palanquin.

"My God!" Aryan exclaimed when he looked at the extravagantly decorated palkis. The showy carriers were decorated with lacquer paintwork and were shaped like lotuses. Carrying the wedding guests to the ceremony in those hideously pompous palkis was a tradition of the family.

"This is just amazing," Vinny said looking at him, "You knew this?"

Rana shrugged. He looked at Ria who suddenly looked very uncomfortable. He wondered if she had ever thought something so ridiculous would happen to her.

"Please sir," the man who had checked their invitation card motioned them towards the palanquins. Rana knew they were holding up the queue. Aryan quickly climbed into one and Vinny took the other.

"I am sorry for this," Rana said to Ria, who smiled uncertainly, but climbed in with Aryan. Rana joined Vinny.

"Rana, you can't be staying in that shoddy flat if your family is this rich," Vinny said as the carriers were lifted by the men and they moved ahead.

When they reached the entrance of the hotel, they alighted from the carriers. There was fifty meters of red carpet filled with people walking slowly as photographers from various media organizations snapped pictures.

"Oh my God!" Vinny squealed, "All of Bollywood is here!"

And it was. Some of the biggest names in the film world walked the red carpet of the hotel. Apparently, his daughter-in-law was a fashion designer who was very popular in Bollywood. Along with the stars, India's who's who of the corporate world were there. He spotted the world's biggest steelmaker, the chairman of the country's largest conglomerate and the chief executives of nationalized banks. Rana knew the family would've invited the politicians and the bureaucrats, too, and he could spot some of the prominent ones immediately.

Vinny and Aryan started pointing out the celebrities and shouted their names. Pretty soon, they ran ahead, trying to get a glimpse of India's biggest movie-stars, leaving Ria and Rana behind.

Rana thought Ria looked very unnerved and regretted asking her to accompany him.

"Ria! Ria Marathe!" Rana heard a loud voice calling her. He thought Ria flinched when she heard her name.

A bald man, who, Rana thought, had actually polished his hairless pate to a shine, cut through the crowd with a big smile on his face. Up close, Rana realized he was a top filmmaker who had produced some of the most enduring blockbusters. He was actually quite old, but it seemed had taken a generous dose of Botox. Rana couldn't recall his name.

"Where have you been, Ria? I have been so desperately looking for you!"

"Hello, Khanna sir," Ria said.

"Well, you look good, my child. Why don't you come over to the studio? We have been discussing something exciting," he said.

"Uh. . ." Ria stuttered.

"Well, don't tell me you are busy with other projects. I will be disappointed if you say that. I would've expected you to call me when you were out of your self-imposed exile," the man said. Rana had an unbearable urge to slap the man for his callousness, but he restrained himself. The wedding hadn't even started, and he was already on the verge of imploding.

"No, sir–it's nothing like that. I have retired," she said, without looking at the bald man.

"Retired?" the baldy made a face and looked at Rana as though noticing him for the first time.

"Yes, sir," she said.

"Well, what a shame," the man said and walked away, making a big show of being angry.

"Who was he?" Rana said.

"Jayesh Khanna," she said.

"The film producer?"

She nodded.

"You worked with him?"

"For my first film," she said.

"Which one?"

Ria told him the name. It had been the biggest hit three years ago.

"You wrote that movie?" Rana asked.

Ria nodded as though she was a little embarrassed about it.

"What an as . . . unpleasant man, I mean," Rana said correcting himself in time.

Ria smiled and nodded, as though agreeing with the unspoken word.

They rounded up Vinny and Aryan before they entered the hotel's banquet hall through a massive, flowery arch created for the wedding.

As they went through the arch, Rana saw the family. His brother, who was just three years older than him, but looked at least seventy-five, stood at the entrance to the hall with hands folded in a Namaskar. He smiled at everyone as he welcomed them. There were a few more family members with him, perhaps his nephews.

Rana felt a faint throb in his chest.

They reached the entrance.

The clan looked at them. Their smiles froze. His brother clenched his jaws. The boys whispered into each other's ears.

"Pratap," Rana said to his brother as he drew closer to the entrance, "Don't look so happy to see me."

His brother refused to speak. Rana thought Pratap wanted to say something nasty, but couldn't.

Rana smiled at him and folded his hands in a Namaskar.

"Convey my regards to your wife, Pratap" Rana said, "And tell her to stay away from me."

Rana moved ahead before Pratap could say anything.

"Who was that man? He looked a little like you. Your brother?" Vinny asked him.

Rana nodded.

"Then why was he trying his best not to hit you?" Vinny said.

"Good job, bucko," Aryan said to her.

The floor was covered with what seemed like a million rose petals. There was a sixty-piece orchestra, led by the greatest percussionist of the country. There were several giant television screens broadcasting the wedding.

Now that he was inside the wedding hall, Rana had no idea what he would do next.

"Could we move around?" Vinny asked.

"Stay together," Ria said to her.

Vinny and Aryan disappeared in the crowd. For a moment Rana thought of calling them back, wanting them around. In a place swarming with his own family, he needed the support of strangers.

"They will be okay," Ria said.

Rana nodded and didn't tell her that he had been more worried about himself.

Someone put a hand on his shoulder and he turned around. It was his daughter, Divya.

"I had thought you wouldn't come," she said with a smile that was so much his own. The family used to comment that Divya had inherited her father's smile, but thankfully, nothing else.

Rana felt an overwhelming affection for Divya, his eldest

child. She had always been close to him, even when she was a little girl. But then his wife and his family hatched a conspiracy and she was torn away from him. He could never forget that, as a girl of twelve, she had refused to stay with him when he had begged her to do so. His beloved daughter, whom he had believed would never leave him, had deserted him like everyone else. Now, at thirty-five, she resembled her mother. Her face had puffed out slightly, like his wife's had after the pregnancies.

"Why wouldn't I come?" he said.

"Well, considering you haven't even spoken to us in the last three years, it was safe to assume that," she said, trying to be sarcastic like her father, something she had never been able to. It was Rohan who had staked claim to Rana's sarcasm.

Rana thought his daughter even sounded like his dead wife now, as she spoke in a tired, sighing voice.

"How are you?" she said, trying to sound concerned.

"Alive, if that's what you are asking," he said.

She looked at him for a few moments with hurt clouding her eyes. He felt miserable for saying it but he said nothing further.

"This is a very happy day for all of us," she said.

"What does that mean? Are you trying to say I don't understand even that much?"

"No, Papaji," she said in a whisper. Papaji was the first word she had ever learned to speak.

Rana suppressed an urge to apologize to her for all the terrible things he had said to her in the past and pat her head, as he used to when she was four. That was the extent of affection he had shown to her. His wife had held that against him when she had turned their children against him.

"Will you ever forgive me?" she asked.

"I am nobody to forgive you, Divya. You are an adult now," he said.

She stood there staring at the petal-covered floor for a few moments before walking away.

Rana looked at Ria, who in turn looked at him as though she had witnessed something deeply disturbing about him.

"What has your daughter done to deserve this cruelty from you?" Ria asked.

"I wasn't cruel to her," Rana said quietly.

"You weren't? I saw her almost in tears, Ranasahab. I haven't seen a crueler parent than you," she said, her mouth set in a hard line.

"You have no idea about my life," Rana said and was surprised at the vicious tone in his voice. Ria actually took a step back, as though she had seen a stranger in him.

"And I am glad that I don't know anything about you," Ria said, "What kind of a father talks to his daughter like that?"

"The kind who has been betrayed," he said.

"Betrayed?"

"They all betrayed me, Ria," he said.

Ria looked at him and said, "I think you should sit down."

"I am fine," he said.

"Well, well, well," he heard a voice, "Who do we see here? The prodigal returns! To what do we owe this privilege?" Pratap's wife Padma asked sarcastically.

"It's my son's wedding, if you didn't notice," Rana said through clenched teeth, suppressing the urge to say something nastier. He had promised Ria and Aryan that he would go through the wedding without an incident.

"Yes we did notice. And we notice many other things too," Padma said and looked at Rana and Ria. She rolled her eyes and the women with her laughed.

"I asked Pratap to tell you not to cross my path," Rana said.

He thought Padma looked like a pantomime actor, with her gaudy makeup—perhaps the only way she knew to avoid looking older than she was. Ironically, it made her look like a clown.

"Well, you haven't changed your ways at all, I see," she said, looking at Ria.

Rana wanted to physically assault her. Perhaps she sensed something in his eyes and said, "That's fine. I, too, never wanted to cross your path. It's just that you keep coming back into our lives."

Like a comet that brings destruction.

"Get away from me," Rana said in a whisper. The pantomime act moved on, to find another victim.

"What happened with you, Ranasahab?" Ria asked, in a whisper.

He told her, as India's greatest percussionist conducted a soulful orchestra.

When Rana had informed his father thirty-nine years ago that he wanted to be a writer, his father told him to grow up and then told him he had always known about the woman he had met in college, a commoner with whom he had supposedly fallen in love. She had surely corrupted his mind. Didn't he realize who he was? He was the scion of the Rathod family, for God's sake, and it was time he started acting like one.

Rana had heard his father out very patiently, even when he had ridiculed Nina. He had deserved every humiliating admonishment. Two years. Two bloody years had disappeared. And the biggest shame was he had used the family money. He hadn't even had a second thought while spending it on the drugs and alcohol and women.

What are you if not the son of a wealthy man?

His father had told him to straighten his act, come back to India, get married and help his brothers in the family businesses. Or else, face the consequences. When he asked his father what consequences he meant, the patriarch had told him he would be thrown out of the family. They would have nothing to do with him. Rana had laughed long and hard. Everyone, his three brothers, their wives and two sisters had already labelled him the black sheep of the family. He knew they secretly hated him, especially Pratap and his wife Padma, for he had done things they could never imagine doing. Being the black sheep had its advantages too.

Rana had told his father he didn't need the family. He was sorry he had squandered so much of their money and there was no way he was going to repay it. His father had told him he needn't bother seeing him ever again. Rana had said he was sorry it had to come to this. He also told his father he was regretful for disappointing him.

That was the last time he ever spoke to his father. The old man died after two years. But his final act was creating a trust for his errant son. The man had known his son far too well. In that final act of his, he had condemned Rana to a lifetime of shame.

Rana was silent for a long time after he told this story to Ria. The wedding festivities went on unabated around them.

"That trust is the biggest shame of my life, Ria. I came back from London with a bunch of novels I had written. I kept the promise I made to Nina. I was drunk and high all the time, but I was also writing. They were all detective fiction," Rana said with a chuckle. "Those books sold like hot cakes for many years. But I knew I was finished as a writer when fifteen years ago, my publisher stopped reprinting my novels. I hadn't written anything new five years before that. That was when I started using the trust money. Pretty soon, I got used to living the life of a leech. You have seen those ridiculous things in my flat, haven't you? That espresso machine, that television and that refrigerator? I bought them out of spite, just to squander the money my father had left me. Twenty years of living on someone else's wealth is a long time, isn't it?" he asked bitterly.

Ria said nothing.

"The thing is, I have proved my father right after all," he said, "He knew I was good for nothing. And I would need the family money forever. Everyone here resents it, Ria. They think I am the freeloading bastard who has had it very easy in life. I think they are right."

"Why do you think your children betrayed you?"

He refused to answer that. She waited for him to answer, but didn't press him when he remained silent.

The MC of the event announced that the bride and the groom had reached the entrance and were walking towards the hall, where they would be wed.

Rana got up. It wasn't long before he saw his son. The boy hadn't changed. He still had the same curly shock of hair that covered his forehead so annoyingly but endearingly when he was a little boy. He was smiling and holding the hand of his bride. She was a pretty girl and looked radiant in the family jewels. Rana thought he had seen old photographs of his mother wearing those jewels.

His wife, Leela, had also worn them. Leela who had

betrayed him and had taken his children away. She had told him he was a useless father; an alcoholic and a big failure; pining for a long-lost love and ignoring his family and his responsibilities, while refusing to grow up. Sometimes Rana thought he didn't even remember why he had married her. He had met her at a friend's place. He had loved her enthusiasm for his writing. And he thought he had liked her. Liked her enough to get married in a month and regret it for the rest of his life.

The charade of their pointless marriage had carried on for ten years, before they separated. She told him she always thought he would outgrow his dream of becoming a writer, as she had married him because he was a Rathod. And if her sacrifice of marrying him didn't yield what she thought was rightfully hers—part of the family wealth—then what was the point of it?

He had never divorced Leela. He hadn't felt it necessary to do so. Every moment of the year he had spent with Nina was etched in his memory forever, but the decade-long marriage was a foggy nothingness made up of endless days of quarrelling and intense hatred.

Leela had died ten years ago. She had been bitter to the very end, never forgiving him for the crimes he was always going to commit. Had he cried for her? He wasn't entirely sure. They hadn't even talked for fifteen years.

Rana had never forgiven her for poisoning their children's hearts against him. And he had never forgiven his children for refusing to heed his persistent pleas to come back, leave what didn't belong to them and stay with their father. His children had refused, even as adults. He wrote to Divya and Rohan, when she was eighteen and he was sixteen, telling them that the wealth, to which they had grown so accustomed, wasn't earned by their father. They should come live with him because he was their family and not his brothers.

They had refused. Rohan had even called him an escapist and a fool for forsaking a life of comfort. His brothers and his wife had then told him never to write to them as he was causing them a lot of pain.

Rana watched Rohan and his bride walk slowly,

acknowledging the people. Rana's eldest brother and the entire family walked behind them; Divya too. The black sheep, as always, stood outside. He was the commoner as his father had said, one amongst the ordinary people who had dared to defy the family and had failed spectacularly.

Rohan saw him. Rana thought his smile faltered for a very brief moment. His son didn't acknowledge him. Rana hadn't expected him to. The boy looked through him. Rana thought his daughter-in-law saw him too and she slowed down. Perhaps she had wanted Rohan to stop, to talk to his father. Rohan didn't stop, and for a brief moment, dragged his wife in his wake. The family looked at him, their expressions, disappointed, angry and sad, as he had expected.

His son's wedding ceremony was performed while he looked on as a part of the crowd. He did not realise it, but he was weeping, the tears flowing down his cheeks, wetting his untrimmed beard.

"Do you want to go home now?" Ria asked.

He refused, turned back and walked to the bar.

He asked the bartender for a drink and was about to down it when Ria held his hand.

"You can't do this today. You touch it again and I will never meet you, Ranasahab," she said.

"You have to let me do it, Ria," Rana said, "I am not worth whatever you are doing for me."

"What are you fighting? Happiness? Can't you see how happy they are?"

"Do you know what my son told me when he was nine? That I was a loser. And he told me he feared he was going to be one too. It was Leela, my wife, who taught a nine-year-old to talk like that to his father. Can you imagine that?"

She said nothing.

"My wife taught my children everything they needed to know to hate me. And those smiling faces you see, the royal family, they took her under their wing. My eldest brother gave them shelter. That's the word he used, as if I had driven them out of our house. My wife gladly accepted this charity as long as she got to live in a palace."

"Drinking is not going to bring those days back," she said.

"She said she couldn't live the life of a middle-class loser with an average writer, when she knew she had married into a royal family."

They were silent for a few moments. Rana didn't want to have the drink any more.

Ria chewed her lip as though taking a decision before she said, "I never believed in an afterlife. But I want to now. There is this maddening hope I have of meeting Varun. And all you need to do is walk fifty steps and talk to your children. But you choose to turn your back on them and drown yourself in alcohol and hate. It is never too late to take those fifty steps, Ranasahab. You think you have paid the ultimate price, but you are so wrong. It will be too late when you know it was far too easy to walk up to them and forgive and seek forgiveness."

He looked into her eyes for a very long moment. She had said it, and she knew she had said it, that she was going to die.

That was when Rana knew what he had to do to make her stop from killing herself.

"It is strange, you're asking me to do this," he said, steeling himself for what he was going to say next.

Ria looked sharply at him and said, "What do you mean?"

"You want me to forgive them and forgive myself," he said, "But did you forgive yourself for what happened to your son and husband?"

Her lips trembled. She reeled as if she suddenly found the ground she was standing on shaking. He didn't hold her, fearing his resolve would break if he did that.

"What are you going to do, Ria, to forgive yourself?" he asked, "And what would your son do when he meets you in the afterlife if he knew you never forgave yourself?"

Her eyes remained closed. He waited for her to recover, to let the pain in her heart torment her till it had had its fill.

When she opened her eyes, he said, "I am sorry if I crossed any lines there."

She said, as she watched the ceremony conclude, "I promise you I will do as you say if you forgive your children."

"As expected, Rana Singh Rathod is at the bar," Rana heard the voice of his eldest brother, the current lord of the Rathod Empire, Vijay Rathod. "If you drink a drop of that swill, I promise you I will evict you personally."

Rana turned at him and thought his brother looked so much like their father.

"You won't have to worry, Bhaisahab," Rana said, "I am not going to drink."

Rana thought his brother was surprised at his reply.

Rana walked past him, through the sea of people, up the stage where his son and daughter-in-law were thanking the guests. Rana walked up to the front of the row.

"Rohan," he said to his son, "Thank you for writing that letter. At least you wrote it. You are a far better man than I can ever be and I am proud of you. My blessings will always be with you and your bride. And I am sorry for all the pain you've endured because of me. I hope you forgive me."

He walked back, leaving his son with his mouth open.

Rana walked up to his daughter and said, "You don't need my forgiveness, Divya. It is I who has to apologize to you. You have my blessings."

He walked up to Ria and said, "I have kept my promise. I hope you keep yours."

She nodded mutely. Rana wanted to hold her, to tell her that everything would be alright, as he had told Nina when she was dying. It hadn't worked for his one true love. He nodded back at Ria.

"What has happened?" Rana heard Vinny's voice.

He turned to look at her and Aryan. The boy had a worried expression as though Rana was going to collapse, like he had after that depressing night in the bar.

"Time to go," he said to them.

They walked out of the hotel, leaving the family behind. Rana thought he would never return to wreck their lives anymore.

Aryan had the best day of his life. He saw all the heroes and heroines he had seen on the screen in real life. They were just like real people! Some of them looked very different from their on-screen versions. Like his mother. She looked a lot prettier on TV than in person. She was transformed on TV into a smiling person who you thought never had a single worry in her life. He knew otherwise. They hadn't waited for the wedding reception, which was a big letdown, because apparently the best chefs from the city had been asked to cook for the wedding. His mother had refused because she had to shoot the next day's programme. Her hospitalization had piled up the backlog.

Ranasahab was unusually quiet when they were going back. Gone was the restlessness and anger that was evident on their journey to the wedding. Even Ms Ria seemed very silent on the way back. It was as if something strange had happened at the wedding that had made them so quiet.

Apparently Ranasahab had done some weird stuff during his daughter's wedding. It seemed he had gotten drunk and accused everyone of turning his children against him. He had been physically evicted from his daughter's wedding. Aryan and Vinny had heard some people talk about it. They were talking about it as though it had been very amusing and they were even hoping for a repeat for his son's wedding. Vinny had called them sick bastards, making him laugh. She swore a lot for a girl. He had never thought girls would swear. None of the girls in his class swore, he was sure of that. They were too uptight and so uncool, unlike Vinny.

He knew he loved Vinny. He wasn't sure what kind of love it was. It was nothing like the movies. He didn't feel like breaking into some song and dance routine with her. Maybe he was a bit too young for that. He was just starting his teens, as Vinny said. He had decided not to tell her how he felt about her. He was sure she would laugh at him for saying something so corny.

When the car stopped in front of his house, he said bye to Ranasahab and Ms Ria.

"Bye bucko," Vinny said. They were in the backseat of the car, and a few times his hand had inadvertently touched hers.

He didn't know why an electric sensation flowed through him every time it had happened.

"What does it mean?" Aryan said, about to open the car door.

"It means you need to go home now."

"No, I meant what does bucko mean?"

"Well . . . I don't know. But you are a bucko, so you should know," she said.

Then she did something he loved and was disgusted by too. She kissed him on his cheek.

He thought she was as surprised as he. She gave him an awkward smile.

"I will see you tomorrow morning," he said to Ranasahab, hoping Ranasahab and Ms Ria hadn't noticed his embarrassment. He got out of the car and didn't even look at Vinny again. Ranasahab winked at him before turning the car around and then drove away.

Aryan needed to focus now. The race was just a week away and school would begin the next day. He knew he was going to beat Samar. Ranasahab had told him he had become a good runner. Aryan thought he would be always grateful to Ranasahab for telling him to challenge Samar and helping him with his running.

Chapter 17

# The Three Make Promises

When Rana stopped the car in front of Ria's house, she thanked him.

He nodded at her. She opened the door, got out and walked to the gate of her housing society. Rana put his head on the steering wheel. The rubber cover on it was clammy with the sweat from his palms.

"You alright?" Vinny asked him from the back seat, touching his shoulder.

"No," he said.

"If you want to tell her something, now is the time," she said.

"What would I want to tell her?"

"The truth about your stupid cancer," she said. He knew Aryan would've told her about it, and Vinny would've guessed he had lied to Ria.

"How did you know I was lying?" he asked, without moving his forehead from the steering wheel and glad that he didn't have to look at her since she was in the backseat.

"Rana, I am an adopted child," she said softly, "I was eight months old when my parents brought me home from an orphanage."

Rana looked back at her. She was staring at Ria, who was walking away from them both.

"For many years they didn't tell me about it. Some nasty children used to call me an orphan when my parents weren't around. I don't look like either of my parents. But they kept on lying to me, thinking I wouldn't be able to handle the truth. Finally, they told me one day—it was the happiest day of my life. I love them to bits. But their constant deflection taught me how to identify a lie when I hear one," she said looking at him. "You have to tell her. Trust her that she can handle it."

Rana tapped his head on the wheel a couple of times and said, "Wait in the car."

He got out of the car and called out to Ria. She looked back, a little puzzled. Rana walked up to her.

"I need to tell you something," he said.

"Okay," she said.

He had no idea how to make it sound less awful than it was. Maybe just mention it as if it had been a joke all this while. *The cancer was just me trying to be funny. I had even thought of shaving my head for the chemo effect.* He had always planned it to be said casually in the coffee shop while he was reading his novel to her. *And, by the way, I don't really have the cancer, Ria. Should I read that chapter again?* It would be just one of those things you move on from, like telling someone you had liked a movie or a book and then telling them later you hadn't, not really. Inconsequential, trivial little thing, that one.

"I am not suffering from cancer," he said.

It sounded as if he was admitting to murder.

"I am not sure I understand what you're saying," she said, her eyes narrowed, clouded.

"Well, I am not suffering from cancer," he said feeling stupid for repeating, "I mean I never have had cancer."

She was quiet for a long moment.

"I see," she said. The inadequacy of her reaction was even more damning. He wanted her to lash out at him, call him vile things and make him feel miserable.

"Well, it was just one of those things, really," he said and was perplexed what he meant by that. One of what things? Terrible lies?

"Is that your usual pick-up line?" she asked, her voice even.

He felt naked, like a man caught in the middle of a disgusting act.

"Is that the way you get women?" she asked. He sensed the

first quiver in her voice.

"No, Ria. I am sorry. It was . . . I didn't think you would even talk to me," he said.

She was quiet for a few moments. He couldn't look into her eyes.

"You thought I was a fool, right?"

"No," Rana said. It would have been far better if she had just made a scene. Called him a liar and got it over with. "I told you, Ria. I never thought you would even talk to me. I am sorry."

"That's what everyone says, isn't it? I am sorry. A magical phrase, as if everything will be fine after saying that," she said with the saddest smile Rana had ever seen.

Rana said nothing.

"I will leave now, sir. I never ever want to meet you again," she said, turned around and started walking.

"You have to remember your promise, Ria," he called out to her, "As I have fulfilled mine."

She paused and looked back at him, "Go home, Ranasahab, please. I am done dealing with liars in my life."

She turned and walked away from him, her steps steady and determined.

Rana walked back to the car. Vinny spared him any more shame by not even looking at him.

"Don't you have something to say?" he asked her, bitterly.

She said nothing and stared out of the car window.

"Come to the front seat, Vinny," he said.

"May I sit here in the back?" she asked in a whisper.

"Bloody hell, what have I done?" he wondered aloud and drove back to their building society.

The next day, Ria got a call from the lawyers telling her that they had done all they were supposed to do. They asked her if she would come in the afternoon, as they needed her signatures on a number of documents. She looked at the date marked on the calendar. It was a promise she had made to herself. Then, there was the promise she had made to Ranasahab yesterday and the one she had made to Aryan's mother. It was as if those three promises were made by three distinct people. She knew she couldn't fulfil all of them.

Forgiveness. She had used that word a lot recently. But Raj's sin wasn't forgivable. Some things are just not done: like betraying your wife ... like making love to her while thinking about another woman. In many of her scripts she had liberally used betrayal as the theme. The characters had to react in a certain way to create the impact. There used to be a lot of theatrics, a lot of gesturing and screaming at each other in her scripts. She had written all the possible scenarios, always believing that's how one reacts when someone close to you betrays you.

And how had she reacted? She hadn't done any of the screaming or gesturing. She had done nothing, other than standing under the shower for an hour to soothe the terrible pain she had felt in her heart when she had known what Raj had done. There was no way to confront him about it. He was long gone.

Six months before the day her world went dark, the signs of his infidelity were quite obvious. When she had asked him about the sudden spurt in his late-night appointments, he had said there were some scripting sessions that weren't going as planned. He had spun a tale that depicted him as a victim at the hands of unsympathetic producers and egotistic stars. It sounded very strange even then, but she hadn't pursued it. She had never pursued such matters with him. Raj had always told her how lucky he felt he was, because she did not nag him about the trivialities of life. His betrayal was not just physical or emotional. She had been taken for a ride, treated like a fool. She had always disliked fools and then Raj had proved she was one.

His clothes smelled strange, the way they used to in the first year of their marriage, when they couldn't keep their hands off each other. She had ignored that too, because he had flattered her by telling everyone how much she trusted him. Ria Marathe, the eternal fool, she thought.

She had ignored many other signs. His dress sense had improved—he bought clothes he'd never have looked at earlier. He had also begun to take care of his looks and buy gifts for her, such as perfumes and clothes. She later realized that those gifts were given to her either because he felt guilty about hurting her or because he did not want to leave her out when buying gifts for the other woman. That's what she had become after three decades of togetherness—an afterthought. She had heard that familiarity breeds contempt. She would've taken contempt from him, but being reduced to a caricature who could be so easily hoodwinked had scalded her soul.

The day she learnt about his relationship with another woman was an ordinary day—just like the several she had lived through after the accident. She was sitting in the darkness of her home when the doorbell rang insistently.

A woman she vaguely remembered meeting earlier was at her door with a suitcase in her hand. Ria recognized that suitcase—it belonged to Raj. He told her it had been misplaced after he had returned from a shoot in Bangalore. And then she knew what the woman was going to tell her. Everything made sense in that instant—the long absences, the smell of sex, the expensive gifts and the missing suitcase.

The woman had told her frankly that she and Raj had had an affair that went on for several months. Ria couldn't hear her clearly for the loud ringing noise in her ears.

"I am so sorry," the woman said.

Ria said nothing.

"There are some things of his with me. They didn't just belong to him. They belonged to you too," the woman said.

"Okay," Ria said.

"I know you will never forgive me, but I had to tell you. There was no other way. Please don't hate him. He was a good man," the woman said.

"Okay," Ria said.

An unknown woman was pleading with her not to hate her husband because he was a good man. This was a man who bought things for the woman and then bought some for her too. Perhaps that was the goodness the woman was referring to.

"Are you alright?" the woman asked worriedly.

She hadn't understood the question. Alright with what? Alright with Raj sleeping with her? Or alright with the woman reassuring her of his goodness? She wasn't sure.

"Can you hear me, Ria?" the woman said.

Hearing her name from the woman's mouth had made Ria flinch.

"I am fine," she said.

The woman put the suitcase on the floor and said, "It wasn't his fault. Things just happened. I have done a terrible thing to you and I will never be able to forgive myself. But I hope you do."

Ria said nothing.

"I am so sorry," the woman repeated.

Ria felt a mild annoyance. People who repeated things were fools, according to her, and she was never good with fools. She had felt like laughing at that thought. It was as if every single fool she had derided in her life was laughing at her. She was the biggest fool of them all!

"Is that it?" she asked the woman.

The woman was surprised. Ria wondered if the woman thought it was so easy to say sorry and move on. Did she think they should have come clean while he was alive? She wondered how she would have reacted if Raj and she had come together and said to her, "Hey, by the way, we have sex behind your back. It wasn't anyone's fault, really. We are basically good people. Things just happened. And oh, sorry for whatever it may do to you."

"You guys could've told me even when he was alive," Ria said to the woman, "It would've mattered then, wouldn't it? Now you can't do anything about it. He is dead. Maybe we could've parted ways and dropped the charade of living together. I wouldn't have asked him to get my son home. Maybe he wouldn't have driven the car like the way he did that day. Maybe my son would've been alive right now."

The woman's mouth fell open. Perhaps she had known Ria would never forgive her.

"I am not sure what forgiving you now would achieve. It

isn't as if you are going to end your relationship, are you? That has been taken care of."

"I am so sorry," the woman said.

Ria had smiled and said, "You know I hated people who repeated words like sorry. I still do. Goodbye."

She had closed the door as the woman had walked out of her house in a state of despair.

That was the day, two weeks before her birthday, when the thought of killing herself had taken root in Ria's heart.

When Ria reached the offices of Lakhani and Shah she saw Ranasahab standing in front of the entrance. She decided to walk past him, without a word.

"You can't do this," Ranasahab said when she reached the entrance.

"It's my life, Ranasahab, and I can do what I want to do with it," she said and hated the way she sounded so petulant and petty.

"You told me about forgiveness yesterday, Ria," he said.

She said nothing.

"So what are you punishing yourself for?" he asked.

"I am not punishing myself. I did nothing wrong," she said.

"But you are about to," he said, "This is not the way."

"Well, now I have to listen to a selfish alcoholic who has neglected his children forever," she said.

Ranasahab's face turned dark before he composed himself and said, "Yes. You have to listen to him because you made him a promise. I know I am not the man you thought I was. But that doesn't mean you will disregard what you told me yesterday."

"Please get out of my way, sir," she said.

"I won't. You didn't get out of my way yesterday," he said.

"What do you think you are, sir? My knight in shining armour? I don't need saving."

"I am not here to save you, Ria. I am here to save myself. In a way you are right. I am selfish. I didn't think I would say this to anyone, but you have saved my life. It is because of you that I have started writing again. It is because of you that I can get rid of the shame I have lived with for twenty years," he said.

"What do you mean?" she asked, perhaps sensing what he was going to say.

"That moron Lakhani won't help you. I have told him not to take your case ahead," he said.

"You what?"

"I am sorry. But not for what I have done here," he said.

She walked past him, entered the lawyer's office and demanded that the receptionist permit her to meet Mr Lakhani. When she entered the lawyer's cabin, he had her papers ready.

"Ms Marathe," he said handing the papers back to her, "I can't do it."

"There is something called professionalism, Mr Lakhani," she said.

"Not when you are getting what you always wanted," he said.

"What has Mr Rathod done?"

"I don't know what you mean to him, but he has agreed to dissolve his trust if I don't take up your case," he said.

"What?"

"Yes, Ms Marathe. Isn't it incredible! Now I can go and tell the Rathod family that I have saved them so much money every year."

She felt a kind of blinding anger she had never felt before. There was a glass with water in it on Lakhani's table. She picked it up and threw the water on his smug face.

"What the hell!" Lakhani screamed but couldn't lift himself from the chair he was wedged in.

Ria stormed out of his office.

Ranasahab was still standing where she had left him.

"There are other lawyers in this city," she said without looking at him.

"And I will stop them too," he said.

She started walking away from him without saying another word.

"Ria, think about Aryan!" Ranasahab said, "He looks up to you, thinks the world of you. He keeps telling me he has learnt so much about writing from you."

She stopped in her tracks.

"You have helped him come out of a tragic phase in his life," he said, "Are you going to push him back into the shell from which he just emerged?"

She wanted to tell Ranasahab to stop talking, to stop torturing her anymore, but she could not speak—her throat was so constricted that the words on the tip of her tongue were not given voice. All that escaped was a painful sob.

Ranasahab walked up to her, held her shaking hands and said, "What would you tell Varun when you meet him in the afterlife? That you left another boy like him in the lurch?"

Ria put her head on Ranasahab's shoulder, and wept unashamedly. She said, "I miss them so much, Ranasahab."

"Aryan and I don't want to go through the hell you have endured, Ria," Ranasahab said, "The hell of losing someone you are deeply attached to. Please."

"You won't," Ria said to him.

When Aryan looked at himself in the mirror, he didn't think he looked like the boy he had been before the Diwali vacations had started. He had no clue how his fellow students in school were going to react to his new look. He thought he was being paranoid about things that he shouldn't be worrying about. As Ranasahab had said, a boy of his age need not worry about certain things in life, such as recession and what others were thinking of him.

He had a fitful sleep in the night and was woken up by his mother in the morning. This was the first time she had done so in a long time. In the last week, he and his mother had made a pact — have breakfast together every day no matter what. A few nights when she had returned from the restaurant a little early, she had cooked some of her favourite dishes for him too!

They didn't talk a lot, apart from him telling her how fast he ran that day and what Ranasahab had to say about it. He told her how Ms Ria was very interested in knowing about his writing. His mother had looked at him a little strangely when he told her about Vinny. She had asked who Vinny was and he had said, "Oh, some girl who stays in Ranasahab's housing society." She had smiled and asked him to stay away from girls till he was at least eighteen or nineteen.

"Aryan, the vacations are over," she said when she woke him up on the first day of the school after the vacations.

He knew that. That's all he thought about the whole night through. As a result, he felt very tired when Jeevan dropped him in front of the school gate. He walked with his head down to the prayer ground and got into line with the rest of class seven B. The boy in front of him, someone who had never even noticed him before, glanced at him, looked ahead and turned back again.

"Aryan? Is that you?" he asked in a bewildered voice.

"Yes," Aryan said, "I suppose so."

"Hey, what have you done to yourself? Where is your oversized shirt and what have you done to your hair?"

"Nothing much," he said.

The boy looked at him as though he was seeing him for the very first time. He looked ahead after a few moments. The girls' row was right next to them and some of them whispered in each other's ears and pointed at him. A few even smiled at him. Aryan hoped they weren't mocking him.

After prayers when they reached the classroom, for a very brief moment, the entire class became silent when they looked at him.

"You can't be Aryan," Sanjay said to him when he sat on the bench.

"I am his evil twin," Aryan said and sat down.

Sanjay looked at him as though he was seriously considering that possibility.

"What's the name of that girl?" Sanjay asked.

"Which girl?"

"That scary one who made Samar almost pee in his pants," Sanjay said in a whisper.

"Her name is Vinny," Aryan said.

"Is she your girlfriend?"

"Yes," Aryan said with a smile.

Sanjay turned his lips down and raised his eyebrows in

mockery. "Are you lying to me?"

"Why would she do it for me otherwise?" Aryan asked, as much to himself as to Sanjay.

Sanjay fidgeted for a few moments before saying, "Point taken."

Aryan wondered how he had never noticed that everything about Sanjay was wrong. From his hangdog-like hair, to his oversized shirt, to the way he walked. It was as if Aryan had copied him all this while. Or was it the other way around? He wasn't sure.

"Well, look who is looking like a hero," he heard Samar's voice. This time, his body didn't kick into the familiar reaction of intense panic followed by resigned acceptance of Samar's abuse.

"Ponchu, you look as though you have had plastic surgery!" Samar said. Several children laughed dutifully.

Aryan smiled at him and said, "I hope you are focussing on your running, Samar, because I am going to beat you."

The class was silent for a few moments. Then the laughter started.

Samar looked at the class and screamed, "Shut up!"

"He is going to beat you, Samar!" someone said.

"Go, Aryan, go!" Another said.

Aryan liked what he was hearing. They were noticing him! And he didn't think it was just because he had changed his hair and the way he walked. He didn't know what exactly it was, but for the first time he thought he didn't feel out of place. He belonged.

"You are going to lose, Ponchu," Samar said pathetically, "And this time, that girl isn't going to be around to help you."

"Well, we will see," Aryan said. The children hooted some more.

Aryan thought Samar looked like a little boy whose lollipop has been snatched from him. He knew he was going to beat the idiot in the race.

That evening, when Aryan reached home, he was surprised to see his mother sitting on the reclining chair with a glass in her hand. She hadn't touched alcohol after her return from hospital. She had darkened the living room by closing all the curtains. Aryan felt a cold dread in his heart. He knew it was something about his father.

"Are you alright, Mom?" he asked softly.

"Oh yes, I am fine. I haven't been better in fact," she said in her characteristic drunk and slurred voice. *Haffent been betah infac.*

"You don't sound fine," he said. She wore her favourite black dress, and was just a silhouette in the darkness.

"Your father called me today. He said he would be divorcing me. He has already filed the papers," she said and laughed, "Imagine that! The second best thing he has ever said to me after fifteen years. You know what was the first? It was when he had asked me to marry him. Isn't that awesome? Nice symmetry there."

She raised the glass and took another swig. They were quiet for a long time.

"Will we go to Jaya's tomorrow, Mom?" Aryan asked.

"But don't you hate it?" she said in a surprised voice.

"But you don't. So that's okay. I will like it one day," he said.

"We didn't deserve you, Aryan," she said.

He didn't want to tell her that he knew the story about his birth. When he was eight or nine, he had heard them fighting in their bedroom over who would visit his school to collect his report card. The teachers had insisted that everyone's parents had to visit that time.

They had quarrelled for a while over who was busier and it didn't take them long to say the things they had always thought he never heard. His father said, "I regret that you became pregnant." His mother responded with, "I hate that you made me." His father shouted, "It was your mistake! I had told you we weren't ready for a child." "You were never going to be!" his mother responded in kind.

Aryan had always believed his birth was a mistake, and if one day he just disappeared from their lives, they wouldn't even notice his absence. But he didn't think it was so anymore. Not after meeting Ms Ria. He was sure if he were to die, his mother would be just like Ms Ria, wanting to kill herself. If she liked going to Jaya's, he wouldn't mind it any more. He would take her to the *sthan* every day if she so wished.

"We will be alright, Mom," he said.

She smiled. He didn't see her smile in the darkness, but he knew she had.

"I think so too," she said and put the glass down.

She rose unsteadily and hugged him.

Chapter 18

# The Circle of Three

When Ria entered the film studio, it was, as always, filled with sweaty men carrying spotlights, cranes and chairs to various sets. She had always wondered why there were so many chairs in the studio. She had rarely seen anyone sit. She felt assaulted by the familiar smells of cigarettes, gutkha and coffee. The sounds were like visiting an old friend you had forever taken for granted— people cursing each other using the vilest words (none of which were truly meant), the dancers rehearsing noisily and the extras indulging in gossip.

That had been her life for a long time. That had been their life. Raj and Ria Marathe—the most happening scriptwriting duo.

Ria saw the woman. She was engaged in a very animated discussion with a ponytailed and bearded man. The woman saw Ria and her mouth fell open. The ponytailed man was saying something to her, and when she didn't respond, he shook her shoulder roughly. She disengaged herself from the man and walked up to Ria.

"Can we talk, please?" Ria asked.

The woman nodded mutely.

They walked side by side and entered the dressing room used by the dancers. The room was full of make-up kits and stained bras. Discarded clothes were flung on plastic chairs. The room reeked of talcum powder and cheap perfume, both of which were strangely intimate and feminine.

Ria thought she saw intense fear in the woman's eyes, as

though she knew this conversation would end badly. Ria thought the woman had beautiful dark eyes. Did Raj love those eyes? Did he praise them every time he met her? Did he tell her that his wife's eyes weren't as beautiful? She feared her tongue would form some terrible words and spit them out.

"When did you resume work?" Ria asked instead.

"More than a year ago," the woman said, sounding guilty, as if she was ashamed that she had got back to her life after the death of the man they both had loved.

"How has it been?"

The woman looked at her, perhaps trying to sense if there was some kind of mockery in Ria's question. She took a deep breath, as though convincing herself there was none and said, "It was horrifying for the first few weeks. As if I was somehow betraying him by getting back to work so soon. But he would've wanted me to."

She paused. Ria thought the woman knew she had spoken about Raj in a way only his wife was supposed to.

"I am sorry," she said.

"No. Go on," Ria said.

"I cried nonstop. Every opportunity I got. It had seemed the only right thing to do when I wasn't writing. Write or cry."

The woman had been a newbie when it came to writing for the movies. Ria always called her the woman, but she was just a young girl, really. She couldn't be more than twenty-five or twenty-six. She remembered the first time she had seen her. She had been ecstatic to have finally met Ria and Raj Marathe, her heroes. The way she had looked at Raj wasn't hero-worship though. It had been a deep longing. Ria remembered chiding Raj to stop losing his hair as it was making him look a lot older than he was–something young girls loved.

Write or cry.

"Did Raj talk about Varun when he was with you?" Ria asked.

The woman had stark fear in her eyes before she said, "Ria, I hated you and your son with such an intensity that I am ashamed to admit it now. Because he was in love with you two. When we were together, all he talked of was his . . . your son."

Ria nodded.

"After they died, I hated myself, believing my hatred towards you had caused that horrible accident," she said.

They said nothing for a long time. The sounds from the studio were seeping through the door, valiantly trying to fill up the silence.

"I haven't come here to make you defend yourself," Ria said, "I have come here to apologize."

The woman was shocked.

"I have behaved in the most terrible way with you," Ria said, "You showed great courage when you came to my house with Raj's belongings. You could've easily hidden them forever from me."

"Do you forgive me, Ria?" the woman asked with a sob.

Ria remembered her name was Juhi. She thought it was a pretty name.

"Yes, Juhi. And I hope you forgive me, too," she said.

Juhi walked up to her and held her hand. Ria hugged her.

"I don't deserve it, Ria," she said crying.

"You do. So do I. And so does Raj," Ria said.

When she walked out of the studio, she knew which one of the three promises she had to discard. The sounds of traffic on the road were strangely soothing. She felt light, as if she had suddenly discovered the beauty of breathing deeply. The sky looked beautiful–blue and clear.

The race was just two days away and Aryan knew he had to concentrate on training. He thought he had become a very good runner, a far superior runner to Samar. He had practiced hard in the evenings, too, and had missed out on visiting Sakhumai for several days. Aryan promised himself to visit her on the evening before the race.

For the last three days, since his son's wedding, Ranasahab

had been busy writing his novel almost non-stop. Aryan and Ms Ria listened enthralled as he read all he had written that day to them every evening. Aryan thought Ms Ria looked very calm and at peace, as though she had forgotten what he had read on her notepad. A deep anxiety about her still bothered him every now and then, but he knew Ms Ria wasn't going to kill herself. He had always known that her son wouldn't let her do it. Aryan liked to think that perhaps Ms Ria cared for him and Ranasahab too much to do something so terrible to herself. In the last three days, she had even told him that after Ranasahab's novel was done, she would love to have Aryan read his novel to the two of them. Aryan had embarrassedly replied that his novel was not even ten percent as good as Ranasahab's and he wouldn't waste their time. Ranasahab had sighed deeply, as though relieved by his answer. However, Ms Ria had told him she would judge whether it was any good or not. That was when Aryan knew she was going to be fine.

Aryan had dithered over how to ask Vinny to come and cheer for him on the day of the race. He thought about it for a long time in school. It was the only thing he thought about, and so, when Samar tapped him on his head he was startled.

"Day dreaming isn't going to help you," Samar said.

Some of the Rebels scowled and a few others laughed. It was as if Samar's gang could not decide how to interpret and react to his words. Samar looked at the ones who laughed. They soon began to scowl like him.

"But the practice will," Aryan said.

"Practice? You think running in the jogger's park with that old man is going to help you beat me?"

"Yes," Aryan was surprised that Samar knew about it.

Samar laughed. This time he was joined by the crew.

"You think so? When he laughs at you mockingly while you are running with your head down?"

"What?" Aryan said, all the time telling himself not to listen to the bullying idiot.

"Oh don't tell me you think he is there to encourage you, Ponchu," Samar said.

"He doesn't laugh at me!"

"Everyone laughs at you. We all laugh at losers, Ponchu. And that old man laughs the hardest. He shakes his head when you are running. He thinks you are going to lose very badly. I think he hates you," Samar said.

"Shut up!" Aryan screamed.

"Oh . . . look who is going to cry now," Samar said making a fake frightened expression with his arms raised.

"I will see you on the track, Samar," Aryan said and walked away.

He is lying! He is trying to mess me up because he is scared.

When he reached home that evening, he wasn't so sure. He stayed awake, wondering if he should call Ranasahab and ask him if he truly meant it when he had said that he, Aryan, could beat Samar.

He didn't sleep till his mother was home well past midnight.

"Do people laugh at me, Mom?" he asked her as she was taking her shoes off.

"No! Who said that?" she asked, frozen in position.

She looked as if it had been a very tiring day at work. Since she had told him about his father's decision to divorce her, Aryan had seen the old lustre return to her face. He had even heard her hum, as she used to when she had just been promoted as head chef at the restaurant.

"Aryan, who said that?" she said, walking up to the water cooler.

"You believe I am going to win, don't you?" he asked.

She didn't reply immediately. She poured a glass full and gulped it, all the time looking at him through the glass.

She let out a sigh and said, "Well, winning isn't everything, is it?"

He waited.

"I think you are doing a great thing by taking part in the race," she offered.

"Mom, am I going to win or not?" he asked, hoping she would give him a straight answer.

She leaned back on the kitchen table and said, "I don't know."

"You don't know?"

"I don't know, okay?" she snapped, "I am very tired and I don't want to talk about this race right now."

"Okay," he said.

"I am sorry, Aryan. I think winning isn't everything," she said more calmly, "You are practicing so hard and I think everyone is going to appreciate what you do in the race."

"Which is to lose it," he said.

She raised her hands in the air and said, "What do you want me to say?"

"The truth," he said.

"Well, I hate being a parrot, but I am repeating myself here," she said, walking towards her bedroom, "You are competing and that's everything."

"Mom, do you mind if I say something?"

She stopped and raised her eyebrows impatiently.

"When you told me a year ago that you weren't very sure if you were going to get promoted or not, I told you that you were going to get the promotion. You asked me if I truly believed that and I said yes. You asked me to speak the truth and I said I never lied."

Her lips trembled.

"I believed in you, Mom, and I spoke the truth. I hated your job. I rarely saw you after you became the head chef. But I still wanted it to happen."

He walked to his bedroom and closed the door.

A day before the race, Rana waited for the boy at the jogger's park but he didn't turn up. He had stopped picking him up from his housing society as the boy had insisted he would run all the way to the park. For a brief moment, Rana hoped the boy had finally realized he had no hope of winning the bloody race and had decided not to pursue the lunacy any more. Then he wondered if everything was alright with Aryan.

He called up Aryan's home but his call was picked by the

voicemail. He left a message asking him to get to the ground as soon as he got the message. Unable to shrug off the feeling that something had happened to Aryan, he drove down to the boy's school. The schoolboys looked so alike in their blue shorts, white shirts and red ties that Rana almost called out Aryan's name when he saw some boys in uniform walking by.

It struck him that he had never bothered to remember what class Aryan studied in. Was it sixth? Seventh? It had to be the seventh, but there were many sections of the seventh class and all had a lot of children.

When he reached the school's playground, he saw Aryan sprinting with all his might. Rana thought the boy looked quite swift. Had he really improved in the last few days? Or was it just an illusion?

Aryan saw him and stopped. Rana thought he must've been running for a long time. The boy was sweating so profusely that his clothes were stuck to his body.

Rana walked up to him and said, "What are you doing?"

"What does it look like?"

"Okay, you need not be a smart-aleck with me," Rana said.

The boy didn't answer. He wiped his sweaty face. His hair was matted on his forehead.

"Why didn't you come to the jogger's park?" Rana said.

"I wanted to run here."

Rana looked at the defiantly staring boy and wondered what the hell had gone wrong with him.

"What has suddenly happened now?" Rana asked.

"I have a question for you, Ranasahab," Aryan said, "Did you ever think I could win or were you just humouring me?"

Rana laughed and said, "Is this what you are sulking about? Whether I believed or not? How does it matter?"

"It does to me," Aryan said.

"Honestly, no. I never believed you could win," Rana said, angrily. He had no idea where the boy had suddenly got these thoughts. He wondered if Vinny had told him something about what he thought about Aryan's running in the race.

"Then you shouldn't have wasted your time on me, Ranasahab," he said.

"I never said it was a waste of my time," Rana said lamely.

"It was," Aryan said and walked away.

Aryan didn't run to Sakhu-mai's hut. He wanted to conserve energy for tomorrow. He had read about routines followed by great athletes like Usain Bolt and Justin Gatlin—they believed that you shouldn't tire your body on the day before a race. Although his mother and Ranasahab didn't think he could beat Samar, he had no doubt he could do so.

When he reached Sakhu-mai's hut in the slums, he found it was locked. He had never found it locked in the last six months. A man was sprawled on a metal cot in front of the neighbouring hut.

"Are you looking for that old woman?" the man asked Aryan without changing his position. Aryan had never spoken to anyone in the slums. The man was reed thin, as if he had been starving for a long time.

"Yes," Aryan said.

"I have seen you many times here. You are very late though," the man said with a big yawn.

"What do you mean?" Aryan asked, a cold dread taking root in his heart.

"The old woman died two days ago," the man said stifling another yawn, "We cremated her immediately. The poor woman had suffered a lot already. Her niece packed all the things in the hut and left for her village."

Aryan felt all the energy drain from his legs. He walked unsteadily towards the closed door of Sakhu-mai's hut. This was the woman who had been more than his grandmother. He sat down heavily on the solitary step to the entrance of her house.

"Are you alright, boy?" the man asked.

Aryan leaned on the door. He had been so busy with his life that he forgot about Sakhu-mai. She had fed him, lain awake at night when he was ill, and told him stories of Rama and Krishna when his parents were late coming home. Sakhu-mai had raised him. She died alone and in pain. He hadn't been able to do anything when she suffered through her cancer, and he wasn't there when she said goodbye to this world. He bent over on his folded hands, and he cried for the woman who had loved him so long unconditionally.

After a long time when he looked up, the man was staring vacantly at the sky. A woman stood next to the cot and was looking at Aryan, as though waiting for him to finish his crying before she spoke to him.

"Are you Aryan?" she asked.

Aryan nodded.

"Sakhu-mai's niece gave me this for you if you ever turned up. She waited for you yesterday, but then left for the village this morning."

The woman handed him a piece of paper. It was a letter from Sakhu-mai's niece written in broken Hindi.

"Aryan, Sakhu-mai died yesterday. She was in a lot of pain. It was cruel of God to make her suffer so much. I know she is in heaven.

Whenever you were with her, I always thought she suffered less. When you weren't with her she used to cry out in pain frequently. You meant a lot to her. I am going back to the village. I wish you all the best with your race. Sakhu-mai's blessings will always be with you."

Aryan folded the letter and put it in his backpack. He stood up, touched Sakhu-mai's door tenderly.

"Goodbye, Sakhu-mai," he said softly.

He ran all the way home.

Aryan couldn't sleep the whole night. He knew he would never forget Sakhu-mai for the rest of his life. He heard his mother come home late at night. He battled with the thought of telling her about Sakhu-mai's death, but then decided against it. She would ask all sorts of questions—how he continued to stay in touch with her and why he went to the slums when he knew going there was unsafe.

Aryan said a silent prayer for Sakhu-mai and thanked God for ending her terrible pain.

He fell asleep in the early hours of the day and woke up

with a start when the alarm went off.

The house was empty. The sound of water leaking from the kitchen faucet made the house seem emptier. He saw the note on the kitchen table.

"All the best, kiddo! I know you will do well."

His mother hadn't said that he was going to win, and the note meant she wasn't going to be there for the race.

There was great tension in the class when he entered. A few children, mostly girls, looked at him and looked away as though fearful of even acknowledging him. The other children made a big show of ignoring him. Samar had a nasty smile on his face, the kind which generally preceded someone getting bruised.

"Hello Mr Loser," Samar said. The rebels tittered.

Aryan ignored him and sat on his bench next to Sanjay, who made a big show of ignoring him too.

"What's wrong with you?" Aryan asked.

"I am not going to talk to you," Sanjay said in a whisper and looked back at Samar's bench nervously.

"Why?"

"Samar has threatened that he will beat anyone to pulp if they dare to support you today," he said.

Aryan started to laugh.

"Why are you laughing? Are you mad?" Sanjay whispered.

The entire classroom was looking at him as Aryan bent over on the desk, holding his stomach.

"He is afraid of me!" Aryan said and laughed harder.

The race was at five in the evening. During lunch break at twelve, Aryan decided it was time to go and pee one last time before he started his warm-up. The warming up techniques taught by Ranasahab were brilliant and they made him feel energized every single day. Remembering Ranasahab pained him—he thought of him as his only true friend. He didn't know how to slot his feelings for Ms Ria—perhaps he would know when he grew older. He'd had no doubt about his relationship with Ranasahab. They were friends, even if Ranasahab would hate to acknowledge it. Thanks to Ranasahab he had met Vinny, whom he wanted to keep meeting forever.

Aryan was thinking of these things while peeing in the dirty school lavatory when he felt a hand on his back. Before he could turn around, he was pushed hard into the lavatory bowl. He tried to stop his fall but it was too late. The bowl had choked and he hadn't flushed after urinating. He banged his midsection painfully into the contours of the bowl and the urine splashed on him.

He heard laughter behind him.

When he turned around, he found that Samar and the Rebels had surrounded him. He blushed, feeling ashamed.

"Ponchu, you thought I would let you run just like that in the race?"

Aryan said nothing and looked at the exit. There were a few more boys in the loo. They quietly put their heads down and filed out. One of the boys in Samar's gang closed the door and leaned on it.

The piss on his clothes was seeping through and he could feel it on the skin of his stomach. He felt like vomiting.

Samar held his shirt and raised his hand to hit him.

Aryan felt a kind of rage he had never felt in his life.

"Your father wants to divorce me."

"You are participating in the race and that is enough."

"You need to get real, boy, you can't win."

"Sakhu-mai died in a lot of pain."

Aryan arched his head back and rammed it hard on Samar's mouth. He heard a sickening crunching sound. Samar's head snapped back. When Aryan looked at him, blood was gushing out of the bully's mouth.

"Aaaa . . . aaaa," Samar made shocked noises and spat on his hand. Two bloodied teeth landed on his palm. The boys with Samar flinched and took a step back.

"You bastard!" Samar wailed.

Aryan felt blood dripping from his forehead. He screamed and kicked Samar with all his might between his legs.

"Gaaaaaw . . . gawww," Samar held his crotch and squealed like a pig. He landed on his knees and then rolled over on the filthy floor screaming in pain.

Aryan looked at the other boys. They were shell shocked to see their leader bloodied.

"If you touch me ever again, Samar, I will kill you," Aryan said.

He walked to the door of the lavatory and looked at the boy leaning on it. The boy moved away and Aryan stepped out. The area on his forehead which had crushed Samar's teeth hurt.

He heard the loud crying of the bully as he walked away from the loo.

Rana didn't want to see Aryan's humiliation. The boy was going to lose badly and Aryan wasn't going to take it well. Rana thought Aryan had never even paused to think about a defeat. It was as if he was going to run alone and it was a no-brainer that he wouldn't win.

So when he found himself in the car, ready to drive down to Aryan's school, he was a little surprised. He heard a knock on his window and saw Vinny. He rolled the window down.

"Are you going to the school?" she asked.

"Yes," he said.

"Well, you can't," she said folding her hands and arching her back.

"Why?"

"Because you would stand there in the crowd with that smirk on your face. If Aryan sees you like that, he will surely lose," she said.

"Vinny, don't be ridiculous. My face has nothing to do with his winning or losing. The boy is delusional if he thinks he can beat that bully."

"You are wrong. And as you say, bloody wrong."

"Watch your tongue, young lady."

"Thanks, old man. But you aren't coming to Aryan's school unless you promise me that you will cheer for him."

Rana thought for a few moments before he said, "Vinny, I know what it means to lose. And I don't want Aryan to go through the hell I went through."

"You can't stop him from running the race. All you can do is stand there and encourage him."

"Vinny, how old are you, really?" he asked.

"Sometimes I think I am older than you," she said.

"Get in the car. I am sure Aryan is at least waiting for you," he said.

She smiled and got in the car.

He couldn't stop Aryan from running. That was the truth. And if he did lose, then so be it. The boy had to start running in his life and Rana was sure he would lose a lot in the beginning, but maybe one day he would start winning.

When Rana and Vinny reached the school, they walked straight to the school ground. It was full of children screaming their throats hoarse. The ground was split into areas dedicated to various competitions—long jump, high jump, obstacle race and kabaddi. There was an announcer who was updating what was going on in the sporting extravaganza: "And we have a winner in the class five kabaddi competition! A new school record in the high jump!" The children were sweaty, covered with grime and animated. It was as if the entire school had been transformed into one big cauldron. The sheer noise was daunting.

It struck Rana for the first time what it would mean to run in front of so many children. It can't be labelled competing, as he had told Aryan. It meant something deeply primal. The children were actually hoisting the winners on their shoulders and the losers were roundly jeered at. It was the most brutal judgment a thirteen-year-old could be subjected to. Just the day before this event, the school ground was empty. Now, it was a place where heroes were hailed and losers were derided. Rana realized there was nothing more animalistic than the competitive spirit of children. For a few moments, he felt a faint shiver run through his body.

They tried to find Aryan but couldn't. Vinny told Rana he belonged to class seven B. But it seemed all the children were dispersed around. They asked a lot of boys. None of them knew Aryan. Finally, they met a boy who was bespectacled and was standing alone near a bunch of hyperventilating and yelling schoolmates.

"Aryan Khosla is my bench-mate," the boy said, pushing his glasses up his nose.

"So you are Sanjay," Vinny said. Rana was surprised Vinny knew that.

"And you are Vinny," the boy Sanjay said, "He only talks about you nowadays."

Vinny turned crimson when the boy said that.

"Well, where is he?" Rana said.

"Don't know," Sanjay said, "Something happened during the lunch recess."

The boy avoided looking at them.

"What happened?"

"I don't know for sure," the boy said, "but everyone says that Samar tried to beat him up in the loo."

"What?" Vinny shouted.

The children around them turned their heads to look at her.

"That's what everyone says," Sanjay said guiltily, as though he had made a mistake by telling Vinny about it.

"I will beat the hell out of that bastard!" she screamed.

"Let's first find him," Rana said, "Do you know where Samar is?"

Sanjay mutely pointed in a direction. They saw a bunch of boys sitting on the stadium stairs, with scowls on their faces.

Vinny almost ran to them. One of the boys saw her and pointed her out to the others. Rana thought he saw their scowls turn to fear in an instant, like a kaleidoscope. One of the boys had a huge dressing on his mouth.

"You," Vinny pointed at the boy with the burst up mouth, "where is he?"

The boy looked at the others, as though trying to deflect the question. He looked older than them. Rana had no clue how Vinny knew so much about Aryan.

"That maniac hit me," the boy said, moaning loudly.

"What?"

The boy pointed at his mouth. Rana knew he was Samar.

"Aryan did this to you?" Vinny said, her voice full of disbelief.

The boy nodded shamefacedly.

Vinny started to laugh. The boys got up and walked away.

"Can you believe that?" she asked Rana.

"No I can't," Rana said.

"Hey! Where is he?" she asked the boys, who were slinking away.

"The principal told him he can't be part of the school sports after doing this to me. He is going to be expelled!" Samar said with a snotty chuckle, "You tell him he is a big loser!"

The boys ran. For a moment Rana thought Vinny wanted to chase them.

"We are just three hours away from the biggest event of the day! The hundred meters race for all the classes!" they heard the announcer say.

Rana and Vinny looked at each other. Rana knew what needed to be done. They ran.

Rana drove maniacally to the five-star restaurant where Aryan's mother worked. As he drove, he called up Ria and told her to reach Aryan's house. She had arrived at his school for the race and, like them, was trying to locate Aryan.

The restaurant where Sheila Khosla worked was the most expensive and snobbish place to eat a meal in the entire city. Rana stormed through the entrance and was greeted by a beautiful maitre d' with a dazzling smile.

"Where is Sheila Khosla?" he asked the woman. Her smile faltered but she didn't answer.

"Come on! I don't have much time," he demanded loudly.

The restaurant was bathed in artificial moonlight in the afternoon. There was a Beethoven symphony playing softly in the background. The patrons were dressed expensively and talked in hushed tones.

Everyone looked at Rana when he shouted.

"I am sorry sir," she said, "Do you have a reservation?"

"Bloody hell, lady! Didn't you hear what I just said? Where is Sheila Khosla?" Rana demanded.

"Sir, if you don't have a reservation, I will have to ask you to leave," the woman said in a hiss.

Rana walked past her, followed by Vinny in tow. The woman tried to block his path with as much fake grace as possible.

"Sir, you can't just barge in like that," she said.

Rana had visited the restaurant several times and knew where the kitchen was. He brushed aside the woman who was trying to get in his way and marched in the direction of the kitchen.

When Rana opened the soundproof door to the kitchen, the difference between the restaurant's seating area and its kitchen could not have been starker. Chefs were running around the sleek kitchen as though everything was on fire. Some of the food was actually on fire. Sheila Khosla was standing in the middle shouting orders like a sergeant. She was screaming at the chefs as though they were in a war zone. Rana thought there was little difference between her on-screen persona and her real self.

Rana walked up to her.

She looked at him in bewilderment and asked, "What the hell are you doing here?"

"It's a question I want to ask you," he said, "What the hell are you doing here feeding these unknown people when your son needs you most desperately?"

"How dare you talk to me like that in my kitchen?"

Rana laughed and said, "Are you still in the TV mode? This is real life, ma'am. And your son was almost expelled from school today."

"What?" she asked. She banged a pan she was holding in her hands.

"He hit a boy in school, Sheila. The boy had been bullying him all this while. The principal has told him he can't participate in the race."

"My God," she said with her hand on her mouth.

"He needs you today, Mrs Khosla. It is just a stupid competition for you and me. For him, it is much more," Rana said softening his voice, "If you don't go home right this moment and pull him out, you will lose him forever."

"Has he done something to himself?" Sheila Khosla asked in a terrified voice.

Rana shook his head and said, "No! But you need to come with me."

They ran out of the restaurant.

They reached Aryan's home in fifteen minutes of maniacal driving. Ria was at the door of Aryan's house. She shook her head, her face pale.

Rana banged the door and pressed the doorbell. Aryan didn't open the door.

"Aryan! Open the door," Rana shouted.

"Aryan, open the door, please!" Sheila screamed.

The door didn't open.

Vinny called out Aryan's name repeatedly

The door remained closed.

After five minutes of continuous banging and calling, they heard Aryan's voice from inside.

"Go away," he said.

Rana felt relief coursing through his body. This time, he hadn't accepted the worst. *"I did it, Papaji! I crossed the parapet wall without touching!"*

"Aryan, you can't do this," Rana said, trying not to sound breathless.

"It's okay, Ranasahab. I am fine. I really am. Anyway, nobody thought I had a chance."

"You are right," Rana said, "I didn't think you could win. But you know what? You already have! The race doesn't matter anymore. What matters is you decided you could beat the bully at his own game. And you became so good that he seriously thought you could beat him. He isn't going to trouble you any more, Aryan. You have won."

Ranasahab looked at Sheila and nodded.

She walked very close to the door and said, "I believe in you, Aryan. I know you are going to win this race. You are not a quitter."

No sound came from inside the house.

"Aryan, you need to complete what you started. You can't

leave it like that," Rana said.

"And we are all going to cheer for you from the sidelines! You are going to win, kiddo," Sheila said.

The door opened.

Their first sight of the crying boy was terrible. There was a nasty wound on his forehead. Blood had crusted around it. Rana embraced him in a tight hug.

Aryan then embraced his mother.

After a few long moments where Sheila fussed over his wound, Rana said, "Are we ready?"

"But he is hurt!" Sheila said.

"Not so bad that he can't run. What do you think, Aryan? You can run, can't you?"

"Yes," the boy said, sniffling.

They ran down the building stairs and got into the car.

"Don't get us killed, old man," Vinny said.

"Shut up, Vinny," Rana said as he speeded. Ria and Sheila dressed Aryan's wound as best as they could with the first aid they had in their purses.

When they reached the school after almost knocking over a couple of bikers along the way, they ran to Dr Ahuja's office. Sheila begged the man to pardon her son and let him run the race. She promised him free dinner for a week, whatever he wanted, no questions asked, in her restaurant. The Principal put on airs about how Aryan had almost killed the other boy and how much blood the boy had lost. Vinny laughed when the Principal said that. Rana glared at her, after which she laughed harder.

It was ten minutes to the race when the Principal made his demand.

"I agree," Rana said through clenched teeth after hearing what Dr Ahuja wanted.

The principal smiled and said, "Well, thank you, sir! I will be forever indebted to you."

The principal had agreed to let Aryan compete in return for a personal reading of two of his favourite novels by Rana. They rushed to the school ground where the race was about to start.

The announcer said on the microphone: "The moment for which we have waited for so long is here! The hundred-meter race for class seven B is about to start!"

Sheila Khosla nodded at him and Ria after the announcement was done. Aryan's mother and Vinny stepped back a little.

Rana knelt in front of Aryan. Ria stood next to him.

Rana asked Aryan, "Ready?"

"I haven't done my warm-ups," Aryan said unsurely.

"That doesn't matter. You are ready," Ria said.

"I am ready," Aryan said looking into their eyes.

"You are going to win this," Rana said, for the first time believing it with all his heart.

Aryan smiled. It was the most charming sight in the world, Rana thought.

The boy ran to the starting line-up and took his position.

Aryan looked to his right and saw the shocked expression on Samar's face.

"What are you doing here, Ponchu?" he said.

"You call me that and I will break your teeth again," Aryan said.

Samar swallowed hard. Aryan thought he looked scared. All the children were looking at them. Aryan knew everyone saw what he saw that day. Something had changed fundamentally in Samar. It was as if he was a new person–timid and unsure.

Aryan thought, regardless of what happened in the next one minute, he belonged. Nobody could take away the sheer joy of running from him, ever.

Epilogue

# Three New Beginnings

Rana couldn't remember the last time anyone had come to his home to wish him on his birthday. And this time, his house was buzzing with people. Sheila Khosla had prepared a buffet meal that made him dizzy. He had asked her how she could whip up so much food in such a short time and she had said that she wasn't just a bimbo on a TV show as he always thought her to be.

His daughter was there with her husband. She saw him looking at her and smiled. She didn't look like her mother, Rana decided. Divya raised her eyebrows at him quizzically. He shook his head and smiled back at her.

Vinny and her parents were there. As was Anju and her new boyfriend. She had already announced that the new man in her life was on the way to becoming her third husband. At which Ria had laughed embarrassedly. Aryan had invited several of his buddies, as he called them. The boys were in awe of Vinny, who was lapping up every moment of it. They had marvelled at and fiddled with the things in his house, like the espresso machine and the giant television. Rana had kept those things in the house, mainly because Aryan had gotten so used to them.

Rohan wasn't there. Rana and his son were still far apart, but they met from time to time. Divya was their go-between. But Rana was okay with it. They were learning to tolerate each other, which was more than enough.

A lot had happened in the last ten months, since the day of

the race. He had polished the novel endlessly and had requested Ria to write the last line.

"The sun was setting in the horizon and he knew everything was going to be alright because tomorrow was a new day."

Ria had pulled out her fountain pen. It was slim and elegant. She had written it on the last page.

"Tomorrow is a new day," she had said.

"Yes," he had replied.

When Ria told him he had to give the novel to a new publisher, he had done so. The new publishers had loved it. They were so excited about it that they had paid him a huge advance, which was enough to last at least a year. There was a buzz that the one-time great pulp fiction writer Rana Rathod was back in a new avatar.

Rana looked at Aryan, who had changed the most since that momentous race day. He dressed and spoke like a normal fourteen-year-old. Rana was quite surprised to know that the boy had an amazing sense of humour. He smiled a lot now. It was as if there was an unknown person who had existed under his skin, waiting to break out. Rana didn't know if he was as fond of the new Aryan as he was of the old, but he knew the boy was going to be fine. He was sure about it the moment he saw how the boy took his defeat in the race. Aryan had come fifth out of twelve. Two behind that bully Samar, who had lost the race for the first time. Apparently, Samar stopped bullying Aryan after that. Aryan once told Rana that children in the school noticed him a lot more and he even had a lot of friends, besides Vinny, of course. Rana knew the boy was still smitten by her.

Aryan didn't come to his house as often as he used to earlier. He came rarely, if at all. Rana thought that was okay, although he missed playing games with Aryan and Vinny on the XBOX.

Rana thought Ria had yet to get over the deaths of her husband and son—perhaps she would never recover from the tragedy. She had resumed her career as a scriptwriter and was going to write the new movie for the bald producer they had met at his son's wedding. When she had told him about it, he had smiled and told her he would certainly see the movie.

She had thanked him. Rana had thought she didn't mean to thank him just for his promise to watch the movie. She was helping Aryan finish his novel. The boy had some real talent.

They had repeated their reading sessions at their circular table for three in the coffee shop for Aryan's novel. Rana had felt envious of the boy, for realising at an early age where his talent lay. Tomorrow onwards, Ria would read her new script to them.

He was sure they were both in a better place than they were a year back. And so was he.

Divya got a cake with just three candles on it. Everyone whooped and clapped. And Anju's voice was enough to drown all the other voices when she said, "Happy birthday, you three! Ria, Aryan and Ranasahab!"